I couldn't believe I was actually doing this.

I was parked outside of my dead husband's mistress's office at twelve-fifty-five p.m., trying to look casual. I could only hope Cherry James would walk back into her office any moment now. I finally saw a group of four women, laughing and walking into the front of the office. I had no clue what Cherry looked like. All I had seen on her LinkedIn profile was a tiny, gritty avatar of a woman with blonde hair. The only woman in the group who relatively fit that description was much plumper than I expected, and she was pregnant.

Damn, damn, damn. If that did happen to be Cherry carrying my dead husband's baby, then this drama was way too much for me. I was going to have to sell our townhome and retire to Mexico much sooner than I anticipated. Still, the overall evidence was inconclusive. I sat outside for another good half-hour, catching up on my reading in *Vogue* until I was so bored I couldn't stand it. I would obviously never last as a professional detective.

Drumming my fingers nervously on the steering wheel, I tried to decide what to do. Option A, I could drive away and pretend this whole thing never happened—except April would question me incessantly about whether or not I saw the mistress.

Option B, I could wait until five p.m. when Ms. James would probably be leaving her office. But the main problem with that was I wasn't sure what she looked like.

Option C, I could march into Cherry's office and ask for an appointment with her so there would be no doubt about who she was or what she looked like. Option C seemed like the best choice by far. I got to take action and didn't have to throw up the white flag or even sit in an office parking lot for the rest of my afternoon off.

Option C, it was!

Danielle thinks that the worst is behind her, but she couldn't have been more wrong...

As a beauty editor of Denver's hot new *High Life* magazine, Danielle Starkey didn't have becoming a widow on her to-do list. Then nine months after her husband's death, she discovers he booked a vacation with another woman. Suddenly, Danielle sees Adam's death in a whole new light and has to get over it - for the second time.

Hit with the truth when she least expects it, Danielle brings a fresh, funny, and honest approach to the grieving process as she struggles through online dating, stalking her dead husband's mistress, and, hopefully, finding the man of her dreams. With her stubborn and sassy best friend April by her side, Danielle refuses to let sleeping dogs lie. Will she finally face the truth about herself and her marriage? Or will she succumb to one of the five stages of grief?

KUDOS FOR 5 STAGES OF GRIEF

5 Stages of Grief—sounds like a self-help book, right? Wrong. Think Chick Lit, surprisingly good Chick Lit. I say surprisingly because I had no idea from the title I'd be so impressed with the story. Bethany Ramos has littered her tale with the kind of feisty and sassy humor that had me laughing aloud and thinking of same situations in my own life….*5 Stages of Grief* portrays Danielle's journey with more than smart humor. There's some pathos, self-reflection, a generous dose of scheming from our plucky heroine, that will have you in fits of laughter, and a hilarious look at the perils of on-line dating…Bethany Ramos has excelled in her debut novel with a fresh style that makes her characters engaging and vulnerable. The reader wants Danielle to be happy, to find her peace, and above all, have a successful date! – *Taylor, Reviewer*

Normally I don't read Chick Lit. It's just not my genre. I'm more in to action and suspense than Women's Fiction or Chick Lit, so I wasn't exactly thrilled when asked to review *5 Stages of Grief* by Bethany Ramos…However, to my surprise, and delight, I thoroughly enjoyed 5 Stages of Grief...I liked her humor and the realistic way she viewed things. I also liked the hilarious look into the world of online dating. I've never tried it, but Ramos gives us some delightful insights on what it must be like to do so. I know I certainly look at eHarmony commercials differently now. Ramos has a fresh and interesting voice. This is her debut novel, and while she still has a bit to learn about writing, for the most part the book is well written and definitely worth taking time to read. *— Regan, Reviewer*

5 STAGES OF GRIEF

By

Bethany Ramos

A Black Opal Books Publication

GENRE: Chick Lit

This is a work of fiction. Names, places, characters and incidents are either the product of the author's imagination or are used fictitiously, and any resemblance to any actual persons, living or dead, businesses, organizations, events or locales is entirely coincidental.

5 STAGES OF GRIEF
Copyright © 2011 by Bethany Ramos
Cover Design by Janine Alvarado
Copyright © 2011 All Rights Reserved
Large Print ISBN: 978-1-626941-28-1
First Publication: SEPTEMBER 2011

Published by Black Opal Books
http://www.blackopalbooks.com

DEDICATION

To my best friend and husband Mark. You have inspired me to be my best self, and without you, this book wouldn't be possible!

PROLOGUE

Ma'am, this is a suicide hotline. We can't give you advice on how to kill yourself."

"If you don't tell me, I'm just going to Google it."

I wasn't really sure why I said that. I'd never known myself to be the irrational, making-wild-threats, fly-by-the-seat-of-my-pants type of gal. Still, desperate times called for desperate measures, or however that saying goes.

"I was simply asking how many pills a person needs to take to kill themselves," I continued. "I didn't necessarily say that I was going to be the one doing it."

Also not true. But again, I was desperate. I wasn't sure why I thought I could trick the Suicide Hotline operator into telling me the best way to off myself. She was obviously a professional. But I figured anything was worth a shot—especially since this whole ordeal was anonymous. The anonymity of the call charged me with a newfound boldness, probably classifying me as, "This crazy lady who called up the hotline today and asked me how to kill herself," that the operator would tell her boyfriend about later over dinner. So be it.

"Ma'am, can I please have your first and last name?"

"No." I absolutely loved this new, rebellious, anonymous version of myself.

"Ma'am, unless you give me your first and last name, I'm afraid we can't continue on with this phone call."

Shit. I tried to think of a totally anonymous name off of the top of my head. "Heidi Klum." Ah! What a horrible fake name! That's what I got for watching hours on end of *Project Runway*.

"Ma'am, with all due respect, I don't believe that is your actual name. So can you please tell me your first and last name?"

The Suicide Hotline operator sounded exasperated. I actually started to feel a bit of compassion for her. After all, she was wasting ten minutes of her precious evening trying to help an unreasonable caller like myself when she could actually have been helping someone much closer to death by their own hand.

The truth was that I wasn't going to kill myself. I simply wanted to dabble with the idea as an option after the shocking/horrible/stomach-turning news I had recently received.

I promptly hung up on the patient, Suicide Hotline operator so she could progress to the more important callers of the evening—and maybe actually save someone's life. That thought made me feel quite pleased with myself. For a moment, I almost believed I had done a good deed. Twisted thinking, yes, but I would take a pat on the back where I could get it.

I returned to my previous activity of watching—you guessed it—*Project Runway*, eating a bowl of tepid ramen, and placing mental bets on when the fish in my husband's aquarium were going to die since I hadn't fed them in a full week. I was thinking the angelfish would probably last another week without food, but all of the colorful guppies were looking positively green around the gills. I assumed that meant their numbers would be up soon.

I never used to be the type of person that would starve her pets and watch them suffer before her eyes. But again, shocking news will do strange things to a person.

This shocking news came in the form of discovering a secret about my husband, which was made all the worse because he was dead. Finding out this secret made me unspeakably angry—full of boiling rage I couldn't do anything about because the person who did this to me was dead. And I'd been wasting my time grieving over him for the last nine months.

When your spouse dies unexpectedly, it is literally the worst thing you could ever imagine happening to you—especially since I'd only been married for three years. Three years is that magical-in-between time where you are just settling into the rhythms of your marriage, thinking about having a kid or two, and feeling pretty darn happy that you'd made it. You'd been able to create a solid relationship that looked like it would last well into the future.

So when death became a factor, it seemed like a horrible, cruel twist. Which could pretty much be summed up by every *Lifetime* movie ever created. I was such a sucker for that channel—pure addiction.

My husband passed away in a typically cliché fashion. He was driving home on a rainy night, his car fishtailed, and he went into on-coming traffic and died instantly.

I could say this now with such clinical candor because I was over much of my sadness regarding the situation—simply because of the aforementioned secret that punched me in the stomach and made me start to hate the man. Of course, admitting *that* made me feel like a horrible person who starved her fish and watched them die—which I obviously was. It was also difficult to admit you hated your late husband when all of your friends, family, coworkers, and even dry cleaner had been showering you with sympathy because of your tragic loss.

So that left me in a bit of a pickle. Did I reveal the horrible secret I found out about the jerkoff and let everybody else hate him, too, or did I let his memory live on angelically and continue to receive false sympathy that was becoming more and more difficult to swallow?

I found out about this gut-wrenching secret roughly nine months after his death. I had just recently returned to work as the beauty editor for the hit Denver magazine *High Life* that had newly launched their online publication. This was the sweet, cushy job I'd always dreamed of, but I'd only been able to enjoy it for a mere six months before the husband-killing car accident occurred.

So basically, I got my awesome job as a beauty editor for a hip Denver magazine. I started enjoying my new position. My husband was killed. I was forced to take six more months off of work because I could barely leave the house, since I looked ghoulish from grief—to put it nicely. And when I felt I was finally ready to return to work—like a semi-normal human being who recently lost a spouse—BAM! I found out the secret that took my "grief" to a whole new level.

I had been back at work for about two months when I learned this secret. *High Life* was a newer, albeit highly successful, publication that started in Denver but soon had a national reach. *High Life*, true to its name, represented the typical outdoorsy, granola, nature-loving woman often found in the Mile High City. So all of our features, articles, and columns related to this natural, healthy, and independent career woman you might find walking about the streets of downtown Denver at any given time.

For some reason, this image appealed greatly to the entire country. Women everywhere were snatching this magazine off the racks to read more about the latest organic, fair trade, faux fur lined boots that were en vogue for the season, or to find a homemade beauty mask recipe made from organic yogurt, papaya, and honey that would revitalize tired and dry skin so that you instantly looked five years younger.

The job itself was fantastic—everything that I had been hoping to achieve after working in freelance PR for a lowly beauty supply store in south Denver for more than five years. I always felt like that crappy job was my steppingstone to something greater and much more fabulous, so I kept chugging along. Even when I had to create flyers advertising weekly specials for exclusive made-for-TV products like the Bump It or Smooth Away.

I was just starting to ease back into my role at the magazine. I had my own small but adequate office, which, for me, merited quite a celebration since I was used to being crammed into a long desk with four or five other PR reps who constantly chatted on the phone with anyone and everyone they knew with such fervor that I could hardly think straight.

My assistant buzzed my phone at ten a.m. I was expecting this since I had placed calls to a few popular beauty bloggers in the hopes they would review the beauty section of *High Life* to give it a little more Internet buzz as we proceeded to launch the online version of our magazine. Thinking that one of these said beauty bloggers was giving me a ring back, I jumped on the call right away.

"Hello. Danielle Starkey."

Yes, I still had my husband's name. I just wasn't ready to face going back to my former Danielle Black just yet.

"Mrs. Starkey? This is Meredith calling from Classic Vacation Caribbean Travel regarding your recent reservations booked by a Mr. Adam Starkey. I'm afraid we have a little bit of a problem. We have reservations for two at the Grande Royal Antiguan Beach Resort for August first through August ninth, which was five days ago. We were concerned since the hotel alerted us that you never showed up for your vacation."

I struggled to suppress the tears that immediately welled up in my eyes. "I think there must be a mistake. My husband never told me about a vacation he booked for us. Unfortunately, he...passed away, which is why we never went on that trip."

Even though the mention of my husband's name felt like a sharp poke into an open wound, I also felt a little bit of pleasure knowing he had booked a surprise vacation for both of us so far in advance. He was always the thoughtful type. This was just one more of his surprises I got to be reminded of after his death.

Meredith was clearly embarrassed and at a loss for words. "I am so sorry for your loss, Mrs. Starkey. We had a reservation here for Adam and Cherry Starkey, so I'll try to see what I can do to get your deposit back for you since you missed the vacation altogether."

"Sorry, that must be a mistake. My name is Danielle, so the reservation would have been under Adam and Danielle Starkey."

Meredith hesitated. "No, it says right here that it was under the name Adam and Cherry Starkey. Mr. Starkey also faxed us copies of both of your passports, and the other traveler's legal name is Cherry James. Is that correct?"

"Cherry? Like Cherry, not Sherry? Are you sure it's not Danielle, or even Dani?" I asked lamely, although Dani and Cherry sounded nothing alike.

"Yes. Mrs. Cherry Starkey. Is that correct?"

I was simply stunned. Why would my husband book the wrong name for our surprise vacation? How could he make a mistake with his own wife's name? And whose passport did he fax instead of mine? I wasn't necessarily the brightest crayon in the box, but I wasn't slow either. The only answer I had for why it took me so long to connect the dots was simply due to my overwhelming disbelief mixed with some residual grief. How could my husband stab me in the back from beyond the grave? It just didn't make sense.

When I finally grasped the reality that my husband had booked a secret vacation with a mistress—who had a stupid, slutty, stripper name, I might add—I wrapped up the call with Meredith from Classic Vacation Caribbean Travel as quickly as possible.

"Thanks for the information, and if you could get the deposit back, that would be great. Oh, and can I ask how you got this number?" Since I wasn't the "Cherry" in question booked on the vacation, I was wondering how Meredith had gotten ahold of me so quickly.

"Yes, we called the home number left by Mr. Starkey. The voicemail had your work number listed, so we called you here."

Damn my overly-informational voicemail covering all the bases for me! "I see. Thank you."

I slammed down the phone with both hands and immediately started puking the stomach acid that had risen up in my throat into the trashcan under my desk. I had always heard—and seen on *Lifetime*—that when women were faced with the truth of infidelities, they would cry, go into a rage, or cut all of the sleeves off of their husband's nicest shirts.

I really thought that Mary J. Blige would have been playing in the background as I tossed all of my husband's clothes into trash bags and threw them out onto the lawn for him to find when he got home from work.

Still, in my cheater-revenge fantasies, I had never thought about the fact that Adam would be dead and long gone, and I would have to find out about his mistress nine months after he passed away. I hadn't seen a *Lifetime* movie that covered this scenario just yet and really was at a loss over what to do.

STAGE 1: DENIAL

CHAPTER 1

After the vomiting-into-the-trashcan-underneath-my-desk episode, I decided to work through lunch and finally call the webmaster of a popular beauty blog to see if she would do a feature on our Winter Best of List for the career-minded mountain beauty. This was a call I had been putting off for quite a while. I absolutely hated to chase down seemingly important people who acted as if they didn't have time for me. Granted, this was a fear I needed to shake if I wanted to be successful at *High Life*, and today seemed as good a day as any to shoot for a career victory.

I was able to leave a voicemail with the bigwig-beauty-blogger's assistant, who kindly told me I could expect a call back late tomorrow afternoon. Hey, at least they gave me a time frame for the point of contact this time, instead of letting me lie in wait, all the while unsuspectingly answering calls from my cheating husband's travel agent—

Nope. Not going there. I tried to push those creeping thoughts from my head. There simply wasn't anything I could do about a dead cheater. I felt exploring the issue brought a whole new meaning to "beating a dead horse"—pun intended.

I honestly had never heard the name Cherry before in my life. *There I go again!* These thoughts absolutely had to go, or I wasn't going to get any work done in this century.

I pressed the fingertips of both of hands lightly against my temples to stop what appeared to be the beginning of a monster headache and ran my fingers through my hair as I tried to think of what I could do this evening to distract myself from this overwhelming bubble of despair that threatened to pop and rain down on me at any moment.

I could only imagine Cherry was a thirty-six/twenty-four/thirty-six type of gal, as often idolized in nineties hip-hop songs. She probably had a perfect stripper type of body with extension upon extension that rivaled even my best hair days with my all-natural mane.

As this thought threatened to send me into a tailspin, I decided that the only way I could have an enjoyable Wednesday evening after what the travel agent revealed was to phone my sister. Maybe her husband was willing to watch her son Jackson for a few hours so we could go out and play together.

I gave her a quick call as I was wrapping up the last of my work for the day.

"What up, girrrl?"

"Lacey, that hood vibe totally suits you."

She laughed way too hard and way too long for what really wasn't intended to be a joke to begin with.

"Sorry!" She sounded like she was trying to catch her breath from her own hysterics. "I've had hardly any sleep because Jackson stumbled into our room and puked on my legs while I was sleeping, and then I figured out that he already puked all over his own bed, so there wasn't anywhere to sleep. I think I'm going totally bonkers."

"Wow, if I felt bad about not having kids before now, you just made me feel so much better."

Immediately I felt that sudden, familiar rush of sympathy on the quiet phone line. I knew Lacey was thinking about her poor sister with the dead husband, and I contemplated whether or not to drop the cheating bomb. But, really, what did it matter? Adam was dead now, and there was no undoing that. I decided to stay quiet.

"Oh, Danielle...I wasn't thinking. I'm really sorry."

I ignored her condolences, since they meant nothing to me as of today, and cut to the chase. "Do you want to meet me downtown at Lodo's at seven? They have retro drink specials for anyone who dresses in 'sixties, 'seventies, or 'eighties clothes. So we could just make fun of all of the college kids that look like *Saturday Night Fever* if you want to?"

"Oh...I'm so sorry, Dani. I really can't tonight. I can hardly keep my eyes open, and I'm positive that my jeans still smell like vomit, even though they weren't puked on. How about we try for two weeks from Saturday?"

"Sure, that'll work."

"A'ight, peace out, sistah!"

I ended the call in the middle of Lacey's next round of hysterical laughter. I figured I was better off not spending an evening with someone who appeared to be more out of their head than I was, family or not.

I wasn't sure exactly what to do with the night ahead of me, so I decided to do what any girl trying not to think about her cheating significant other would do—wander aimlessly around the mall and window shop. I guess I could have technically blown some cash, but for some reason I couldn't face trying on clothes, jewelry, or shoes. Whether I wanted to admit it or not, something was definitely wrong.

I finally decided to go into Express, figuring I could pick myself up something in "business-casual" for work to lighten my mood. I started mindlessly thumbing through trousers in white, off-white, tan, fawn, khaki, dark khaki, olive khaki, deep brown, gray, charcoal gray, and black, but I quickly grew bored with that rack. Before I knew it, I found myself on the men's side of Express. This was definitely a line in the sand that no angry widow should cross.

The odd thing was that Adam absolutely loved Express for Men, although he never wanted to admit it. It all started with the first Christmas we spent together when we were dating about five years ago. I was peppy, upbeat, and pretty darn cute—all qualities I would never be accused of having these days—and I was more than elated to finally have a serious boyfriend to buy a Christmas present for.

Of course, Adam and I had just graduated from college, so we were broke as a joke. We decided to each chip in fifty dollars to "take each other out" to a fancy Christmas Eve meal at the Brazilian Steakhouse next to Union Station. There, apparently, men sauntered by your table with different types of meat on a stick throughout the evening, and you simply had to point at them and say, "Good sir, I want that meat."

Or at least that's what I heard. I didn't really know why I envisioned myself talking in proper Elizabethan English, but I figured my first Christmas celebration with my first serious boyfriend in a long time was as good a reason as any.

Those few weeks before our special Christmas meal passed in a whirlwind since I was still in training for the PR company I had started working for as a beauty rep. Lo and behold, I had an evening free to myself, and I found myself in pretty much the same place—wandering aimlessly around Cherry Creek Mall and waiting for Adam to get off of work so we could try to undo the horrible decorating job his roommates had done to their lonely and scraggly Christmas tree.

And then I spotted it. In the store display window of Express for Men, there was a beautiful—in a manly way—and soft-looking white "skinny" winter scarf wrapped jauntily around the neck of the creepy, faceless male mannequin. I just knew it would look perfect on Adam, especially since he had a face.

I went into the store, grabbed the skinny scarf, and made it to the register, only to discover I was out a cool seventy dollars. I blinked. *Seventy* dollars? *Seriously*? Still, it would have been more than embarrassing to have backed away from the register and laid the white scarf down on the floor in defeat. So I just put it on my credit card and hoped the charge would somehow disappear in the not-so-distant future.

And then the day of our Brazilian Christmas Eve dinner finally arrived.

We started our meal relaxed and casual, joking around with each other and trying to talk in forced British accents when we ordered our various meats from the men with the sticks. As the meal started to wind down, and my holiday cocktail dress grew tighter, I decided it was almost time for the gift I had snuck into the restaurant in my large Coach handbag. It was always good for smuggling something. I began to grow nervous, even though it was just a little—seventy dollar!—skinny scarf that I was giving to Adam. I still felt kind of bad for breaking our no-gifts-on-our-first-Christmas-together rule.

I suddenly realized Adam was saying something to me. I tried diligently to tune in and push all white-skinny-scarf thoughts out of my head.

"Danielle, I know we've only been dating about eight months, but these have been the best eight months of my life."

Oh my God, what was happening?

"You are everything I've looked for in a girlfriend. 'You're smart, beautiful, funny, compassionate, and I have to say you are truly my best friend."

What was he talking about? Was he saying what I thought he was saying? Adam started to shift, and yes, he really did get down on one knee. Holy shit! He totally one-upped me by proposing when all I got him was a lame, white skinny scarf! I happily accepted his proposal—taking a moment to gawk at my giant engagement ring—and gave him a huge, passionate kiss, even with all of the bits of Hawaiian barbecued pork ribs stuck in between my teeth.

Fuuuuck! I wasn't exactly sure why I went down this delightful road on memory lane, but I knew it wasn't good. I needed to get my mind off of all of this Adam-turned-cheater drama, so I marched furiously through the mall, looking for something to buy.

I made my way quickly past the pretzel stand, since carb loading wasn't going to do it this time. I briefly paused at a jewelry store, but that was way too close to my engagement ring memory for comfort. In fact, I was still wearing my engagement ring and wedding band at the moment, which was pretty weird, and something I would have to address later.

Moving on, I finally stopped dead in my tracks in front of the perfect answer to my now-deceased marital problems. The Pet Emporium. The window was full of all of the roly-poly, adorable, fat, squishy puppies I had always wanted as a girl and even as the twenty-nine-year-old I was now. I'd always had everyone, including Adam, tell me how horrible it was to buy puppies from pet stores. They came from a puppy mill. They were ridiculously marked up in price. They probably had kennel cough.

My logic was, if I didn't buy them from the evil, capitalist pet store, wouldn't someone else do it instead? Or would they just die? If you thought about it, I was really saving their lives. The thought of my good deed spurred me on, directly into the pet store, where I immediately picked out the tiniest and most feeble looking Chihuahua. It resembled a bobblehead doll fit for the dashboard of a car.

A quick eight hundred dollars later, and I was the proud new owner of Madam, my tiny teacup Chihuahua with an all-black coat, a white belly, and white paws. Hooray! I don't know why, but that moment of retail therapy weakness really did erase all the bad memories I was having. Maybe there was something to be said for a shopping addiction.

I didn't think much about the name I had chosen for my precious new bundle of joy until I called up my best friend April to tell her the news.

"Don't you think it's weird that you pretty much named your dog the same name as your late husband's, except for one letter?"

Shit. What was I thinking? "No." I said in my snottiest tone as I tried to buy myself some time. "Actually, I named her Madam because she is so dainty and beautiful, and I also bought her her own bed she will sit on like a throne. So there."

I knew saying "So there" immediately made me sound guilty and quickly changed the subject. I knew just the thing.

"Doooo youuu knooow whoo shee looks liiiike?" I hissed in my best Japanese accent.

"Oh my God, seriously. Don't even start this."

April's full name was April O'Neill. For anyone raised in the 'eighties who grew up watching Ninja Turtles, you would immediately recognize her as the hot reporter love interest who always wore yellow.

"It's Spliiiinter, Apriiiil."

April absolutely hated it when I did my Splinter impression. It was normally reserved for times when I was drunk, but I figured this was the perfect chance to deflect her from my creepy post-mortem issues.

"If you don't stop, I'm going to hang up on you."

"It's not my fault you have a thing for turtles, and ninja fighting, and happen to live above an antique shop..."

I heard her sigh and make noises like she was going to hang up the phone. "Okay! Sorry! We can move onto another subject, but I do think Chihuahuas in general really look a lot like Splinter—just saying."

I assumed by April's silence that she agreed.

"Why don't you come over and see Madam? She's absolutely adorable, and I think she could literally fit inside my coffee mug."

April only lived about five miles away in Lakewood, where she was an event coordinator at the Lakewood Country Club. By Denver standards, that was pretty darn close to me. It normally only took her fifteen minutes to get here, if she didn't have to battle with insane traffic.

"Well, actually, it would be a good idea if I came over since I have a little bit of news for you."

I tried to browbeat the news out of her, but she wasn't having it. I guess I would just have to wait fifteen more minutes to find out what was going on in her life. To be honest, any news or drama related to anyone other than myself was a welcome distraction.

Sure enough, less than twenty minutes later, I heard April ringing the doorbell of my townhome, luckily or unluckily for me, located just west of the Cherry Creek Mall on East Cedar Drive. Adam and I thought the townhome was an excellent purchase for our first—and last—home together. We bought it for two hundred thousand dollars three years ago when we got married, and it had now increased in value to a half a mil. I guess I should count that as one good thing about being the widow of a cheater since I now owned a bit of valuable real estate should I choose to sell it on a whim and retire to the beaches of Mexico.

I opened the door for April and immediately noticed she had a small bottle of Bailey's in her hand. This meant she couldn't have been too upset at me for torturing her with my Splinter impression over the phone. Bailey's was our "talking beverage" and always had been as long as I had known her. April and I actually met, working at a restaurant together as hostesses, directly out of high school. And we had been best friends ever since.

We bonded over our mutual hatred of our manager who had not only a lazy eye but a stereotypical love for young, just-out-of-high-school hostesses. He was also difficult to read since you never knew exactly who he was looking at. On top of that, Gino's, the restaurant where we worked together in South Denver, seemed to have a never ending array of plumbing issues. They ranged from an overflowing toilet—that the hostesses were told to take care of because the busboys were too busy—to frozen pipes in the winter, causing the sinks to leak in the bathroom, to the especially mysterious issue with the general plumbing that caused booths one through four on the left side of the restaurant to always smell slightly like a dirty diaper.

If you ever thought the job of a hostess wasn't challenging, think again. We were forever trying to think of creative ways to please the servers who had the section that smelled like a dirty diaper, fondly called the "Toilet Bowl" by the staff. We would do everything in our power to encourage families to sit in that section, especially if they had babies wearing diapers, thinking that perhaps they would think the bad smell was coming from their own children.

Nine times out of ten, we ended up having to move the family away from that section just as they started to get their appetizers because they simply couldn't stand "that horrible smell" any longer. This would inevitably lead to a fight between the wait staff when a "Toilet Bowl" table moved to another server's section, and the original server wanted to keep that table since no one wanted to sit in her section anyway.

You get the picture.

Luckily, that job only lasted two years until the both of us moved on to a series of other random restaurants throughout college. But that was when we started our tradition of drinking Bailey's together when we wanted to have a serious talk about life. Whether it was if April should date the new busboy or not, if April should date the lazy eyed manager to get promoted to a server—absolutely not!—or if April should date her married colleague at the Lakewood Country Club, Bailey's was the beverage that loosened our lips and brought us together.

After we had both gotten settled on my warm and comfy faux suede couches with a Bailey's on the rocks in hand, and after I made her admit how adorable Madam was, I forced April to spill the beans.

"Tell me all of your secrets." I always thought the direct approach worked best with April. She had a tendency to waffle back and forth and dance around the actual point of the conversation. Given the day I had had, I was not in the mood for that tonight.

"Fine." She glared at me. I guess she was still a little upset about the earlier teasing. "Good news and bad news in no particular order: I lost my job, and I have a date."

"Whoa! Start from the beginning, please!"

While her job as the event coordinator for the Lakewood Country Club was by no means making her rich or famous, it was still a good, steady job in the field she was interested in and it could advance her further in her career over time. I'd had no idea she was even having issues with her job, so this came as a major shock. While the second tidbit of news would have seemed run-of-the-mill for many, for April, it was also a big shocker.

I previously mentioned she was once considering dating a married colleague who worked with her at the Lakewood Country Club. Against all of my best advice, which eventually amounted to begging her not to, she decided to do it anyway. April had always been the type of person who did exactly what she wanted to do, but in this particular situation, I felt it was a trait that steered her wrong.

April's coworker, Roger—which was an entirely lame name in itself—made it very clear to her he was interested, although he had *four*, count them, *four*, children birthed to him by his living and breathing wife who he was still married to. If that was not enough to turn you off of someone, then I don't know what would.

April proclaimed she tried to resist his advances. Then she gave the tired excuse of so many who had affairs—Roger simply wasn't happy in his marriage and had wanted a divorce for a long time. Oh, please.

I tried to steer her clear of the situation as nicely as I could, especially since I was a newlywed at the time and believed in the sanctity and value of marriage. Little did I know how wrong I was about that, too.

April promptly began an affair with Roger due to their "undeniable chemistry." They were caught by his wife in a matter of months. Roger decided to divorce his wife—he really had no other choice because she left him—give her custody of his four children—all between the ages of six and twelve—and move in with April, ultimately proposing to her six months later.

By the time the ink was dry on his divorce papers, Roger and April were married in a small ceremony with only three hundred of their closest friends. Of course, I was her matron of honor as she had been my maid of honor the year before. Yet this time, I felt awkward and forced to go through all the motions of throwing a bridal shower, bachelorette party, and a full-blown wedding for a relationship I thoroughly disapproved of.

If I didn't say we had grown apart during their marriage, I would be lying since I so obviously disagreed with the infidelity that birthed their union. I tried to gently, and not so gently, tell April over and over again the statistic that even more marriages ended in divorce that started from infidelity, but she would have none of it. She absolutely "knew" she and Roger had a connection, and he was simply in the wrong relationship at the wrong time.

Still, I didn't think she was ready to be an instant step-mom to four young children, which definitely started to take its toll on her after a year of marriage. Ultimately, Roger ended up telling her he didn't think he was ready for a second marriage so quickly—code for the fact he was probably dating a different coworker yet again—and he decided to end their marriage of a little over more than a year.

Yes, it was certainly difficult for April to deal with this sudden loss and even admit she was wrong about him. And after months and months of bitterness, crying, and drinking Bailey's together, she finally decided she would be open to dating someone new. Granted, she hadn't taken the plunge yet. Other than giving out her number to a few weirdoes at the bar from time to time—only to screen their calls when they called her in the sober light of day. But at least she claimed she was open to the whole dating scene.

Then Adam died, and it seemed to put a huge wrench in our young and carefree friendship. I highly suspected April felt guilty about meeting someone new and falling in love until I had gotten over my grief. And now here we were today.

"Basically, the Country Club decided the current PR manager could also handle the event coordination since our business has been dwindling," she said. "And fewer and fewer weddings have been booked over the past two years. They decided to make my job obsolete since it was an extra. So now I'm out of work, and that bitch PR troll Rosalyn has double the workload and ten thousand dollars more per year."

Rosalyn and April had a long-standing feud as the two highest-paid women at the Country Club. Although April would like to believe she was mature and way past that catty, high school phase, she was still always checking out Rosalyn's clothes, hair, and clients to see who was doing better than the other in the Country Club politics. Pretty much your run-of-the-mill female rivalry in the workplace. Oh, and add to that the fact Rosalyn had discovered the big secret of Roger and April having an affair, outed them, and ultimately got Roger fired since it was against company policy. Although that hardly matters now, since Roger was April's ex-husband.

"Oh, God," I cried. "I'm so sorry! What are you going to do? Do you have any savings? Have you been job hunting?"

"That's the thing. I kind of had a hunch things were going bad over the past month, so I've been secretly sending out a few résumés, but I don't even have a nibble so far. I'm just thinking if worse comes to worse, I'll have to waitress or go to a temp agency."

Wow. If April was even considering waitressing again, then things were much worse than I had anticipated. When we both quit our final waitressing jobs after graduating from college and moving into the real career world, we literally burned our uniforms and aprons in the fireplace in a ceremonial ritual. Unless you have been a waitress, dealing with asshole after asshole, you wouldn't understand. Unfortunately, the ceremonial fire stank so much of garlic from our rancid work uniforms that were so rarely washed, it had to be immediately put out with some Fresca I had in the fridge. But the thought was still there.

"Well, if there's anything I can do for you," I said. "You know I'm here for you. That really sucks. I'm so sorry. Dare I ask about the good news? Where did you meet this guy, who is he, and when is your date?"

April had a smug smile on her face. "You are never going to believe it. You're really going to laugh at me. I decided to join eHarmony."

"*What*? No way!"

April continuously bashed all of the pathetic people that used online dating services, although I was always a sucker for those delightful eHarmony commercials with the happy couples who finally found each other after all these years. Of course, as she was quick to remind me, those were all paid actors and online dating services were for creeps who had no actual social skills.

"What made you decide to do that after all this time?"

"Well, I decided to finally swallow my pride since a coworker, *ex-coworker*, of mine just got engaged to this guy she met on a dating site. I thought about it a little, and it really seems just as good as meeting someone in a bar. Except you don't have beer goggles on, and you can read their profile to see their values and hobbies and all that stuff. I still think there are creeps on those sites, but it's probably the same odds of meeting a weirdo at the bar, which I do every time I go out."

Couldn't argue with that logic. "So who's the lucky guy? How long did it take to meet him? When are you going out?"

"Well—again, don't laugh since I seem to have an attraction to guys with pedophile-inspired names, but his name is Ralph. He's a teacher in Westminster. He's also divorced with no children, and his profile picture actually looked fairly normal and decent. We've e-mailed each other a few times, and he's pretty fun to talk to so far, so we set up a coffee date—which is what the website recommends for your first date—next Saturday at Starbucks off of Speer. I have to make sure to tell you exactly where I'm going and with whom in case I disappear and end up in a body bag in his trunk."

"Ha ha," I said sarcastically. "That's so exciting! I'm sure it's going to be really fun, and at least you're putting yourself out there!" I added encouragingly. "All you have to do is get the ball rolling until you find someone you actually like."

Suddenly I was struck with a great, albeit totally random, idea. "Hey! I have an idea!"

I jumped up off the couch and startled April enough to make her dribble a little bit of Bailey's onto her chin.

She put her hand to her heart, dramatically. "What? Stop jumping up and scaring me like that! What's your amazing idea?"

"Okay. I didn't say it was amazing, but my assistant is being promoted to a beauty researcher and writer for the magazine, and since you've done tons of administrative stuff in your lifetime, what if you worked as my assistant? It pays about thirty thousand, which isn't the best, but it's definitely enough to live on for a while until you decide what you want to do."

Now that I got the idea rolling in my head, I couldn't stop. "You would work eight to five, Monday to Friday, and you get five vacation days a year and five personal days, and it's actually way easier than you think because we have a database designed for scheduling appointments and organizing my schedule, which really isn't that difficult. And I could probably train you in like a week. I think my assistant is getting promoted in like three weeks, so you could probably start in two weeks." I paused for a breath. "So what do you think?"

"Whoa, slow down, missy. This seems like a pretty good idea, and I definitely need a job, but don't you think it's a little much? You really don't owe me anything. I don't want you to give me a job just because I'm your friend if I'm actually under-qualified. Maybe you could just put in a good word for me and see what happens?"

"Nope." I was firm and confident in my decision. "You're going to start in two weeks, after I clear this with my boss, of course. And I promise you you're going to love it!"

CHAPTER 2

My boss actually thought the idea of April working as my assistant was utterly fantastic. She hated screening applicants for a new position, and April had PR and admin experience from her time as an event coordinator. It was the perfect fit.

I decided to give April a call during lunch to tell her the great news—she basically had a new job handed to her on a platter, and all she had to do was come in for an interview with my boss as a formality to make sure she wasn't a total psycho or very ugly.

Yes, as unpleasant as it sounded, it seemed to be an unspoken fact that my boss, Gwen, only liked to hire fairly to very attractive employees. I had not once seen an employee walk through the doors of *High Life* who was overweight, balding, or not perfectly polished from head to toe. That put a little bit of pressure on me in the morning to make sure I looked as glam as possible, but at least I had the extra time to put the finishing touches on during my rigorous commute.

I knew April would be a shoe-in since she was tall, voluptuous, and exotic due to her half-Hispanic heritage. April was one of the only women I knew who never expressed guilt about eating or felt pressured to be thin—which was a good quality to have when working at a magazine full of trendy, bitchy, skeletal women. She always thoroughly enjoyed her meals where the food seemed to magically go to all the right places. Mainly her boobs.

I, on the other hand, always struggled to eat a balanced meal that was less than five hundred calories because when I "thoroughly enjoyed my meals," it looked like I immediately gained ten pounds from head to toe. Damn you, DNA.

"Heyyyyy!" I drawled to April when she answered the phone.

"Did I get it?" she squealed. She had as much enthusiasm as if Ed McMahon had visited her doorstep. It appeared she was much more desperate for a job than she'd let on. Well played, April, well played.

"Well, I talked to Gwen, and she looked over your résumé. We talked a little bit more about your hours and your salary-"

"Seriously, stop it. I hate it when you do this. I hate it. Tell me whether I got the job or not right now!"

Geez, what a bully. I smiled. "Of course, you absolutely got it! Didn't I tell you that you would?"

"Thank God! I didn't want to freak you out or anything, but I was really thinking about donating my eggs, or at the very least, selling all of my furniture, because I didn't know how I was going to make rent next month. This is so, so helpful. When can I start? I could seriously come in tomorrow if you wanted me to."

After I told her she could come in the following Monday and instructed her on the basics of the hip-mountain-chic wardrobe that was the prerequisite for working at *High Life*. I suggested we go out and celebrate this Friday, since she finally got a job and didn't have to worry about selling parts of her body for money.

"We could go to Lime downtown," I said. "And then maybe hit the bars afterward? I know how you like the free tequila shots in a lime they give you at the beginning of the meal. If you want, you can just stay at my house, and we can take a cab from there. What do you think?"

"Best idea you've had all day. See you Friday, bitch!"

Um, it's *boss* now, I thought. I guess we'd have to work on that Monday. I did have a small amount of concern about having my best friend work as my assistant, especially since April was nothing if not outspoken. She had steadily matured as she'd gotten older, but she was fired from three restaurants in a row in college because she refused to do one thing or the other. Whether it was wiping the crusty ketchup out from underneath the cap or taking a ten-top of frat guys a half-hour before the restaurant closed, if she didn't want to do it, she wouldn't.

I pushed that thought away with the rest of the thoughts I wasn't thinking about these days. Like a cheating spouse, and whether or not I needed to explore that further. Right now, my thinking was that what was in the past should stay in the past. There was no sense crying over spilled milk. Another alarming trend was I kept talking in worn out figures of speech. Which could potentially be a symptom of a deeper emotional problem. But who was I to look a gift horse in the mouth? Obviously, I hadn't fully mastered the art of using my figures of speech correctly yet.

Since it was only Wednesday and the next fun thing I had to look forward to was painting the town red—there I went again—with April on Friday, I spent the next two nights distracting myself as best I could. Think massive amounts of reality TV and attempts at training Madam to at least piss on the tile floor as opposed to the carpet.

Although I owned our, I mean, *my* townhome, I really didn't want to have to steam vac every night of the week because of little doggie accidents. That was one thing I didn't think about when I made the impulse buy of an adorable teacup Chihuahua. Even worse, she was so little it was hard to tell if she had peed on the beige carpet or not. I had to resort to sniffing suspicious spots on my hands and knees or even sticking a finger into the carpet to see if it was wet. And I thought I would only have to succumb to such humiliation if I ever had kids.

But don't get me wrong—Madam was truly the light of my life. She was absolutely nothing like Adam, and she made a much better companion, if you asked me. Sure, she couldn't control her bladder wherever she happened to be, and she bit me with her little pointy teeth while I was sleeping, but I'd be hard pressed to discover she ever cheated on me since she was so ferociously loyal and loving. Now I truly understood why a dog was man's best friend.

ↄ၁ↄ၁

By the time Friday finally rolled around, I was more than ready to get my drink on. I even made the mistake of pre-gaming a little bit at home while I waited for April to get there at nine o'clock. Normally, I was quite a bit of a lightweight, so I just stuck to drinking at the bars—except for that brief phase in college where I lived within walking distance from downtown, and my friend Regina and I would drink forties and walk to the bars. But I digress...

Now, I was a big-time grown-up, so I paid for my drinks at a real bar like a real person when I wanted to go out.

But, for some reason, since it had been such a stressful week, I was really feeling in the mood to party. I didn't want to admit the cheating husband news hit me so hard, but it felt like a burr under my saddle—excellent use of a figure of speech!—all week, pestering me and poking at me when I least expected it. Why wouldn't it just go away? Adam was dead, so you'd think all of the drama would have died with him. But I just couldn't get all of the questions surrounding the news out of my mind.

So many times I stopped short of Googling his stripper girlfriend's name, but I had always thought it was a little bit crass to resort to Internet stalking. April, however, was a whole other animal since she would stalk anyone and everyone online, sometimes total strangers out of sheer boredom. She previously admitted to me if she was on the phone with a bride for a long period of time, planning her event at the Country Club and dying of boredom, she'd Google her and look up her Facebook profile just to see what she looked like. If she was fat or ugly, all the better. If she happened to be beautiful and thin, then she was probably a bitch with a bad personality.

Made sense to me.

I, on the other hand, normally didn't use and abuse the search engines to find out about random people. Even if that random hooker may or may not have slept with my husband.

So to keep myself away from the temptation of the Internet while I waited for April—who you could always count on to be late—I started my night early with a few homemade lemon drop martinis. Of course, mine were the ghetto version with Absolut Citron and sugar-free lemonade, but they tasted like the real thing if I put a little bit of sugar on the rim of my juice glass!

Besides, no one was home to judge me on my drinking habits, which made it all the more tempting to have not one, but three, pre-Big-Night-Out martinis.

By the time April arrived, I was definitely feeling good, if you know what I mean. I tried to hide it because I didn't want her to think I started without her. I told her I was working on my first martini and offered her one.

"Nah, let's just grab some dinner at Lime and get crackin' on those free tequila shots. Plus, I want us to be able to chat for a bit so I can get the scoop on all the office gossip!" she said mischievously.

I groaned silently. This was just one more dreaded issue I had hoped wouldn't come up with April as my assistant. I really felt strongly about not spreading gossip or being a part of any work drama since I wanted to get promoted as quickly as possible. Let's just say being in the restaurant business taught me a thing or two about keeping my trap shut, and I hoped the alcohol wouldn't loosen my lips enough for me to air all of our company's dirty laundry to April over dinner.

Since April had wisely thought to call ahead for a reservation, we were seated surprisingly quickly at Lime for a Friday night. As we gorged on the chips, salsa, and free shots of tequila, she pumped me for office gossip right off the bat.

"So who's sleeping with who?"

I tried to play dumb, like I was too caught up in my work to care what anyone was doing at the office, but April wasn't having it.

"Seriously, you absolutely have to know. Does Gwen hook up with any of the guys in the IT department? They're pretty cute."

I remained silent and tried to divert attention by cramming my mouth full of food so all I could do was shrug my shoulders and look innocent.

"Wait, does she like girls? Her hair's pretty short, and she definitely has a masculine energy. I'll have to watch my back if she plays for the other team."

I swallowed my food so fast the salsa burned my throat. "No, no, no, nothing like that. Um..." I tried to think of something to get her mind off of the work gossip. "How are things going with Ralph?"

"He was a freak. He showed up wearing really short gym shorts to our coffee date, which was a total turnoff. Not only does that outfit choice make absolutely no sense for a coffee date, but short shorts are *never* flattering on a man, no matter how you slice it."

I agreed with her on that one. "So do you have any other online dates lined up? Are you getting tons of messages?"

"Yeah. We'll see," she said, brushing me off. "What about you? Are you thinking you want to meet someone in the future? I know it's been less than a year, but where are you at with the idea of dating?"

I was totally floored by her question. I had hoped people would continue to ignore my love life and never really force me to move on since Adam's death was so painful. Now, I actually didn't know how I felt. I would have been at a loss for words, except for that extra tequila shot. Suddenly, I was talking and talking and couldn't seem to stop.

"I actually got this really weird call from a travel agent who said Adam booked a vacation he was supposed to go on last week with somebody else. I thought it was me at first, but it wasn't me because the travel agent said they had a copy of her passport. Her name is Cherry James, so obviously, he hired, like, some escort or something. I guess it's not a really big deal since he passed away, but it's still kind of weird news."

After that verbal diarrhea, I glanced up at April. She was staring back at me with a stunned expression on her face. She had a chip in hand paused halfway to her mouth as she sat frozen like a statue.

"Say something," I said.

"No, *you* say something. Keep explaining! That's some crazy shit! What are you going to do?"

"Well, nothing, I guess. I mean, there's nothing I really can do about it since I can't bring him back from the dead to yell at him, can I?" I laughed lamely at my not-so-funny joke.

"No way. You absolutely need to Google this girl, hunt her down, find out exactly what she was doing with your man, and then boil her rabbit."

"I don't think so. Google's your solution for everything. But I'm not you. Let's just enjoy the rest of our meal and then try to get ugly guys to buy some drinks for us. Sound like a plan?"

We concluded our meal with superficial conversation, since it seemed like both of us were a little too shocked to talk about what was really happening in my life. By the time I got up to go to the bathroom at the end of the meal, I realized I had had much more to drink than I thought. I had to grab onto the wall for a bit of support as I escorted myself to the toilet. I didn't think I'd been that far gone in a restaurant since I was in my early twenties—when it seemed like a great idea to always get a little bit drunk before going out in public.

If I took some time to think about it, it was kind of obvious I was doing worse with this Adam thing than I realized. But isn't that what alcohol was for? The three martinis, the half shot of tequila in a lime, the Grande top shelf margarita on the rocks...they all seemed to take the hazy edge off of this messy emotional turmoil biting at my heels that I really didn't want to deal with right now.

Luckily, I didn't have to. Within ten minutes, including a little lipstick touchup of my blurry reflection in the low-lit bathroom mirror, we were ready to rock and hit downtown Denver in style. We walked, or rather stumbled, around the block to Mynt on Market Street, an upscale mojito lounge that was as hip as they come. I wasn't sure what an upscale mojito lounge was, but I knew I liked upscale, and I knew I liked mojitos, so...you do the math.

As April and I sauntered down Market Street, we passed the usual gang of random homeless people. One grubby man in particular stood out since he made jerking hand motions in our direction to show how attractive he thought we were. Nightlife in Denver was just so fab. Since we were out slightly earlier than the majority of twenty-somethings, we were able to grab a few seats at the bar and pick our poison.

The bar was dimly lit with fluorescent lights. There was a strange mix of Michael Jackson's "You Are Not Alone" set to a fast techno dance beat playing on the Muzak. Not something I would've dreamed up in my wildest imagination, but also not a combination I was necessarily opposed to.

I started nodding my head in time to the dance-mix, even though techno music always made me uncomfortable. Like I was the awkward sixth-grader that couldn't dance in front of her friends. Seriously, can anyone who isn't on ecstasy dance to techno? I still had yet to find someone who could.

I waved my hand flirtily at the female bartender, which really didn't make sense because I liked men. But it also seemed like a great idea to do whatever I could to get her attention. It appeared to work since she sauntered over right away in her leather bustier to ask what type of mojitos April and I wanted. We went with a pitcher of raspberry since it seemed like a go-big-or-go-home kind of night. It probably wasn't the first bad decision we were going to make for the evening anyway.

By the time we finished that first pitcher, a couple of older, cocky looking men at the bar were willing to buy us a few more drinks, so we kindly obliged. I got into a conversation with a man named Russell, who appeared to be about twenty years older than me and, oddly enough, owned a hair salon. He claimed he wasn't gay and was also happily married, yet it seemed a bit fishy that he was out on the town with another guy, hanging out in a bar without his wife.

But who was I to judge? Since I was in the beauty industry too, we immediately fell into a conversation about whether or not mineral makeup was on the way out. Russell vehemently disagreed since he had a huge, new display selling Bare Minerals makeup in his salon in Westminster. It was a little strange he felt so passionate about makeup, but it was always a fun subject for me to talk about, so I went with it.

After what felt like a mere five minutes but was probably more like twenty, I turned around to see whether or not April was ready for yet another drink—preferably purchased for us by the men we were talking to. She had taken a seat with man number two on what looked to be an end table next to a couch a few feet away. By that time, the bar was absolutely packed, so I was lucky to have kept my barstool.

I was sitting backward on it, facing away from the corseted bartender, sandwiched between Russell to my right and a tall blonde Amazonian type, who appeared to be having difficulty ordering herself a drink, to my left. *If only she was smart enough to flirt with the bartender like I did, she'd have a drink in her hand right now.*

I waved April over from her conversation with Russell's friend, to ask her what drink she wanted next. Since there was such a crowd, she had to push past several people to get to me. Customary for any nightlife bar scene in Denver. But the tall, blonde Glamazon next to me obviously hadn't been briefed on busy bar etiquette. The next thing I knew, she shoved April, hard, with her shoulder, trying to stake her claim on her bar space, and pushed April into me with such force I would've fallen off of my barstool if Russell hadn't grabbed me by the back of my skimpy top. Luckily, it wasn't too skimpy, or else it would have ripped right off me, leaving me planted face-first on the floor.

As I tried to gather my bearings, the only thing I could hear being shouted over and over again was, "I'm spicy! I'm spicy! I'm spicy, BITCH!"

I had no idea what "I'm spicy" meant. I just assumed I misheard whatever April was shouting since it was probably lost in a drunken translation. But, no, that was exactly what she was shouting, word for word, as she chest-bumped against the Glamazon repeatedly.

It finally dawned on me, April was trying to express the depth of her Latin heritage and why said Glamazon shouldn't mess with her. She was using the *Bad Girls Club* approach of bumping into the offending girl over and over, without actually punching her, shouting one phrase again and again at the top of her lungs until her opponent backed down.

The Glamazon must have also seen the same episode of the *Bad Girls Club*. She was doing the same rigorous chest-bumping against April, while shouting, "What? What? What? What, BITCH?"

Hmm...I only gave her a two for originality. She could've at least thrown in a few more creative insults or just skipped straight to the hair pulling. Not even a split second after I thought that, the Glamazon had apparently had enough. She shoved April with brute force and sent her sprawling on her back on the floor in the middle of the bar, exposing all her "goodies" to the whole room, although that was probably the least of her worries at that moment.

I tried to do the good-friend thing and jump in there to help her. Unfortunately—or fortunately—Russell held me back like a rag doll. So I just sat there lamely and sipped my mojito as I watched the show. It'd better be good.

The entertainment was pretty much over as soon as it had begun since the bouncers in downtown Denver had the stealth of ninjas. They hoisted April up by grabbing her underneath her arms, so her feet weren't even touching the floor, gently carried her out and deposited her on the pavement outside. Not even a scratch or a hair out of place!

When I saw April being ejected, I quickly thanked Russell for the many, many drinks he'd bought me—which I also felt I deserved since I was his beard for the evening—grabbed my purse, and raced out the door.

April was already storming down the block about twenty feet ahead of me.

"Hey! Hey, April! Seriously, your legs are way longer than mine, so slow down a minute please!"

I broke into a swift high-heeled jog and finally caught up with her at the corner of Fifteenth and Market. I grabbed her by the arm, and when I did, she whipped around with an enraged expression on her face.

As soon as our eyes met, I started laughing uncontrollably and repeating, "I'm spicy! I'm spicy!" over and over again. It was so hysterical it was bringing tears to my eyes.

April tried to keep glaring at me, but she eventually gave up and started laughing too. "God, that girl was such an evil bitch. *She* was the one who shoved *me*, so where did she get off pushing me on the ground? Luckily, I was all waxed and groomed when I flashed everybody, but still."

"I know!" I said. "She was like eight feet tall anyway, and her roots were embarrassing. Besides, I thought it was lame she couldn't think of a better insult than 'What?' That is *so* played."

We continued to trash the Amazonian she-bear as we walked on toward our next destination on Market. We finally made it up to the Purple Martini in the Sixteenth Street Mall, where it got unrecognizably fuzzy and very ugly from that point on.

April and I got into one of those drunken bonding conversations that seemed so deep at the time yet made absolutely no sense when you reflected on it later. The only point of clarity I remembered was when I kept repeating, "I can't believe I'm a widow," again and again. I startled the other unsuspecting bar patrons when I slammed down my fist on the bar for emphasis and said, "You know what? I really need to *do* something. Like do something. Do something big! What should I do?"

April halfheartedly lifted her head from the bar, where she was resting it between sips of her drink. "I already told you," She muttered, slurring her words. "You need to Google the bitch that cheated with Adam and let her know you know so she finally knows what you're all about."

I had a difficult time following that train of thought, so I just kept going. "You know what's weird?"

"What?"

"The word 'widow.' It just sounds, like, really funny, and whenever people call me a widow, I always think of a spider." I covered my mouth with both of my hands and giggled hysterically.

April laughed, too. "Yeah, I can totally see that. You're just like a big spider. You're a widow, you are a widow, you're a widow." She chanted along with me.

If this kind of behavior didn't freak out the other people in the bar, then I didn't know what would. Still, Denver had its share of weirdoes, so people were normally pretty tolerant. I slapped the bar again as I had an utterly brilliant idea. "Oh my God!" April looked up at me in surprise. "Now I know what I have to do!" I declared. "I have to get a tattoo. Tonight."

Adam was pretty straight-laced and had never liked tattoos. He always thought they ended up looking horrible and wrinkly as you got older. Yes, I would give him that. But the truth was now he was dead, he would never see me get older. That definitely hurt, but even more importantly, if Adam were still alive, we would probably be in the same boat since he was a big, fat cheater anyhow.

That ominous train of thought spurred me on. Seconds later, I closed out our tab and started Googling the closest tattoo parlor on my iPhone. "Oh my God, it's like a sign," I squealed with delight. "There's this place called Celebrity Tattoo around the corner on Market, and they're still open!"

I had the short walk to think about what I wanted branded on my body forever, but when we arrived at the tattoo parlor, I still hadn't made up my mind. I'd always heard the rumor you weren't allowed to drink before getting a tattoo. Many, many of my friends in college had really crazy tattoo ideas—like Gary Coleman, for starters—on a night of heavy drinking that never came to fruition because they were kicked out of the tattoo parlor due to inebriation. It appeared Celebrity Tattoo did not have such a policy.

I didn't see how anyone could have mistaken me for being sober. But the tiny, heavily pierced tattoo artist with her hair in pigtails didn't seem to care one bit. Maybe she was drunk too? I signed a slew of paperwork illegibly to get the process started. When the tattoo artist finally asked me what I wanted and where, I garbled back, "Got any recommendations?"

This was met with a strange look, although not a refusal of services, so the show still went on.

"Hey, I know!" April shouted, since it was often difficult to control the volume of your voice when you had been drinking, "You should totally get a black widow spider, like on your hip or something, because that's what we were just talking about!" She looked as triumphant as if she had just won a spelling bee.

"You're one hundred per cent right. That's what I would like, please," I said as I closed my eyes and settled back in the chair, waiting for the tattoo artist to begin. I thought maybe I could take a quick nap and sober up, but that shit was more painful than laser hair removal!

I still didn't understand why they wouldn't let you get a tattoo when you'd been drinking. That needle would kill a buzz in a few seconds flat.

I wrapped up our field trip by paying the hefty two hundred dollars for the tattoo and hailing a cab so that we could get back home in one piece before all of the cabs were taken at bar-close. April flopped face down on my couch the moment I opened the door, even though I had to move her around a bit to make sure she hadn't crushed Madam in her wake. Luckily, Madam was curled up in a little ball next to my pillow on my bed, where I immediately joined her and passed out.

CHAPTER 3

I always felt suspicious of anyone who claimed they slept well after a night of heavy drinking. I normally found myself up all night using the bathroom, drinking water, and trying to keep my vomit down. And today was no exception.

I woke up bright and early at seven a.m. and started cooking a few eggs to make breakfast tacos for April and myself. Geez, my side was really hurting, and I wasn't sure why. I tried to reflect on the evening we had last night. I remembered a semi-dramatic fight at Mynt with a little bit of shoving, so maybe someone had knocked into me and elbowed me in the ribs?

I rubbed my right side absentmindedly, and the pain got even worse. What the hell? As I lifted my tank top to inspect my possible injury, I saw a full, four-inch tattoo of a large black spider making its way up from my right hip toward my ribs. I was so shocked I almost dropped the spatula. I raced the few feet into the living room and shook April awake. Apparently, she was one of those people who could pass out and have a wonderful night of sleep after insane drinking—but I didn't have time for jealousy right now.

"Oh my God, April! April! This is serious!"

"What? Give me a few minutes, okay?" She wouldn't even give me the respect of opening up her eyes to acknowledge my crisis.

"April, I must have gotten totally crazy last night because I have a huge spider tattooed on my ribs! What happened? Do you remember? I have no idea why I would do that!"

April obviously didn't feel alert enough to open her eyes, even for this important topic of conversation. "Yes, we were at Purple Martini, and you insisted you needed a black widow spider tattoo to make you feel better about the whole Adam situation. So we went to Celebrity Tattoo on Market, and you got one." She buried her face back underneath the pillow.

"April!" I hissed and tried to pry the pillow off her face. "This is *not* okay! Why wouldn't you stop me? What kind of friend are you? Seriously!" The blame game was unfortunately my go-to move whenever someone wouldn't respond to me when I was upset. I used it all the time with Adam, and it drove him crazy. April, however, was much more resilient. She simply ignored me and tried to go back to sleep.

I went back to cooking breakfast, but I was in a complete state of shock. All I could think about was tattoo cover-up options and tattoo removal, which I had heard was even more excruciatingly painful than the initial tattoo itself.

I was *so* screwed!

Of course, April felt coherent enough to eat the breakfast tacos I made for her, but she insisted the entire debacle was not her fault.

"I never told you to drink, like, ten martinis and ten more mojitos when we went out, did I? You just need to deal with the problems you're having," she said, smiling sweetly. "And stop trying to take it out on other people."

As much as I didn't want to admit it, she was right. Stuffing down all my emotions over the horrible news about Adam was getting me nowhere. Except perhaps into mountains of debt for all of the tattoo removal I would have to pay for. I mean, *really*. I'd heard of people getting drunken tattoos before, but who ever got one four inches in diameter? *Of a spider?* I was thinking of calling up that tattoo artist to give her a piece of my mind, but then I remembered I broke the rules anyway by being utterly wasted when I was there. My arguments would probably fall on deaf ears.

I spent the remainder of the morning on a diet that consisted mainly of vitamin water and ramen. It felt more like a throwback of my college days, and I wasn't sure exactly why I was in this place again at the age of twenty-nine. Luckily, it was a Saturday, so I had the entire day to regain my composure. When I just couldn't take one more *Real Housewives of Beverly Hills* episode, I decided to aimlessly surf the Internet.

Of course, I started out innocently on Facebook. But there was really nothing interesting there, apart from a few posts from college girlfriends bragging about their babies cutting their first tooth, rolling over, waving, etc.

What had life come to?

When Facebook got boring, I decided to move on to my usual Internet regime of checking out makeup websites, perusing a few beauty blogs, and finally catching up on shameless tabloids on People.com.

I had to admit I was more than tempted to Google the elusive Cherry James, who was most likely five-nine and one hundred-twenty pounds with huge, faketastic boobs. Or at least that was how I pictured her. It was then I had a brilliant idea I wasn't exactly sure I was ready to execute. Maybe, just maybe, it would be a good idea for *me* to join an online dating website like April had.

I was sure there were more than enough fish in the sea on eHarmony for both of us, and I didn't really have to fall in love or meet the man of my dreams or anything like that—since I probably wasn't going to anyway. It would just be something fun to take my mind off of this strange situation that was torturing me every night before I went to sleep. At the very least, I could probably find a semi-good looking guy to take me out to dinner a few times or even go to a work function with.

The more I thought about it, the more it seemed like an utterly fantastic idea. Suddenly, it was urgent I join eHarmony right away. I mean, all of those dates were out there waiting for me. So I'd better set up an excellent profile to make sure they could find me, take me out, and make my life a little bit better ASAP.

I typed eHarmony into my browser with fingers shaking from adrenaline and excitement and started out by registering on the website. This led me to a lengthy survey with hundreds of questions, which seemed like a daunting task in itself. The first few questions were easy, like my gender, birthday, education, and...marital status. I wasn't sure about posting the whole widow thing online since it made me think of an old woman with a Cruella DeVille inspired white streak in her hair. I went ahead and checked the single status since it was partially true.

I sailed through the rest of the questions like an expert test taker, listing my personal beliefs, personality traits, and even a self-description that basically told the world that I was a total catch without saying so in such plain words. I tried the tactic so many people use on job interviews when you're asked the sticky question of listing your top three weaknesses, which I was always trained to list as my strengths in disguise. How tricky...

'Oh, my weaknesses? I guess you could say my weaknesses are that I often overwork myself, I thrive on competition, and will do whatever it takes to complete a project, and I'm a perfectionist.'

Any interviewer who tried to get past my rock solid answer was always met with more strengths disguised as weaknesses to coerce them into giving me a job. All I could say was it had worked so far since I was still gainfully employed. This was the same stealthy approach I used with eHarmony, making sure I put my best foot forward by describing myself as "intelligent, funny, compassionate, and a lover of animals."

I thought saying I loved dogs was a little too hokey, but I wanted any potential date out there to see I was strong and edgy with a bit of a soft side. I concluded the profile creation process by awkwardly uploading a photo of myself and Adam, whom I had obviously cut off the side of the picture. Unfortunately, there just weren't many single pictures of me since I had been holed up in my house since his death. A happy picture of the two of us on vacation with Adam cropped out would have to do.

I didn't really know why I was putting so much thought into this profile anyway. It wasn't even a big deal. I just wanted to meet guys that could be friends or casual dates since I definitely wasn't looking for anything serious. Plus, if anyone was really strange, I could set up an emergency call from April to get me out of the date or even pull the widow card to send them running.

After I created an extensive profile to represent my sexy, single, and friendly self—or at least I hoped—I took the next step in the process by reviewing the first five matches automatically sent to me. I liked the fact the website sent a few suggestions my way, making it pretty easy for me to sit back, relax, and reject a few possible suitors each day. The first match I opened seemed about average, but he reminded me too much of my high school math teacher. He had large glasses that were clearly dated, strange feathery hair from the seventies, and a shirt buttoned to the top button. Nope. *Next!*

The next few matches really didn't do anything for me or even seem like people I would want to meet out in public. Since this happened to be the criteria for going on a date, I rejected them too. The last match, however, caught me off guard because he seemed totally normal and attractive. This made me pretty suspicious. I could only assume it was a fake picture or a picture taken ten years ago. But this Jake Altman seemed like he could possibly be a great choice for my very first online date. His interests were music, camping, and food, which were all pretty much synonymous with Colorado. I was comforted by the fact he hadn't listed ritualistic sacrifices or kidnapping children. That fact alone was good enough for me, so I decided to bite the bullet and send him a message.

I was at a bit of a loss about what to say since I hadn't flirted via e-mail or even text with a stranger in more than five years. Of course, Adam and I would send the occasional loving text or e-mail with a cute little note about meeting for dinner or drinks later in the evening, but I was clearly out of practice.

Hey Jake, I began typing. No, scratch that—too overly casual and awkward.

Dear Jake, Again, I quickly deleted what I just typed since that was the way I normally started e-mails to my grandmother. Dammit. I decided to start out simple just so I could get this e-mail out of the way. There was absolutely nothing to be nervous about. Especially since it didn't even matter if he wrote me back because it was only for the purpose of a casual meeting and nothing more.

Jake—much better.
I just wanted to drop you a note
to find out a little more about you

since your profile seemed pretty in-
teresting. I also love camping, but
who doesn't in Colorado? :-) Any-
how, feel free to message me back if
you would like to talk more.
    Danielle

I sat back with a sense of satisfaction as I
sent off the e-mail. A few brief lines making an
introduction were all I needed to see if this
Jake character was a psycho or not. I made a
mental note to ask April for some eHarmony
tips when she started work on Monday, which
brought me to another vexing train of thought
altogether.

I couldn't believe April was starting work
as my assistant in just a few days. I definitely
had some serious preparation to do to get her
trained properly for the job. I decided to spend
the rest of the weekend recuperating from my
way-too-fun-night-out on Friday and compiled
a hefty folder of documents related to all our
management systems at *High Life*.

By the time Sunday evening rolled around,
I felt confident I had created a packet fit to
train any new assistant, April included. As a
reward for my grueling efforts, I took a few
hours off to watch yet another episode of

Bethany Ramos

Bridalplasty, a reality show where engaged women competed for plastic surgeries to ultimately win their dream wedding. Yes, this show disturbed me to the very core. But it was also pretty fun to see grown women cry when they didn't win a syringe that guaranteed them entrance into the injectables party. *Boo-hoo.*

CHAPTER 4

Since I had rested so thoroughly over the weekend, I woke up completely alert fifteen minutes before my alarm went off on Monday morning. That was unusual for me, but it was an overall exciting day since my longtime best friend was finally starting work as my new assistant.

I still had quite a few doubts about how well we would work together. April had a much stronger personality than I did, and I was supposed to be her boss. I quickly swept those thoughts under the rug and tried to remain excited about this new opportunity. Besides, it would do me good to have one more person in my corner at work when it came to the drama circulating at *High Life*.

I arrived at work twenty minutes early as opposed to my usual five and set out organizing the assistant's desk in front of my office to get it ready for April. My previous assistant apparently had quite a bit of crap stored up—old candy wrappers, crumpled issues of *People* magazine, and even a few suspicious looking tissues I picked up with a pair of disposable gloves I found in the supply closet.

By the time I finished my major cleaning overhaul, April was still nowhere to be found. It was seven-fifty-eight a.m. I had hoped she would be at least ten minutes early on her big first day in my office.

I sent her a few questioning texts saying, "Where the hell are you?" but received no immediate response.

I was starting to panic as the clock reached eight-oh-five a.m. I didn't want my boss to see my new assistant, who was also my best friend, was late. Just as I was about to freak out and start stalker-calling April's phone in the hopes she had at least gotten into a minor accident as a legitimate excuse for her tardiness, she breezed in the door with two coffees and a bag of muffins from Starbucks.

"Hey, girl! Happy first day of work! I decided to treat the both of us to coffee and a little bit of breakfast, but it took longer than I thought."

Well, how could you be mad at someone with a reason like that? Still, this couldn't become an everyday habit.

"Thanks! That was really sweet of you," I said. "Since you're already a little late for your first day, why don't you get settled at your desk, and I'll show you how to use the phone and computer systems. I also made up an introduction packet with all of the training materials for you to look over this morning while I catch up on some of my work."

As April got settled into her newly cleaned desk, I went back into my office and logged onto my computer to see what e-mails awaited me. There were the usual e-mails from beauty reps and skin care companies hoping I would feature their products. These I normally deleted since the vast majority of the products out there were copycats of the better selling products anyway. If I had to review one more green tea lip balm with an SPF of thirty, I'd scream.

As I scrolled through my e-mails, that also included a few forwarded messages from my home address, I saw a delightful e-mail title showing I had a response on my eHarmony profile. I'd almost forgotten about that. I hadn't even told April yet! I would save that juicy story for a lunchtime chat since I wanted to make sure she stayed focused on work while she was on the clock.

I opened up the e-mail immediately, even ignoring an e-mail from my boss that was probably about an upcoming meeting scheduled for later in the week to discuss the beauty product lineup for the next four months of the magazine. I sucked in a breath. The e-mail was definitely a response to the message I'd sent Jake on Saturday. *Don't get too excited, don't get too excited, don't get too excited*, I told myself over and over again.

In case you couldn't tell, I had a problem with getting overly excited. This generally ended up in a letdown since what I imagined was normally far more exciting than the actual reality of a situation.

> *Hey Danielle,*
> *Good to hear from you, and I think you have an interesting pro-file too! It was very flattering to get a nice message from such a beauti-ful girl as you, and if you're inter-ested, it would be great if we could meet for coffee sometime. It's prob-ably way too early in our commu-nication to go camping, but I'll*

keep in mind that you love camping too. :-) I hope you have a great week, and I will talk to you soon.
Jake

Hmm, looked like he went with "Hey" after all. I'd have to remember that for next time. I didn't want to admit it to myself, but I was truly excited about this message. It was strange to revisit those fluttery feelings of anticipation over meeting someone for the first time. Still, I had a bit more pep in my step as I went through the rest of the day. At least I had enough sense to remember the common dating rule of not replying right away to avoid seeming desperate. I gave it one full day before I sent Jake an e-mail response.

Hey Jake,
I agree that camping wouldn't be the best first date, but I'd also love to meet you sometime for coffee. I'm free this weekend if you're interested, and I look forward to talking with you soon. ☺
Danielle

It wasn't more than an hour before I received an e-mail back from Jake confirming he would love to meet me Saturday at eleven a.m. at the downtown Starbucks. I quickly agreed since it was relatively close to my house—but not close enough he could figure out where I lived, stalk me, and kill me. It also seemed like the ideal public place to avoid any type of scene, should the date take a bad turn.

Since Saturday was still a good three days away, I tried to bury myself in work for the rest of the week and hoped April would fit in as well as I wanted her to. I said a few prayers she would immediately become the perfect assistant, even my boss would love, so I wouldn't look like an absolute fool for recommending her.

On top of that, if things went sour at work, I could only imagine things would get quite awkward in our friendship. This was something I truly wanted to avoid since I had very few close friends in my life after Adam's death. Even though anyone and everyone extended their condolences to me for becoming a widow at such a young age, they still dropped off after a while when I continued to grieve and didn't get over it right away.

I think a lot of my girlfriends expected me to bounce back and want to hit the dating scene again, when all I wanted to do was to be alone for a while. Like, maybe the next ten years. As for all of our couple-friends, they meant well in comforting me and inviting me to dinner a few times, but it got pretty weird when I was the third, fifth, or even seventh wheel in our usual gatherings. Although I still got invites for drinks from couples Adam and I were friends with from time to time, I would normally just decline to spare them the awkward conversation. How kind of me.

This was yet another reason why I was so looking forward to this coffee date. It could potentially help me reenter the world like a normal person who didn't have a dead spouse. In fact, I was contemplating keeping this whole dead spouse thing under wraps, especially for my first coffee date. I didn't want to spoil my chances of fun flirting with a cute guy named Jake, now did I? Yes, that was definitely the best plan of action for my first real-live-online date.

This was the reasoning I used when I decided to play it cool as I mentioned my date to April at lunch the following day. We still went to lunch together, even though I was her superior. I figured it was the best way to keep an eye on her, catch up, and make sure she got back from her lunch break on time, since she seemed to have a hard time grasping the concept of punctuality thus far. Hopefully, that would be something that was ironed out as she got more familiar with her job.

We were both at the downtown Subway around the corner from our office, grabbing a quick lunch, when I casually mentioned, "I have a coffee date this Saturday. I actually joined eHarmony since it seemed like a good idea." I kept my eyes on my sandwich because I didn't necessarily want to see her response.

She screeched at the top of her lungs, causing a few people in the ordering line to look back at us in alarm. "No way! No *way*! That is so fantastic, and it seems so unlike you. What got into you?"

"Well, after all, I was online researching laser tattoo removal." I was still trying to lay on the guilt for April allowing me to drunkenly get that horrific tattoo. "I saw an ad for eHarmony, and I remembered you set up a date pretty easily, so I thought it would be something fun to try out to get my mind off of all of this drama."

"Sooo...Who is he? What does he look like? Do you have any other dates lined up?"

I took a big bite of my sandwich and chewed thoughtfully. I simply loved to torture April with gossip. She refused to take her eyes off me until I swallowed my big bite of Italian Club and replied, "His name is Jake. He's average height. He has shaggy brown hair, brown eyes, and he loves camping. We're going to Starbucks around the block this Saturday at eleven, so you have to text me during the date to see if I need you to come up with a potential emergency."

When April looked at me skeptically, I added, "No, really, you have to. This is my first date with a human in, like, five years, and if he's a total freak, I don't think I can handle it. Just text me at like eleven-fifteen, and then if I hate him, I can say my assistant called me in to work on an emergency because the system crashed. It's perfect!" I smiled proudly.

She reluctantly agreed to be my get-out-of-jail-free card. Then we promptly steered the conversation on to bigger and better things, like what I was going to wear on this upcoming coffee date. It was definitely a faux pas to wear something overly fancy or very short shorts if you happened to be a man, as April experienced on her previous coffee date.

I decided to take her advice and wear a short fluffy skirt with a tucked-in top, a long necklace, and gladiator sandals. It was the perfect boho chic ensemble any reader of *High Life* would wear. It looked put-together enough to show I made an effort yet not like I tried too hard for this first casual date.

With that out of the way, all I had to do was worry about the actual date until it arrived, coupled with weird dreams of me meeting a man for coffee who didn't have a head, but I didn't want to tell him because it seemed rude. I was going to have to cut back on the melatonin supplements if I kept having such acid-trippy dreams.

⌘⌘⌘

Saturday morning came much more rapidly than I thought it would—as is always the case when you're nervously looking forward to something. During the week, it had seemed like time stood still as I anticipated the date. But the next thing I knew, it was Saturday morning, and I didn't feel prepared at all. My biggest worry was what we were going to talk about. I absolutely hated dead air. Really, I mean that. I *hated* awkward silences to the point of a fault, causing me to talk nervously about the most inane subjects, like a funny trip to the dentist I had a few weeks ago, which really wasn't funny at all.

I actually had an arsenal of funny anecdotes up my sleeve to use in situations peppered with numerous awkward silences. Adam used to call me out on this when we would go to visit his parents. They were a perfectly nice people, but they weren't really into television, Internet, radio, or much of anything. So we would catch up too quickly and end up sitting for hours on end, with the dreaded awkward silence epidemic. In those visits, I was like a long tailed cat in a room full of rocking chairs—there I go again with the figures of speech—spouting off random story after random story simply because I didn't want to sit there in a silence. I feared the same fate for my coffee date. If there were any lulls in the conversation at all, I just knew I'd end up talking about that time I wet my pants at a reggae festival when I was fifteen. Ugh.

I was ready for my date a full fifteen minutes early, wearing the pre-planned outfit with perfectly applied natural makeup and my hair air-dried so each wave looked individually fluffy and effortless. Or at least that's what I hoped.

My hair was actually the asset I was most proud of. It was uncompromisingly wavy, medium milk-chocolate in color, and had natural highlights in the summertime. Seriously, I always had the girls in the beauty department asking me where I got my highlights done and what type of extensions I was wearing—then I had the opportunity to smugly answer, "It's natural."

Wasn't that the most infuriating answer anyone could give you? My hair was literally my only feature where I could blithely retort, "It's natural."

I slathered my lips with lip venom every morning so they puffed up like a blowfish on my morning commute and finally settled back down by the time I got to my office at eight a.m. sharp. Then they looked pretty luscious and "bee-stung" until roughly eleven a.m., when I then had to reapply said lip venom at lunch, struggle with my blowfish lips while I ate a low-calorie salad, and then hope the size of my lips returned to normal by the time I headed back to my office once my lunch break was over. A pretty elaborate plan, yes, but so far I had been given the compliment of having women ask whether or not I had Restylane injections done. I must have been doing something right.

Eyes? For the first few months in my position as the beauty editor of High Life, I went to the elaborate length of applying all-natural, real human hair, individual false eyelashes every single morning before I left the house. Adam used to laugh at me because I would spend thirty to forty minutes on this task alone every day before work, propping up one elbow with the other hand so my arm didn't shake violently as I attempted to attach each individual "natural" eyelash to my own. Of course, post-Adam I decided to give up this ridiculous ritual. Now I normally slapped on a strip of false eyelashes somewhere between Sixth and Fourteenth as I headed north on Downing to my office in downtown Denver. While you might envy me because my commute was much shorter and avoided the dreaded six a.m. to nine a.m. morning rush-hour gridlock of I-25, I assure you that downtown traffic was bad enough. Let's just say that I had enough time to do my own makeup, eyelashes, hair, and even change clothes if I wanted to.

Seeing as I was a beauty editor, it was a given that I had pretty great skin. I got quite a few freebies from the local spas in downtown Denver, starting with The Brown Palace Hotel, which happened to be blocks away from my office. I had my share of facials, microdermabrasions, chemical peels, and IPL treatments "on the house"—just another perk of being a beauty editor—in the hopes I would somehow make a mention of one of these fabulous spa treatments as a "must have" for the beautiful, career-driven, mountain woman living in the greater Colorado area.

My body wasn't fantastic, but it wasn't bad either. I'd like to think I had great legs since I got a thrill out of trail running and hiking—this *was* Colorado, after all. Cliché, I know. Still, my midsection could do with a few sit-ups, although it often had the advantage of being hidden under layers of warm clothing in the colder weather. And I did have the added bonus of the whole after-death weight loss thing that cut a good ten pounds off my weight since I couldn't eat, due to devastation. Quite an advantage that was rarely associated with death.

After this complete head-to-toe assessment of myself, I felt only moderately satisfied, but at least Jake probably wouldn't be embarrassed to be seen having coffee with me.

I tried to kill time before leaving for my coffee date by applying and reapplying different colors of lipstick, eventually settling on a sheer peach shade that made my skin look flushed and healthy. These were all minor details I doubted any man would notice, but they were also the perfect girly ritual to put my nerves at ease. If I could obsess for fifteen minutes over my lip color, that was fifteen less minutes to think about the possible disaster of this impending date.

I jumped into my Honda Fit at ten minutes 'til eleven, giving me just enough time to shoot downtown, grab parking, and hopefully arrive at the rendezvous roughly five minutes late so I looked cool and casual. That was the way I had played the dating game five years ago, and I prayed those rules were still in effect.

By the time I parked and walked to Starbucks, it was eleven-oh-five on the nose. Thanks to my elaborate pre-planning, I felt pretty optimistic. I peered into the window to see the profile of a man with familiar shaggy brown hair and the bright green shirt he said he would be wearing. Since he was alone, I could only assume it was the legendary Jake, although I had yet to see his face.

I opened the door to Starbucks. Jake looked right at me when he heard the bell on the door jingle. He apparently recognized me, too, and gave a small wave as I made my way over to his table. He greeted me with a hug and offered to order me a coffee, which I gladly accepted.

I normally drank my coffee black and told him so. This served as a fun conversation starter that killed just a few moments of our time before the initial meet and greet questions of the first date began. Jake, surprisingly, looked very similar to his eHarmony profile picture, which was a relief to say the least. I had heard so many horror stories, including April's, of people using fake or outdated profile pictures. Essentially false advertising when it came to the face-to-face meeting. Jake was quite attractive, medium height, tousled brown hair, brown eyes, and also appeared to be pretty muscular—but not in a creepy *Jersey Shore* kind of way. From physical appearance alone, he was definitely my type.

Oddly enough, he looked quite a bit like Adam—a thought I pushed out of my mind immediately. "So, Jake, do you live in this area?"

He smiled a gleaming, white smile. "Actually, I live farther north in Broomfield, but I'm pretty close to I-25 and always love coming downtown to hang out," he added endearingly. "Broomfield is a great location since it's close to the mountains, and I already told you I'm a big camper and nature lover."

We continued on with amiable conversation touching upon where he worked—an animal shelter, awww—his last long-term relationship—one year ago, they grew apart—and whether or not he was close to his family. He was.

It was on this last topic of conversation I noticed a slight change in the charming Jake. As I started to ask him more about his family, such as how many brothers and sisters he had, where his parents lived, and how often he saw them, he mentioned he and his kids would normally go see his parents every weekend if they got the chance.

This caused my ears to perk up immediately. "Kids? How many kids do you have?"

Jake appeared to be flushing, although it was hard to tell since he was quite bronzed from what appeared to be a spray tan. He immediately backtracked. "Oh, sorry, that came out weird. I actually meant my brother's kids, but we're so close I usually just call them the kids. All of us will go visit my parents in Colorado Springs as often as we can."

"So you don't have any children of your own?" I looked at him with a piercing, CSI-style gaze I hoped would make him tell the truth.

He laughed nervously. "Not yet, anyway. That's definitely something I'm interested in for the future, but I haven't been fortunate enough to have kids of my own yet."

We steered the conversation on to more neutral subjects, like movies, sports, and travel. But I couldn't get that weird Freudian slip out of my mind. I decided to ask Jake a few more questions about his personal life to see what I could dig up.

"So have you lived in Broomfield for long?"

He smiled dazzlingly. "It's coming up on about four years now."

"Do you have an apartment up there? I actually used to live in that area right after college, so I'm pretty familiar."

"I have a house. I got a good deal on it since it's in the suburbs, you know how it is." I could have sworn he winked at me.

"How many bedrooms is it?" I sounded like a real estate agent, I knew. But I didn't care. I was going to get to the bottom of this if it killed me.

Jake laughed adorably again. "You sound like you love real estate. Well, it's three bedrooms, but we actually have four if you count the office."

"There! You said it!"

I pointed at him like a madwoman. He looked completely taken aback.

"What are you talking about?"

"When I asked you about your house, you said 'we.' Just tell me. Are you married?"

Jake tried to play off the situation by smiling and laughing again, which was starting to become more annoying and less adorable by the minute. "No, no, you've got me all wrong. I said 'we' because I have two beautiful Labradors I consider to be my family. What's with all the interrogation?"

By that point, I had had enough. I didn't know what it was, but I just couldn't tolerate this guy lying to me about his potential wife and children. When I thought about the fact that was probably what Adam had said to "Cherry," a white-hot rage started bubbling up inside of me. I didn't think I had ever felt this angry. Including the time my sister totaled my car in high school when she took it out without telling me. My hands started shaking, my throat felt dry, and my chest hurt.

"You are a douchebag," I rasped.

Jake recoiled as if I'd hit him. "Seriously, what are you talking about? I'm really not married." He shook his head. "You're kind of freaking me out."

"Fuck you, Jake. If you can't tell me the truth, there's really no point in us seeing each other again. I just hope you have the decency to treat your next date with a little more re-spect by telling her you're a cheating piece of shit before you buy her coffee."

I'd always wanted to throw my drink dra-matically in someone's face, but I also felt a little guilty about ruining Jake's nice, green J. Crew shirt with a quarter-full cup of coffee. Instead, I slapped my partially full coffee cup onto the ground, watching it roll underneath a nearby table, dribbling a long trail of coffee in the process. Then I grabbed my bag and marched out with what little dignity I had left.

As soon as I rounded the corner from Starbucks, I broke into a little jog to compensate for some of the adrenaline surging through me. I had to get out of there as quickly as possible. I was also worried about Jake following me and telling me off for humiliating him in public. What had gotten into me? All I knew was this anger was serious. Even though I was ninety-nine per cent sure Jake was a cheating ass, I suspected my rage wasn't entirely directed at him.

At that moment, my phone buzzed with the "emergency" text from April to get me out of my possible bad date. She didn't know the half of it.

STAGE 2: ANGER

CHAPTER 5

I finally managed to cool down as I took the long drive up to my sister's house in Thornton, about twenty miles north of downtown Denver. I texted her I was going to drop by since I knew she and her picturesque family would be doing something adorable on a sunny Saturday, like swimming in their backyard pool.

Didn't it just make you sick?

When I pulled into Lacey's long driveway in suburban Thornton, it was no shock to see her five-year-old son Jackson running through the sprinkler in the front yard with two neighborhood children about the same age. It would have been an absolutely beautiful portrait of childhood in the summertime—if I was in the mood for that shit, which I clearly wasn't.

I walked into Lacey's large suburban home without knocking. I found her cutting up a fruit salad in the kitchen. Again, sickeningly adorable for a happy family on a Saturday morning. As soon as Lacey took one look at me, she knew something was terribly wrong. That was both the blessing and the curse of the bond between sisters.

"What happened?" she said in a patronizing voice as she continued cutting fruit without even pausing to give me a hug.

"Hey, I'm not five. I don't need your sympathy. Besides, it's not even a big deal. I just had a crappy date, that's all."

That got her attention immediately. She stopped cutting strawberries with her knife dramatically suspended in midair. I stealthily grabbed a few of the freshly chopped strawberries from the cutting board and popped them into my mouth without even a reaction from her. "You really shouldn't hold your knife up like that. I think you're supposed to keep it pointed down at all times."

"Shut up, Danielle. What are you saying? Did you finally go out on a date? With who? How did you meet him? This is a really big deal. I can't believe you didn't tell me!"

"Yeah, yeah, yeah, not much to tell. April inspired me to sign up for eHarmony, and I met this guy that seemed kind of nice. Too bad he turned out to be a total tool that cheats on his wife. That seems to be going around a lot lately," I muttered.

Lacey was like a dog with a bone that just wouldn't give up. She wanted to hear every sordid detail of my almost nonexistent coffee date with Jake. And when I got to the part about me accusing him of being married, she was actually on his side, if you could believe that!

"I can't believe you would stick up for a total stranger who is also a cheating pervert!"

"All I'm saying is you have to give him the benefit of the doubt. What if he really was talking about his dogs when he said 'we'? It does seem suspicious, but you've never been the crazy jealous type. What made you jump to that conclusion? Too many *Lifetime* movies?" she asked with a smirk.

"Ha ha, that's absolutely hilarious," I deadpanned. I really couldn't think of anything else to say. So I decided to do the mature thing and talk about the subject of cheating in vague terms as if it had nothing to do with me whatsoever.

"Don't you just think more people cheat than they're willing to admit? Like how do you know Bryan has been completely faithful to you? And what about you? Have you ever cheated on him?"

"Whoa, whoa, whoa. You need to chill out on this whole *Law and Order* act. Why are you accusing everyone you know of cheating all of the sudden?" She paused. "Wait! I knew something was up. Did you cheat on Adam when you were married? Are you having all of this guilt you can't bear to deal with after his passing?"

Damn, Lacey was a total sleuth. This was a quality that normally came in handy when we wanted to find out secrets our parents were hiding from us, like Christmas presents, etc., except she had my dilemma totally backward this time.

"No, that's not what's happening at all. Let's just say I found out about a little situation where someone I trusted wasn't so trustworthy."

Even though I tried to keep my vague act going regarding the subject of cheating, Lacey finally forced me into spilling the beans by nearly threatening me at knifepoint. Or at least that was what she insinuated. The truth was I really did want to share this problem with my sister. Her comfort was invaluable. But I was so angry and bitter, not to mention ashamed, I just wanted to be coerced a little before I dropped the cheating bomb on anyone.

After I told Lacey about the shocking, surprise phone call I received, I added, "Besides, what kind of name is Cherry? That's just so slutty, and I can't believe Adam would pick up a stripper and take her on *vacation*."

"Hey! My name sounds a lot like a stripper name, so you never know. Maybe she's someone he worked with, and she's really straight-laced and professional with a poorly chosen a name?"

"Seriously, if you don't stop sticking up for everybody else, I'm just going to leave. This is total bullshit."

Lacey backtracked and started slinging a few insults of her own at Adam's mistress, calling her a gold-digger—although we were not wealthy in the least—a fat bitch—yet to be proven—and a cross-eyed fuckwit—my favorite insult by far—just to make me feel a little better about my plight.

After we exhausted that subject, Lacey added, "You know, you really need to Google her. Send her a Facebook message or something to tell her you know all about it. Why should she get off totally free just because Adam happened to die?"

I groaned. "That's the exact same thing April said, but I'm not all Google-addicted like you guys. I just don't know if that's a good idea. I don't see what it would solve since Adam isn't even around to yell at for what he's done."

Still, whether I wanted to admit it or not, the Google idea was sounding better and better. I was waking up in the middle of the night and obsessively thinking about what this alleged Cherry looked like. So far, she was a cross between Megan Fox and Reese Witherspoon, which seemed like a pretty weird combination, but I promise you it looked totally-smoking-hot in my head. And that was the problem. I really wanted to know what Adam's mistress looked like so I could at least lay her to rest, pun intended, and get over this whole destructive situation for good.

❧❧

When I finally tore myself away from Lacey's house several hours later, full of delicious fruit salad and several glasses of Pinot Grigio, I found myself in a terrible place. I was in my house—which was actually not terrible since it was comfortable and beautifully decorated—with nothing but time on my hands. I tried to occupy myself with my usual reality television marathon, but it seemed I had already seen all of the recent *Bridalplasty* and *Keeping Up with the Kardashians* episodes, if you could believe it. I kept staring longingly at my computer a few feet away in the dining area and promised myself I wouldn't become just another Google whore who creepily searched online for anyone and everyone I had ever known in my life.

But Cherry wasn't just anyone, was she? That question continued to play in my mind throughout several *Grey's Anatomy* reruns on *Lifetime*—still a solid choice—until I finally justified beyond a shadow of a doubt I owed it to myself to look up this bitch's face and find out what she was all about. If she really did look like a Reese Witherspoon/Megan Fox hybrid, I was definitely going to kill myself. But if she didn't, then maybe I could laugh at her ugly hair, big lips, fat ass, etc. I would take comfort where I could get it.

I logged in to my computer in a few seconds flat. All of a sudden, the white, vast, blank page of Google sat before me. It felt to me like a large plane of opportunity just waiting for me to discover the truth about my past.

Okay, so I laid the soap opera melodrama on a bit thick, but I was feeling pretty inspired at that moment.

I tentatively typed "Cherry James" into Google. Within a second, her Facebook page popped up as the top search result. Who knew this would be so easy? God bless Google. I clicked on the link to Cherry's Facebook page, but her profile was set on private, and her picture was of her dark silhouette from the back, looking out onto a beach at sunset. Shit, shit, shit. I couldn't tell if Cherry's shadow had any Reese Witherspoon or Megan Fox type qualities. I had clearly hit a dead end. Unless I wanted to impersonate one of her friends and trick her into friending me so I could see all of her profile pictures.

Since I wasn't really computer savvy enough to steal an identity, I decided to leave my stalker idea for Plan B as something I could potentially discuss with April later if I was bored, drunk, desperate, or all of the above. Believe it or not, the likelihood of the combination of those three happening was a huge possibility these days.

Not one to be put off by a closed door, I continued to check out the rest of the Cherry James search results on good old Google. The second listing was for an oral surgeon named James Cherry, who seemed quite respectable. But I doubted Adam had booked a lovely dream vacation with this man. So I kept on looking. The next result was an obituary for Cherry James listed in *The New York Times*. Unfortunately, this Cherry was sixty-six years old, and I didn't think Adam had an affinity for senior citizens either. Two strikes.

I continued to scan the results, which seemed to have multiple listings for this James Cherry dentist fellow—reminding me I needed to get my teeth cleaned—until I finally found a LinkedIn profile for Cherry James halfway down the page. Bingo! I'd actually never said "Bingo!" as a form of celebration before, but I really loved the game, and it just seemed right.

Cherry's LinkedIn profile only had a tiny, grainy avatar picture of her. It was still difficult to see if she had any celebrity-like features. She appeared to be a petite blonde with her hair pulled back in a bun, wearing business attire. Her profile also said she worked as a graphic designer at a company in Boulder, which made me think Adam could have met her through his job since they both worked in the same field.

Shit. I'd always felt like Adam and I had absolutely nothing in common when it came to our careers. The Internet was almost Greek to me, other than trolling around on Facebook and now Google, and Adam wouldn't have known a good makeup primer if it hit him in the face. I didn't think having similar career interests had anything to do with a healthy marriage. Yet I always worried Adam would meet some hottie web designer/Internet marketer-type person and perhaps be impressed by her rather than me. And it turned out I was right, from what I could gather from this slut's LinkedIn profile.

I saved Cherry's profile as a bookmark and decided to do what was hopefully the mature thing—give myself some time to think about it before making any rash decisions. Of course, all I could do *was* think about it. Cherry's stupid profile kept me up half the night as I imagined over and over again how she and Adam had met, what they talked about, and how they probably shared stupid insider graphic design jokes I would never understand.

"And then she told me she actually wanted a JPG image instead of a GIF! Can you believe it? A JPG!"

Then they would laugh hysterically as Adam fed her grapes. Or at least, that was what I imagined as anger bubbled up into my chest and made my arms tingle so it became almost impossible to sleep. Luckily, I had adorable Madam to comfort me. Even though I had to sleep in a corpse-like position to avoid crushing her three pound body.

When I finally drifted off to sleep, I probably logged five hours total, when you took into account all of the tossing and turning I did. And I have to qualify that I am someone who absolutely needs her beauty sleep at eight hours minimum or else I am a bitchy, grumpy, ghastly looking mess.

When I woke up to my alarm a few hours later, that was exactly how I would have described myself. My hair was smashed flat against the side of my head, my eyes looked puffy and swollen, and my lips were chapped from anxiously biting them all night long. I managed to somehow arrive at work in one piece, fixing myself up in the car along the way. But as soon as April sauntered in to start her day ten minutes after eight—late as usual—she took one look at me, stepped into my office, shut the door, drew the blinds, and faced me with her arms crossed over her chest.

"April, you really need to start working since you're already a little late," I said weakly.

"No way. I know you're my boss and all, but you look like you've been run over by a truck, and I need to know what's going on with you. Does this have anything to do with how bad your date went over the weekend?"

I'd already brought April up to speed on the horrors of my possible cheater of a coffee date. She hastily agreed he was probably a true douchebag I was lucky to have exposed when I did.

"Um, well, not entirely...The date made me all crazy and angry since Jake seemed to be a total cheater like Adam, and when I got home, I couldn't help myself from looking up Cherry's profile on LinkedIn. So now I know where she works, and, of course, she's some fancy graphic designer and not a stripper, so she was probably really impressive and irresistible to Adam. That's why he cheated on me because all I do is promote beauty products and have no inner intelligence or depth."

April rolled her eyes. "Of course not! You know you're awesome, so I'm not even going to take the time to make your head any bigger. Adam was probably just like every single other guy out there who can't keep it in their pants. Who knows what his real motivation was? The whole point is we need to swing by Cherry's office and see what she's all about. I promise you I had to do the exact same thing with Roger's ex-wife because figuring out what the other woman looks like is all part of the game. You'll never get it out of your head and get over it if you don't check her out."

April's advice seemed wise enough to me. I quickly agreed with her, told her to clear my schedule for the afternoon, and shooed her out of my office to make sure she did some actual work before the day was over. I figured I would just pop up to Boulder and see if Cherry sauntered sluttily out of her office around her lunch hour. That way, I could check out what she looked like and get this whole damn thing over with. Of course, there really was no way to "pop up" to Boulder. It wasn't on the way to anywhere, unless you happened to be relocating to the mountains in the middle of nowhere.

Don't get me wrong, Boulder was a truly beautiful city that had a pretty sweet nightlife. But it was thirty to forty-five minutes away from downtown Denver on a good day. I actually felt a little disappointed I wasn't going to Boulder at night because Pearl Street had some of the craziest people you would ever want to see. I kid you not. I innocently stepped out of a sushi restaurant several years ago, only to see a busker who had a trained mouse on a saddle, riding a cat on a saddle, riding a dog. I was stunned to see such a sight, to say the least. But I didn't even have time to take a picture of the spectacle on my phone since so many people were crowded around the tower of animals, throwing money into the busker's hat. Definitely well-deserved for a street trick.

I finished up all of my work for the morning and told my boss I was taking a half day off for a last-minute dental appointment. She didn't seem to mind. Since I had been back at work as a single window, I had had my nose to the grindstone so much I hardly took any time off. Meaning I had an accumulation of personal days piled up. Hopefully, April could hold down the fort without embarrassing me while I was gone. I kept my fingers crossed.

It only took me thirty minutes to get up to Boulder, which was record time since I had apparently beaten the lunch rush-hour traffic. I located Noble Multimedia & Design, where Cherry worked, in a large business park off of Twenty-Eight and Arapahoe. Pulling my car into a front parking space, I surreptitiously slunk down into the seat and read a magazine. I was sure Cherry didn't know me from Adam—literally. What a morbidly accurate pun—but I wanted to look nonchalant so as to not draw her attention to me if she happened to be walking into her office from lunch.

I didn't have a lot to go on for my detective work. I was parked outside of my dead husband's mistress's office at twelve-fifty-five p.m., reading a magazine, and trying to look casual. I could only hope Cherry happened to be taking a standard lunch break from noon to one and would walk back into her office any moment now. I waited and waited and waited for what felt like a half hour, but was only ten minutes, until I finally saw a group of four women dressed in business-casual attire, laughing and walking into the front of the office. I actually had no clue what Cherry looked like. All I had seen on her LinkedIn profile was a tiny, gritty avatar of a woman with blonde hair. The only woman in the group who relatively fit that description was much plumper than I expected, and when she turned around all of the way, I saw she was pregnant.

Damn, damn, damn. If that did happen to be Cherry carrying my dead husband's baby, then this drama was way too much for me. I was going to have to sell our townhome and retire to Mexico much sooner than I anticipated. Still, the overall evidence was inconclusive. There was no reason for me to freak out about a random pregnant blonde I happened to see in front of an office in Boulder. I sat outside for another good half-hour, catching up on my beauty reading in *Vogue* until I was so bored I couldn't stand it. I would obviously never last as a professional detective. Sitting still for even a half-hour was not my cup of tea.

Drumming my fingers nervously on the steering wheel, I tried to decide what to do. Option A, I could drive away and pretend this whole thing never happened—except April would question me incessantly about whether or not I saw the mistress.

Option B, I could wait until five p.m. when Ms. James would probably be leaving her office. But the main problem with that was I still wasn't sure what she looked like. Cherry may have been the pregnant woman I just saw for all I knew. I wouldn't know how to place her if I saw her live in the flesh.

Option C, I could march into Cherry's office and ask for an appointment with her so there would be no doubt about who she was or what she looked like. Option C seemed like the best choice by far. I got to take action and didn't have to throw up the white flag or even sit in an office parking lot for the rest of my afternoon off.

Option C, it was!

I walked, with what I only hoped was a confident strut, through the glass doors of Noble Multimedia & Design, and marched straight up to the receptionist desk where a petite brunette wearing a name tag that read "Melissa" sat texting on her iPhone.

"Excuse me?"

Melissa looked up at me in surprise. She was apparently engrossed in whatever she was texting or whichever version of Angry Birds she was playing on her phone. "Sorry!" She giggled. "What can I do for you? Did you have an appointment today?"

"Actually, no, but I would like to make one. Is there a Cherry James available I could speak to about graphic design for my company's website?" Good thing I worked for a legitimate and reputable magazine if I were to be questioned any further.

Cute and perky Melissa giggled again and said, "Sorry, she's really, really busy today, and she's in with a client at the moment. Can I book you an appointment for later in the week?"

Hell, no, you can't. "No, thank you. I have some time this afternoon, so I think I'll just wait here until Ms. James is available." I turned on my heel to take a seat in the empty waiting room when Melissa called after me.

"Ma'am? I really don't think it's a good idea to wait today. Ms. James is with our corporate clients, and it doesn't look like she'll be free until her workday is over." She smiled sweetly.

I walked back to her desk leaned into her as closely as I could without spilling the candy dish that sat resting atop her desk, and lowered my voice in what I hoped was a firm and assertive tone—since I'd always heard you need to ask for exactly what you want in order to get your way, whether it was free shipping, an airline upgrade, meeting your husband's mistress...You get the idea.

"Melissa, I don't think you understand what I'm trying to tell you. It's important I see Ms. James about this graphic design project, and I'm not leaving today until I do. Now either you muster up some type of competence and let her know I'm here, or I'll sit in the waiting room for the rest of the afternoon and make your life a living hell."

All of my threats were entirely empty. I didn't even know what I meant by making Melissa's life a living hell, but I thought it would at least light a fire under her ass to see if she would get an appointment for me. I must have underestimated this perky Melissa because she narrowed her eyes right back at me and said, "Look, ma'am. I tried to put this as politely as I could, but you're not getting an appointment with Ms. James today. And because of your attitude and hostility, I suggest you leave immediately before I alert security."

Whoa, I must have laid on my assertiveness a little too thick. I had never had anyone threaten to call security on me in my entire life. I also didn't know how to close a conversation so loaded with threats. I smiled weakly at Melissa and speedily walked out of the large, glass offices of Noble Design & Multimedia before I could find out whether or not Melissa was as tough as she sounded.

CHAPTER 6

On the long drive back to my office, I was deeply shaken by what had just gone down. I had really hoped this whole stalking-my-dead-husband's-mistress-plan would be quick and painless, but, of course, that was wishful thinking on my part. I would have preferred to go directly into Cherry's office under the pretense of this false meeting, get a good look at her, talk to her a bit, maybe confront her, and then close the book on this painful chapter in my life.

But who was I kidding? Really? In a way, I was relieved Cherry wasn't available to take my fake appointment since I had no idea what I was even going to say to her. Knowing me, I would probably go through with the entire bogus meeting, never confronting her, simply because I was intimidated to make such a bold move. I figured I would have to powwow this with April when I got back to my office to see if she had any sage advice on how to handle the matter. Actually, I would take any advice I could get at this point, sage or not. I didn't think I would be allowed to set foot in the doors of Noble Design & Multimedia again, so making another appointment to see Cherry was out.

When I made it back to my office, April looked up in surprise that I had come back at all. I also noticed she quickly minimized a bunch of tabs on her computer. I could only assume she was on Facebook, MySpace, or shopping, all of which were strictly against company policy. No matter, since I didn't have the strength to reprimand my only friend at this point.

April followed me into my office and performed the same ritual of shutting the door, closing the blinds, crossing her arms over her chest, and standing in front of me, waiting for answers. When I let a few moments of silence pass as I looked back at her, she finally said, "So what did that bitch look like?"

"Well..." I stalled for time.

"Oh my God. You didn't even get to look at her, did you? Did you chicken out? Did you sit outside of her office for a few hours and then give up? I told you it was going to take a while to find her if you really wanted to know what she looked like." "Do you have absolutely no faith in me? It was actually much worse than that. I tried to go into her office and demand an appointment, and they kicked me out and threatened to call security on me."

April let out a low whistle. "Well, I guess I never expected that to happen. Sorry I didn't try to prepare you for that, but I really didn't think you would go inside." She ran her hands crazily through her hair obviously tried to think of another idea for me.

"I guess I just have to keep looking up her information online to see if I find anything?" I said sadly.

"No, that's a really bad idea. You've already researched her, and now you actually need to meet with her face-to-face. We just have to figure out how. Maybe you could somehow find her address through her work or her profile, and then we could stake out her house or try to run into her in her neighborhood?"

"That's really not my style. If you want to do some neighborhood surveillance, then by all means, go ahead, but I think I'd rather have some kind of civilized meeting with her. Maybe I could just call her work and explain the situation to her to see if she would meet me for coffee or something? That seems a little weird, but I think the direct approach is my only choice now." I started looking up Cherry's office phone number online as I spoke.

Suddenly April jumped up as if she'd been electrically shocked. "This is so perfect. I have no idea why I didn't think of it earlier!"

Now it was April's turn to entice me to beg her to tell me her great idea. "What is it?" I said flatly. I couldn't even get excited because I had so little faith in a good outcome for the mistress showdown at this point.

"As you know, I am your fabulous assistant, so I do an excellent job of managing your social calendar, right?"

"I guess so." I didn't really see where this was going or what it had to do with Cherry.

"Well—As you already know, we have the Winter Fashion and Beauty Expo sponsored by *High Life* next week, which I am told is frequented by the hottest talent in the industry, like beauty writers, fashion bloggers, PR firms, and even *graphic designers*."

She was right. The Winter Fashion and Beauty Expo was an annual event in its fifth year, created by *High Life* to introduce the hottest beauty and fashion trends for the upcoming season and also scout new ideas for products to feature in the magazine for the rest of the year. It was held in September; far enough in advance to plan out our big winter issue, and fully populated with tons of young Denver talent from every area of the magazine, beauty, fashion, and PR industry. These rising stars were there to try to get their ideas heard, make business connections, and potentially get a leg up on the career ladder. This did seem like the kind of event Cherry would be likely to attend if she was recruiting new clients for her company.

"Yeah, that's true, so what's the deal? Is Cherry James on the guest list? Because if she is, that would be a crazy coincidence, and I'm surprised you didn't tell me that already."

"No, she's not." April said smugly. "But she could be..."

Now it was my turn to sit straight up in my desk as if I had been tasered or shocked with a cattle prod. "Oh my God, that is completely brilliant. Instead of me having to play Magnum PI up there in Boulder, we could just make sure Cherry goes to this event so I could bump into her randomly without having to worry about confronting her or getting thrown out by security!"

This was such a good idea I could hardly believe it. I was also surprised I didn't think of it myself. It must have been all of the stress and shock of finding out the bad news about Adam's infidelity, because I was usually the "ideas woman" in our dynamic duo.

"We have so much to do to prepare for this!" I said. "Can you blast Cherry an e-mail at her office with an invite to the event? Can you also make sure to include a free ticket to the luncheon for the corporate sponsors? Just tell her in the e-mail she's getting a free ticket because we're recruiting new talent, or something like that. She'll probably be more likely to come if she thinks we're interested in her graphic design work."

I myself was in total overload, checking and double checking the event schedule to see exactly what my responsibilities were, where I could potentially run into this slut, and what I could get away with saying to her in a public place that would still show her that I meant business. I figured I could tweak the seating chart for the luncheon somehow to make sure Cherry was sitting at my table—especially if I was using the premise that *High Life* was interested in her services as a graphic designer. *Ha*, I snorted to myself, *as if.*

I didn't have a clear plan of action yet as to what I was going to say to Cherry when I bumped into her at the Expo and later sat with her at the luncheon. This was something I was going to have to brainstorm on, but I figured I had some time with the event being a full week away. Until that time, I decided to distract myself by reviewing a little eye candy on my eHarmony profile. Of course, "eye candy" was a strong word to use since the majority of possible matches sent to me appeared to be trolls that weren't fit to be integrated into normal society. Still, out of fifty or so troll profiles I reviewed each week, I found one or two eligible candidates. I would then pick them apart by scouring their profiles to see if they were cheaters, child molesters, or totally boring. If they somehow happened to jump all of those hurdles, then and only then would I send them a message or respond to a message they sent to me.

The latest candidate I was waiting to hear back from after dropping him a note was named Ryan Jarvis. He seemed normal enough. I was kind of into him because he worked as a chef at The Brown Palace Hotel, which was literally a stone's throw away from my office. I fantasized about meeting him on my lunch break for a decadent four course meal he would lovingly feed to me between sips of sparkling wine. This was probably not something Ryan and I would enjoy every day of the week, mind you, because who has the time to dine that finely in the workweek? But I presumed he would at least be able to whip up a delicious meal for me on special occasions. Like boring Mondays, hump day Wednesdays, and celebratory Fridays—since that was the end of the week and all.

I had already planned out our future, and I hadn't even met Ryan yet to make sure there was chemistry or that he had a semi-engaging personality. Still, if you could judge at all by the e-mails we had exchanged thus far, our meeting for drinks the following night was going to be hot, hot, hot.

Danielle—I liked how he didn't use the "Hey", which seemed to be a good sign.

> *I saw on your profile that you too are lover of animals. The big burning question I have for you is: Is that a blanket statement? Do you really love all animals? What about the emu, which I hear will kick you if you get too close? Or poisonous*

tree frogs? Or stink beetles? Except maybe the last choice is not actually an animal, but an insect...This is all food for thought to stir up some conversation for our date tomorrow night, which I am truly looking forward to.

Until then...

Ryan

Wow, just wow. The fact that he appeared to be witty, sharp, and intelligent definitely got my blood pumping. I tried to think of a few interesting questions of my own to keep the date lighthearted and engaging and also to avoid any of the awkward silences I so dreaded. Still, with such a charmer as Ryan as my date, I highly doubted uncomfortable silence would be an issue.

We were set to meet for drinks tomorrow evening at seven p.m. at a funky little bar called the Candlelight Tavern off of Alameda and Logan in Cherry Creek. It actually worked out well because it was near my house, and we were also meeting early enough to have a relatively tame night since it was a school night, after all. Apparently, this was one of Ryan's only random evenings off on a Wednesday. He worked most nights as the successful and esteemed chef he was. I made a mental note to ask him more about what type of dishes he prepared, what the clientele was like at The Brown Palace, and especially when he was going to cook me a fancy romantic meal for two.

Unfortunately for me, the next day at work was a total shitfest, which also happened to be the day of my big date. I couldn't exactly pinpoint what went so wrong in my workday, but I was boiling over with frustration by the time the clock hit noon.

A lot of it had to do with April. She was having a difficulty keeping my schedule organized and even answering a basic phone call after two weeks on the job. I wasn't sure if she was doing this on purpose, or if she simply was a little distracted. But I had hoped she would have acclimated better to her new position by now.

Everything came to a head when I answered my own phone for the fourth time that morning. I wasn't a total snob who was above answering her own phone calls, but it was just more professional to have my assistant do it for me since that's what she was paid for. Phone call number one went unanswered since April was getting coffee in the break room without even alerting me of her absence. Phone call number two rolled over to my desk when April appeared to be texting on her phone. Phone call number three was answered by yours truly as April appeared to be flirting with a guy from our IT department on another line when she couldn't figure out how to re-start her computer. And phone call number four rang in to me when April was simply slow in answering it. I picked it up after the fourth ring.

After that last and final frustrating phone call from a skin care rep in Utah ripping me a new one since we had not yet featured any of their many expensive sample products they'd sent to us two months prior, I buzzed April to call her into my office for a chat. The buzzing was fairly unnecessary since I could have thrown my shoe at the window that separated my office from her desk to get her attention. But I wanted to put forth a professional air to coax her into behaving and working harder.

She peeked her head into my office and said, "What's up, girl?"

"April," I began in my most boss-like tone. "Would you mind coming in here and shutting the door behind you?"

She looked wildly confused since I'd never spoken to her like that in all of the ten years of our friendship. Nonetheless, she opted to do as I requested by shutting the door behind her and taking a seat in the chair in front of my desk, waiting for me to continue.

"April, you've been doing a great job acclimating as my assistant, but I've been noticing a few areas that could use improvement." I beamed at her, proud of the way I had so professionally phrased what I was trying to say. I surprised even myself since I'd never had to criticize an employee before.

I continued. "Now, I've taken the liberty to make a small list for you of areas of improvement, like being ten minutes early for work every day, letting me know when you're stepping away from your desk for any reason, and answering the phone on the second ring, which is all company policy. If you don't mind reviewing—"

April narrowed her eyes and cut me off in a voice I knew all too well. A tone I called her "sassy voice" she normally reserved for rude telemarketers, waiters who got her order wrong, or annoying people in general. But never for me—until now.

"Hey, I don't really know why you're trying to pull this boss act on me, and I don't see why you're being so nitpicky. Are you hormonal or something? You're totally jumping down my throat about nothing. Chill out, Dani."

I looked at her in surprise. I was utterly shocked she had the gall to talk to me like that in our place of work when *I* was the one who had gotten her a job in the first place. I opened my mouth to respond, but she appeared to be on a tirade I couldn't interrupt.

"Look, I always knew you were really into your work, but there's no reason for you to take it out on me. I try to get here as quickly as I can in the morning, and I'm normally getting coffee for *you*, so I thought at the very least you'd be grateful. I have to say I'm pretty disappointed you even pulled me into your office for this little talk after all I've done for you."

I was sure if you'd taken a snapshot of me at that moment, I would have looked just like a deer caught in headlights, so floored was I at having my best friend and employee tearing into me when I was the one who was supposed to be doing the ripping in this conversation. Come to think of it, I couldn't believe April had the nerve to talk to me like that. I was technically her boss. Our friendship should only have made her respect me all the more.

The familiar rage I'd been struggling with over the past several weeks started to boil up in my chest again. I was feeling all Incredible Hulk about it to the point I could barely control myself. I tried to take a few deep breaths as I thought about what I was going to say. Now I finally understood why people claimed they saw red when they were angry. April suddenly looked to me like the red flag matadors waved in front of a bull in the arena, before they impaled them.

Game on.

"What the *fuck* are you talking about?" This introductory line alone silenced her immediately since I was always the yes-man in these types of situations, going along with whatever she said to keep the peace. Not today. "*I* am the one who got you this job, *I* am the reason you're able to pay your rent every month, and *I* didn't want to tell you this before, but your work performance is less than questionable—it's closer to horrible. You can't answer a phone to save your life, and if you want to keep your job for the next week, let alone have a good recommendation if you get fired, you better kiss my ass, work like you mean it, and pray I forgive you," I growled in a husky voice. "Now get the fuck out of my office."

Great. On top of acting like a wild animal, I now sounded like one too. I didn't know what had gotten into me exactly, but I could have sworn April had tears welling up in her eyes as she nodded, sprang out of her chair, and basically ran out of my office, shutting the door behind her.

I had never spoken to anyone like that in my life, let alone formulated such hateful thoughts before. But it felt good to get it out, good to tell people how I really felt, and good to stick up for myself.

The only not-so-good part of the situation was the simple fact I had emotionally assaulted my best and only friend. I was also a little bit worried about being reprimanded for harassment in the workplace if anyone had overheard our conversation.

But besides that, I was gravy, baby, and I felt like a small weight had been lifted off my chest with that insane outburst. I was fairly confident April and I could work this out later over a glass of Bailey's, as usual, but I wanted to give both of us some time to cool off.

So that was just a small glimpse as to why my workday was a complete shitfest. It was accurate to say I wasn't exaggerating. As I left my office at five p.m., I tried to do a compartmentalizing exercise I had heard about on TV from someone like Dr. Phil or Dr. Laura, by mentally wrapping up my job into a little package and setting it on a shelf to deal with tomorrow. Of course, that mental exercise was a total joke. I had no idea how anyone could just cut the strings on a stressful situation without thinking about it again and again and again. This was also probably why my cheating dead husband problem was affecting my entire life.

But compartmentalizing was the way to go if I wanted a chance in hell of being charming, witty, and intriguing on my date with Ryan in a few hours. I went home and tried to literally and figuratively cleanse myself of all of the drama from my day. I soaked in a long bath with scented oils and candles, diffused my hair into long, loose waves with a few sample products gifted to me from the *High Life* beauty department, and slowly applied my makeup to perfection. Without making it look too overdone, obviously.

After an intense hour of pampering and de-stressing, I picked out a stunning ensemble I thought was entirely appropriate for a nighttime first date: black skinny jeans, a dark green structured top with metal studs along the collar to give me a little bit of an edge, huge jeweled chandelier earrings, and chrome brushed stilettos to give that final pop. And pop was exactly what I was going for. I wanted to knock Ryan's socks off to purge myself of the bad karma associated with my last unfortunate online date.

From what I could tell on his profile, Ryan was a walking cliché. He was tall, dark, and handsome. He also looked like he was of a slight Mediterranean descent, which I would have to ask him about over drinks. Believe it or not, big noses and bushy eyebrows do work on some people. I was hoping Ryan was one of them.

I arrived at the Candlelight Tavern a few minutes before seven. I wanted to play it a little different this time by giving myself the chance to stake out a table, get comfortable, and wait for my blind date to come to me. Luckily for me, Ryan was also quite prompt. I waited for a mere two minutes with a Fat Tire in hand when a man who fit Ryan's description walked into the bar. The place was relatively empty because we were meeting for drinks early, so it was between me—a single girl sitting alone and looking positively sexy— two chubby frat guys playing pool, or a middle-aged couple enjoying a few glasses of wine several tables to my right.

Ryan immediately located me out of the vast sea of competition. I could have sworn I saw his eyes light up when he saw me. That was always a good starting point. I felt my cheeks flush a little at his obvious pleasure at seeing me in the flesh. He introduced himself to me and gave me the European double kiss on both cheeks, which I normally thought was lame and pretentious, but on him, it seemed thoughtful and trendy. He signaled to our waiter to order a beer for himself and rapidly launched into conversation.

He started out by asking me the usual, if I grew up in Colorado—which I did—where I worked, what area of town I lived in, and if I'd been to this bar before.

"Actually, now that I'm here, I think that I've been to this bar once after a very long night out. I couldn't be sure, but it does look kind of familiar to me." I laughed. "Any bar that has Fat Tire on tap is a great choice for me!"

"Ah, so you're a beer girl. That's actually pretty sexy," Ryan said flirtatiously. "So, tell me this. If you could dream up the absolute perfect date, what would it be?"

That question caught me off-guard. It definitely wasn't on the topic of what beers I liked, and it also seemed strangely rehearsed, like a prerequisite question Ryan asked all of his dates. No matter. I wanted to give this tall drink of water, all-star chef, the benefit of the doubt, so I forged on. "Well, that's a tough one. I'd have to say that it would be perfect to go on a sunset picnic in the mountains with some wine and delicious snacks, and then maybe enjoy a fancy dinner afterward. I'm pretty simple, so I'm fairly easy to please." I smiled back, proud of what I thought was an excellent answer to his strange question.

Oddly enough, Ryan looked disappointed at my answer. "Oh. I thought you were going to say a perfect date would be having drinks tonight with me."

I laughed nervously for a little too long. I had no idea what to say to that. I took a few huge gulps of my beer to avoid saying something strange in what was unquestionably an awkward silence.

He tried again, "So you seem like you work pretty hard at your job."

I liked where this was heading. So many guys didn't enjoy talking about my work because it related to beauty. I nodded enthusiastically.

"So after a long, hard day of work, what do you like to do to unwind?" he continued. "Do you like a glass of wine? A bubble bath? Or maybe getting a massage from your partner?"

Um, what the hell was this guy talking about? All of these questions sounded pretty familiar—*like he had read them on eHarmony*! I was fairly certain all of his questions could be found somewhere in the lengthy questionnaire I had to fill out to join the website. What was Ryan thinking, using them as fodder for our first date conversation? I was again at a loss at how to answer such a strange and rehearsed question. I decided to ignore it and attempted to redirect the conversation myself.

"You must work really hard too since you're a chef, right? Tell me more about your job! Do you absolutely love working at The Brown Palace? It's such a gorgeous hotel. I've only had drinks in their cigar bar, so I've never had the pleasure of enjoying a dinner there. What kind of food do you serve?"

He answered quickly, "Oh, it's a great job, very demanding, you know. We mainly cook upscale, fine dining meals, pretty much like what you would find in downtown Denver."

Hmm. He didn't seem as passionate about his career as a chef as I would have thought. I felt like my dream of having Ryan cook me a romantic four course meal was slipping farther and farther out of my reach, but I bravely continued on.

"Have you seen any celebrities there? I heard this hilarious story from a friend who was staying at the Brown Palace for the night and heard someone playing piano in the lobby. It was so good she went to check it out, and it was actually Billy Joel himself! Apparently, his daughter goes to DU, and he was just killing some time playing piano in the hotel lobby. Can you believe it?"

That story was actually one hundred per cent true, told to me by one of the beauty writers at the magazine. Since I was a freakish fan of The Piano Man, I had always felt an attraction to the celebrity vibe of The Brown Palace from that point on. I wondered why Ryan didn't feel the same excitement if he worked at such a fine establishment, frequented by celebrities, in the heart of downtown Denver.

He again brushed me off. "I'm pretty much always in the kitchen, so I don't know if I've ever met someone like Billy Joel at the hotel. Interesting story though."

"So what do you do exactly? Since you're the head chef, do you get to create the menus? Do you make a different menu for every day, or do you rotate seasonally? What's your favorite type of food to cook, or do you have a specialty?"

Now it was my turn to pepper him with questions, pun intended. But at least they were legitimate and heartfelt. Unfortunately, my series of questions caused him to appear very ill at ease. He squirmed on his stool and fidgeted with his beer glass.

"I actually don't get to plan the menus because I work slightly under the main chef directly on the line. So I don't necessarily specialize at this point in my career."

Since I'd put in my share of hours working at restaurants, I was able to cut right through his vague bullshit. "So you're a line cook? You're not the head chef?"

He looked even more embarrassed as he tried to save himself. "Well, you could say I'm an aspiring chef, and I get the opportunity to train on the line at a very popular hotel, which I think is a great career move."

"Yes, but why didn't you just say that in the first place? Why did you lie on your profile?"

I had a much shorter fuse these days for people who kept the truth from me. I had no idea why Ryan would lie about something as mundane as his job and cause me to fantasize pointlessly about him cooking me five-star meals. Seriously.

His expression changed completely as soon as I accused him of lying. "Look, I don't see why you're policing my profile and calling me out about lying. The whole point of eHarmony is to present yourself in the best light. It's not like I really fabricated anything anyway. Besides, you don't see me calling you out about looking heavier and older in person than in your picture, do you?"

Whoa—low blow, buddy. The picture I had posted to my profile was taken a mere year and a half ago. While I may have been younger then, if anything, I had lost, not gained, weight after Adam's death. What an asshole.

"Hey, I thought we were having a pleasant time. There's absolutely no reason to insult me just because I asked for more information about your job." I replied coolly. "I really don't appreciate it."

He immediately realized he'd gone too far and tried to smooth over the mess he had created. "You're totally right, and that came out wrong. I apologize. Why don't we just move on from here and try to enjoy the rest of our evening?"

I grudgingly agreed and spent the next hour essentially re-answering the eHarmony questionnaire I filled out when I joined the website in the first place. It looked like this guy had very poor first date skills, so he stuck to the script provided for him by a dating website.

"Are you a cat or a dog person?"

"Dog."

"Are you a cuddler, or do you prefer to spend time alone after being intimate?"

"I guess, cuddler."

"Do you consider yourself to be passionate and creative or more left brained and analytical?"

"Creative."

"Where do you see yourself five years in the future?"

"Ryan, it's been a pleasure, but I'm going to have to call it a night," I said when I finally couldn't take any more of his dating game questions.

"So soon? I thought maybe we could head back to my place and have a few more drinks? He leered at me. "I live pretty close by."

"I don't think so. I have a long day ahead of me tomorrow."

"Well, can I at least have your number and call you later in the week?"

"Ryan, I'm going to be as honest as possible with you. I don't think this date went well at all, so it's probably a better idea if we both cut our losses and just agree that things aren't going to work out." I scrounged around in my purse for a twenty dollar bill to throw down on the table so I could leave before waiting even a few more painful moments for our check.

But he kept right on going. "A word of advice—you'd probably have a much better time on a date if you opened up and weren't such a bitch when it came to relating to people."

I was completely floored for the second time in the day. *Me*? The person who had bit her tongue throughout the length of this awkward, agonizing date just so I didn't have to hurt this douchebag's feelings? Who the hell did he think he was? I couldn't believe I had wasted even an hour of my life with this guy who obviously was fairly hostile toward women if he was willing to call me fat, old, and a bitch within the course of our first meeting.

"And I have a tip for you, Ryan," I replied angrily. "How about the next time you lure someone into a date based on your false profile, you actually think of a few original questions that weren't copied from the eHarmony questionnaire? Not only are you a self-obsessed tool, but you're also not smart enough to cover your tracks when you're lying."

I spun a full one hundred eighty degrees on my chrome brushed stilettos and marched out of the bar as the heat rose from my chest into my face. I felt satisfied with my exit since I got the last word, but my victory was bittersweet. I had yet another very bad date under my belt. And as of today, I didn't even have a best friend I could call to tell about it.

CHAPTER 7

The next few days at the office were strained to say the least. The silver lining was that April seemed to either have been body snatched by aliens or transformed into a completely new person who now took initiative, was always punctual, and treated me with the respect I deserved. The only downside to all of this was there was no warmth or depth to our interactions. There was still a huge elephant in the room because of my extreme blowup and verbal assault on her a few days earlier.

It was heavy on my mind that I needed to patch things up with her ASAP, especially since we had never gone this long in a Cold War without speaking. Don't get me wrong. April was definitely speaking to me. But she was also using the word "ma'am" to prove the point I was her high and mighty superior, and she was merely my lowly assistant whose sole duty was to serve and support me. She was certainly making her point crystal clear. I just didn't have the time to give her the heartfelt apology she deserved. All of *High Life* was overwhelmingly busy preparing for the up-coming Winter Fashion and Beauty Expo the following Thursday, Friday, and Saturday.

Since it was a three-day conference, it sucked up quite a bit of my time with schedul-ing, confirming vendors, organizing caterers for the sponsors' luncheon and cocktail hours in the evening—and most importantly, making sure Cherry James RSVP'd to our little event so I could finally confront her face-to-face. This was normally a time I would have leaned heavily upon April. But since we weren't speaking as of yet, I decided to go it alone and attempt to plan my attack all by myself.

I didn't know when the Cherry James con-frontation would occur exactly— OPERATION BOOT THE BITCH, as I liked to call it. But I figured a prime opportunity would be when she was seated at my table dur-ing the luncheon. There I would be able to find out more about her life, be warm and friendly, earn her trust, and then strike like a poisonous snake when she least expected it.

My potential plan was to woo Cherry by making her believe we were actually interested in her as a graphic designer for *High Life* since the magazine was growing so rapidly. Then maybe I could set up a meeting with her later to reveal my true identity and put her in her place.

Logistically, there wasn't too much to be done when it came to confronting her. Adam was dead, and I didn't have to tell her to "stay away from my man" or anything like that. I basically wanted to get a good look at her, get to know her a little more to see what made Adam choose her over me, and then tell her the jig was up.

As the Expo grew closer and closer, I was still on the edge of my seat waiting to hear back from her about whether she would be attending or not. I sent April a series of formal e-mails asking her to follow up with Ms. James to find out if she had confirmed for the Expo. To my relief, April received her confirmation on Tuesday, a mere two days before the Expo was to take place.

This set my heart pumping at a whole new level. I hardly slept the next two nights. All I could do was replay dramatic scenes over and over in my head of wives confronting mistresses, soap opera style, as well as a few excerpts from *A Perfect Murder* circa nineteen nighty-eight. Of course, that movie sample was a little bit off since it was Gwyneth Paltrow cheating on *her*—old—husband, who then hired the guy she was cheating with to kill her, much to her dismay. That movie fantasy kept me entertained for a while since I was able to pretend Adam was still alive, and I was the one who was going to hire Cherry to kill him. *If only...*

By the time the morning of the Expo arrived, I was at a bit of a disadvantage. I had yet to formulate a clear confrontation plan, and April and I still weren't talking. To be honest, I kind of thought she would come to me and apologize since I was the one dealing with death, grief, and drama in my life. But no such luck this time. April was stubborn, to say the least. I knew I would have to be the one to come clean and say I was sorry if I wanted our friendship to move forward. Which, of course, I did. I was just distracted with my own upcoming conflict at the moment, thank you very much.

The morning of the Expo was absolutely beautiful—a clear and slightly cool September day. I tried to relax as I drove south toward the

Inverness Hotel and Conference Center in Englewood. The hotel housing the Expo was truly picturesque with a small lake in front of it, gorgeous greenery, a golf course, and an impressive ballroom where our sponsors' luncheon was to be held. On any other day and at any other time, I would have been more than excited to be playing the role of a hot shot beauty editor running a conference at a gorgeous hotel. But today, my mind was more than occupied with what I was going to do when I saw the bitch mistress, what I would say to her, and how long I could keep up my friendly act before I exploded.

I expected I would potentially bump into her somewhere within the main Expo where we had dozens of vendors' booths and displays set up showing the latest beauty products, skin treatments, clothing, and fashion accessories, all vying for a possible spot as features in the upcoming issues of our magazine. Again, I had a very vague idea of what Cherry looked like so I could only be on the lookout for a businesswoman with blonde hair. Luckily, all registered guests at the Expo were required to wear a name tag that also listed their job title and company for the purpose of networking—

and networking hard—with a little ass kissing in between.

To tell you the truth, it was kind of difficult to kiss ass for three days straight, but I guess that was the nature of the biz. Since I started my job as a beauty editor, I had only been able to enjoy my status at one Expo before Adam was killed, and I took a leave of absence. Now I was finally back to help run the conference again.

The last Expo was actually a nightmare. I was new to the business and bombarded by skin care and beauty reps trying to push any and every hot new product concoction in my face. The thought process was that if they were able to get me to agree to like their product, they had a much better chance of having it featured in an upcoming issue, which was essentially advertising gold since it guaranteed women in Colorado and beyond would be likely to buy their product.

This also meant I had to put up with schmoozing, fake compliments, and ridiculous small talk about where I went on vacation last year. This went on until the said beauty rep felt like he or she had an "in" to somehow segue into the great benefits of their toning/firming/ lifting/reversing/ transforming cream that was definitely going to "blow my mind" and would be "perfect" for a future issue.

This year, due to my recent empowerment and outbursts of anger, I had a shorter fuse than ever. It was my plan of action to be blunt and to the point when deflecting the majority of vendors hoping to push their products on me.

It was *so* on.

I arrived at the Expo at nine a.m. sharp, which offered me the decadent luxury of sleeping in for one more hour. Normally, I would have relished this bonus laying-in-my-bed time. But since I'd been so anxious over the past few days, I woke up a full hour before my alarm clock went off.

I sat tensely in bed thinking about when/how/where I was going to confront Cherry until I finally pulled myself out of bed and made some breakfast. This still left me ready for work a full hour early, so I used that time to weed through all of my eHarmony prospects since, due to my track record of phenomenally bad dates, I aspired to be pickier than ever.

I was toying with the idea of coming out and asking a prospect whether or not he was a psycho via email prior to our date. But I also thought maybe that would make *me* look like a psycho, which was not the route I wanted to take.

Was there a test to detect if someone was a weirdo? If there was, it could probably be marketed as an e-course or webinar online, and I'd be able to quit my day job and finally retire on my fat and juicy income at the age of twenty-nine. Still, even if I managed to get through a good first date with someone, there was the whole broad expanse of the future to deal with. How did you ever really know if someone was going to go crazy on you or not? The perfect example being my dead husband who turned out to be a dirty cheater, leaving me with a sticky situation to face all by myself.

This train of thought soured me completely and as I browsed through potential dates on eHarmony, I decided to delete all of my possible dates except one named Kyle, who I planned to Google obsessively, research the hell out of, and save for later to see if I deemed him worth messaging or not. With all of the liars in the world today, you could never be too careful.

Basically, Kyle would have to be a heart surgeon who also simultaneously ran a charity for underprivileged children in his free time *and* ate organically *and* loved camping *and* went to church every Sunday for me to trust him enough to even schedule a date. If he did all of those things and more, I would probably just propose to him myself at our first meeting. He would clearly be a total anomaly I would have to lock down and keep from the rest of womankind before they caught onto his greatness.

With a possible date on the backburner, should he turn out to be Mr. Perfect, I was now ready to bravely face the truth, i.e. slutty mistress, as I walked through the large, gleaming glass doors of the Expo conference center. There was an immediate contrast between the cool, quiet September morning and the inner workings of the Winter Fashion and Beauty Expo. My ears were quickly blasted with yelling, laughing, chatting, and very, very loud ass kissing. Oh, yeah. I was definitely in the right place.

At its best, the Expo sounded like an underground dog-betting circuit, where sweaty men sat in a circle and threw money into the center screaming, "Ay-yi-yi-yi!" At the very worst, it was a recipe for a splitting headache since you couldn't find a moment to yourself to think clearly, unless you happened to hide out in the restroom for a while.

And even then, the restroom was full of crazy chaos. The savviest-saleswomen were still hoping to make deals, rub shoulders with someone important, or just pass out a few more of their business cards. So you could never fully let down your guard.

A true and unfortunate incident happened that first year when I was innocently reapplying my lipstick in the restroom, trying to relax and prepare myself to head back into the beauty jungle. The woman next to me seemed normal enough, attractive, and professional. She was also reapplying her lipstick. She smiled back at me in the mirror, and before I could even return the smile, she had launched into what appeared to be a thirty second commercial about her company's new mineral lipstick that also contained acai berry as an antioxidant to protect lips from sun damage. "Because you know how fragile the thin skin of your lips can be, right?" She beamed at me in the mirror.

I was tempted to drop my lipstick in the sink, half applied, and run for my life. But instead, I did the standard "Mmm," while nodding brightly. I then proceeded to drop my lipstick into my bag and run for my life.

My first order of business at the Expo was to hi-jack the reception area to see if a certain Ms. James had checked in. Another assistant in our beauty department, Alana, was already manning the desk, suspiciously bright eyed and bushytailed for this hour of the morning.

"Hey, Danielle! Excellent turnout so far, huh? We've already had like two hundred people check in, and tons of people arrived even before the doors were open!"

"That's great!" I smiled at her absently as I tried to scan through the guest list on the computer to see who had already checked in. So far Cherry James was a no-show. I instructed Alana in what I hoped was an objective manner to text me as soon as Ms. James checked in since our company wanted to talk to her about her graphic design services. First lie of the day, check. And it seemed to be going well so far because Alana agreed enthusiastically to do as I asked.

I decided to make my way back into the main Expo area to do my actual job of meeting and greeting perspective vendors and wait for the text alert that may or may not change my life. On my way to the Sanitas booth where I hoped to sample the latest papaya and pumpkin enzyme facial scrub I thought would make a good feature for the fall season, I literally bumped right into April, the ice queen herself.

She laughed and turned to grab my arm as she said, "Sorry! My bad!" But as soon as she realized it was me she had bumped into, her cheerful demeanor vanished entirely. She tried to scoot past me with a frosty glare on her face.

"April," I hissed in a low voice. "We really need to talk and get this issue dealt with. You can't just pretend like you're not talking to me indefinitely."

"I'm not pretending like anything. I'm just doing *my* job like *you* asked, remember?" She hissed back in an equally raspy and threatening tone.

With that little snarky remark, I was reading her loud and clear. Just because someone held the role of my best friend for a decade didn't mean they had the right to disrespect me at work and make me jump over hoops to get them to forgive me! April could keep her attitude to herself. This was not anything I was prepared to deal with today, this week, or maybe even this month. Instead of answering her back, I opted to turn on my heel and trot away in another direction—which was unfortunately something I had quite a bit of practice with lately.

The morning flew by as I met skin care rep after skin care rep with a few beauty sales associates and product chemists sprinkled in the mix. The product chemists were a fun novelty at the Expo since I got to chat with them about exactly why they chose each ingredient they put in their products.

But alas, my time with them was limited since they couldn't make any final decisions about comped products that would be sent to the magazine if I were interested in featuring them. The chemists were merely the smoke and mirrors of the day, making the event a little more fun for people like me who actually wanted to hear something interesting about skin care as opposed to more brownnosing.

Before I knew it, it was nearing one p.m., the time that the luncheon was set to begin. I checked my phone for the umpteenth time to see if I had received the all-important text saying Cherry had checked in. Still nothing, and I even had a great signal. I stormed back up to Alana at the front to ask her what exactly was going on.

She giggled at me apologetically and said, "Oh my God, I am so sorry about that. I was just making sure that some of the sponsors got checked in okay, and I didn't have time to text you to tell you Ms. James got here like an hour and a half ago. Sorry!" She shrugged and went back to her work.

What? This was totally unacceptable. I wanted to be completely prepared as soon as Cherry stepped foot in the building. I was also surprised I hadn't somehow sensed she was here, like the Terminator zeroing in on Liquid Metal Man or something. I guess I assumed the atmospheric pressure would change, glasses of water on the table would vibrate à la Jurassic Park, and I would have an existential experience where I slowly floated over to Cherry to give her a piece of my mind.

Now I was *completely unprepared* and also at a disadvantage. I felt like I had been sucker punched with this unfortunate news. My chest tightened, and I grabbed onto the table next to me as I realized I might have already spoken to Cherry without knowing it. I racked my brain trying to think of how many blonde businesswomen I had talked to this morning, but it wasn't something I was paying attention to since I didn't know I needed to be on the lookout yet. I didn't think I'd even taken the time to read a single name tag that day. Who knows if I'd spoken to the mistress in the flesh or not? Thanks a lot, Alana.

I hurried to a nearby restroom to try to freshen up so I'd look like an absolute bomb-shell the moment I first laid eyes upon Adam's woman-on-the-side. I already had my guard up based on my stalker-ific bathroom experience from last year and tried my best not to make eye contact with the woman at the sink next to me, who was also touching up her makeup. Suddenly, her cell phone rang. The startling noise almost made me jab myself in the cornea with my mascara wand.

She answered her phone hastily in an apparent attempt to be polite. "Cherry James."

I sucked in my breath as the blood rushed to my face. Perhaps one of my worst traits was how I got hot and bothered so easily. And not even at the right times, if you know what I mean. If I happened to be embarrassed, scared, stressed, angry, or overly excited, I would get red, sweaty, and blotchy in a matter of minutes. I had hoped this wouldn't be my fate at the first mistress meeting, but really, who was I kidding?

I attempted to be casual and slowly cut my eyes over to Cherry in the mirror as she continued her call. Yes, Cherry did happen to look like a real-life version of her blurry profile picture. Smooth blonde hair swept back into a low ponytail, a young, perky face with full lips that appeared to be natural—dammit!—sweet and soft brown eyes, and a slender frame underneath her stylish pantsuit. I didn't see anything totally spectacular about her. Had Adam had a secret thing for blondes I didn't know about? Could that have been the one trait that derailed our entire marriage, unbeknownst to me?

As I continued to shamelessly listen in on her call, I noticed she also had an animated and unassuming way of speaking that made her appear captivating and adorable, like a small child. Hell, she was probably talking to her dry cleaner for all I knew. But she was absolutely gushing in a way that made you want to hang onto her every word.

"Yes, I absolutely understand! No, no, no, you're so sweet and definitely don't have to do that! All right, if that's what you're going to do, I'm just going to have to make it up to you next time I come in, and don't think I don't remember how you like your latte! Bye, sweetie!"

Holy shit, I was about to be sick. Luckily, I was standing directly over a bathroom sink, so

I was in an ideal location for spontaneous puking. But I was completely floored at the bubbly and sparkling personality of this Cherry James character. Not only was she moderately to very attractive—okay, very attractive—she also seemed like someone I would genuinely like to be friends with and get to know better.

What. The. Fuck?

This was *not* how the big confrontation was supposed to go down. Before I could think of a word to say, Cherry snapped her phone shut, rolled her eyes, and said, "Men."

I smiled back at her weakly since I had yet to experience the stress of juggling multiple men who were madly in love with me, my husband included. Before I could even formulate an intelligent thought, not to mention start an angry tirade in which I would tell off this immoral bitch, Cherry tossed her cell phone into her bag and delicately click-clacked her way out of the restroom on her tall high heels, leaving me in her dust.

CHAPTER 8

My first immediate and unfortunate thought was to call April. I had to get her into the restroom as quickly as possible so she could help me decide my best plan of attack. I mean, I had been totally snowed by this perky, shiny, girl-next-door bitch. What was I supposed to do now?

On top of that, it was definitely going to be awkward to sit down to a luncheon with her since we had already briefly chatted in the restroom. But the whole calling April plan was obviously off the table, so I had to rack my brain and think of a way to handle this situation by myself. Something I certainly wasn't used to doing in the past several years.

As I stood at the mirror in the restroom and tried to formulate a plan—even a weak plan would do—I started to get frustrated at the whole situation. I mean, who did this Cherry think she was, flouncing around adorably for all the world to see when she really was a closet cheater with a dirty heart? I was a total stranger to her, yet she felt it necessary to flirt in front of me, giggle charmingly, and infect me with her vivacious cheer.

What the hell?

As these thoughts rolled along in my mind and gathered steam, I noticed the old telltale signs of some serious anger welling up. That was much better and more familiar than the sense of panic I'd had when I didn't know how to cope with being smacked upside the head by my husband's very cute and very pleasant side dish.

I summoned all my strength and channeled my anger at this pretentious, cute woman— who had no idea she was rubbing shoulders with Adam's living and breathing wife—into a brute force that would hopefully help me get through this unpredictable and volatile luncheon. Then I marched out of the restroom and down the hallway into the ballroom where the sponsors' luncheon was being held. And would you believe it? Cherry was already settled cozily at our designated table, chatting with my boss Gwen about how she got her start as a graphic designer, or some bullshit like that.

I settled into my seat just a few chairs away from her and gave the group a tight and unfriendly smile. The luncheon table consisted of my boss, Gwen Jacobs, power editor-in-chief extraordinaire of *High Life* for five years running, four different department heads of *High Life* who oversaw the fashion, beauty, health, and lifestyle sections, respectively, April, my frigid and potentially ex-best friend and now very ambitious assistant, two male representatives from our PR department, the illustrious Cherry James, prize mistress, and myself. Quite a group.

I said hello to all of the *High Life* staff seated at the table I was already acquainted with and plunged in with both feet by making a formal introduction to Cherry James.

"Hello. Danielle Starkey. I believe we met briefly in the restroom." I shook hands with Cherry and produced more of a grimace than a smile as a greeting.

Not surprisingly, Cherry laughed delightedly as she remembered our brief encounter moments before. "Yes, yes, yes, sweetie, great to see you again! Isn't it a small world that we're sitting at the same table? What do you do at *High Life*?"

Okay, there were quite a few things wrong with that introduction. First off, who feels the need to repeat words like "yes" so many times in a row? It was just getting plain annoying, if you asked me. Second, don't ever call me "sweetie" unless you happened to be serving me a slice of apple pie at a diner in the 'fifties. Third, Cherry didn't even seem to flinch when I introduced myself to her with my full name, showing that she was either entirely oblivious or perhaps had no conscience or soul, or a combination of all three.

I don't know about you, but if I was planning on going on a romantic vacation with a certain Mr. Starkey, I would be on the lookout for any random woman I happened to meet with the same last name. I mean, *come on.*

Luckily, this theatrical meet-and-greet was not lost on April, even though her and I were not speaking at the moment. Gauging from her reaction at Cherry introducing herself in the flesh, April had temporarily forgotten about this entire plotted meeting altogether. Her jaw dropped almost to the floor. Her eyes widened so much I was concerned she would need eye drops to lubricate them in order to blink again.

Still, Cherry didn't bat an eye when April choked exaggeratedly on her water. She simply turned and continued her conversation with Gwen about the need for exceptional graphic design when launching a new magazine online. *Pshhh,* little did she know how truly uninterested we were in her services. The only reason she was seated at this table in the first place was to be a sitting duck in my pond of revenge. Not necessarily the best metaphor to use, but my point was still clear.

I made my way sweetly and professionally through the majority of the meal, starting with a crab cake appetizer, a light spring salad, and grilled salmon with roasted vegetables as the entrée. Was it glaringly obvious we were in hippie-granola-crunchy Colorado? I half expected we would be eating muesli and sipping on wheatgrass. I just felt fortunate to sink my teeth into a legitimate piece of salmon as I mentally sharpened my knives for the confrontation that was sure to ensue. Or maybe Cherry would just choke on her piece of salmon and die right in front of me so I could get my revenge without having to lift a finger?

I could only hope.

Gwen kept trying to bring me into the conversation as her little protégé since I was a newer editor in the beauty department. She continued to praise me for being such a vital component in putting together this year's Expo, when the only true reason I was so interested in devoting extra hours to this event was so I could play the puppet master and make sure I was in the near vicinity of Cherry at all times. I guess if it happened to make me look like a devoted employee, then all the better.

I tuned into the conversation just as Gwen turned to me and said, "Cherry actually works as a graphic designer in Boulder. Did you know that? I was thinking it would be great to have her input on launching the magazine online to make sure it's effective enough to target our demographics nationwide. What do you think, Danielle?"

Well, for one thing, I thought this was my chance to put in my two cents about this bitch Cherry. *Here we go,* I thought happily. "Oh, really? I had no idea! How long have you worked as a graphic designer, Cherry?"

Cherry smiled a million-dollar smile. "I worked at a smaller firm in Fort Collins for a few years, and I've been with my company in Boulder for the past four years."

"And are you familiar with *High Life*? Have you worked with similar clients in the past? What do you think of the online launch of the magazine?"

"Danielle, I'm glad you asked. I actually had some time to research the magazine before coming to the Expo, and I think I could create the fresh and healthy interface *High Life* needs to really appeal to your audience all over the US and help boost your online launch!"

I bet, I thought sarcastically. "And do you work by yourself or in a team? We actually had a few other firms we were considering that you would possibly need to collaborate with. Like Amp Design in Englewood."

That last gem in the conversation was totally off-the-cuff since it was the company Adam used to work for as a graphic designer. I only decided to name-drop his company in the conversation to see if I could make Cherry flinch and possibly find a crack in her perfect foundation I could then chip away at to expose and humiliate her publicly.

April was more than familiar with the name of Adam's company. She again looked up in surprise I had so boldly dropped this information like a stealth bomb into the conversation. Gwen also looked at me with a confused expression since we *never* collaborated with several teams. It was news to her we were even considering Amp Design in the first place—which we actually weren't.

I didn't know how this was all going to turn out, but I did know one thing: I was enjoying this fly-by-the-seat-of-my-pants approach to my first-ever mistress confrontation. *It's go time.*

I had to give Cherry some credit. Her perfectly adorable expression did change slightly, although I couldn't read it. I took that as my cue to jump right in. "Have you worked with Amp Design before?"

She mutely shook her head and looked down at the table.

"Oh, I must have been mistaken. I thought you had been in a very close relationship with their firm. No? You don't know anyone there? Maybe you knew my late husband, Adam Starkey?"

Now all of the cards were on the table. Everyone else seated with us looked absolutely confused, wondering what Adam had to do with this business connection. The only people in the know at the moment were April, Cherry, and myself. I waited with anticipation to see Cherry's reaction.

"No," Cherry answered weakly, "I don't think I'm familiar with an Adam Starkey. I'm sorry to hear about your loss."

"That's funny. I was under the impression that you two were really close. Why else would you have booked a Caribbean vacation together? Is that normally how you handle your business relationships?"

Everyone at the table was frozen with confusion since they didn't know exactly what I was getting at. Could I be implying Cherry and my husband went on a work related trip to Antigua? *Hardly.* Or could I really be saying what everyone else was thinking—this slut played a key role in my husband cheating on me when he was still alive? *Nail on the head!*

"I really don't know what you're talking about," Cherry answered quite softly and without any charm whatsoever.

Gwen finally interjected in an attempt to take control of the strange conversation. "Danielle, you must be thinking about someone else. It doesn't sound like Cherry ever worked with your husband, let alone went on a business trip with him." She laughed at the absurdity of the thought.

I turned to Gwen with a fire in my eyes. "Actually, I think you misunderstood what I said, Gwen. Cherry didn't *work* with Adam; she was actually his mistress, and they had planned a vacation together before he died." I turned to Cherry. "Isn't that right?"

Cherry didn't utter a single word, which, in the limited time I had known her, seemed entirely out of character for her normally effervescent personality. I glared at her some more, expecting her to do the dramatic soap opera thing and yell back at me about how it was none of my business, how she didn't know Adam was married, and how she was the only one he really loved. Or something along those lines. And then throw a drink in my face.

Strangely enough, she seemed to fold into herself and completely shut down, refusing to respond to my last question. Her gorgeous blonde fringe had fallen partially over her face, which was why it was difficult to see at first that she was wiping tears from her eyes.

Wait. This wasn't supposed to happen at all. I was supposed to get angry, and then Cherry was supposed to get angry, and then we would have it out and be done with it. I was so overwhelmed with frustration I had no idea what to do about a crying mistress throwing a wrench in the confrontation. Suddenly, I felt April put her hand on my arm from across the table. That single touch jolted me back to reality as I realized how entirely sad this entire circumstance was.

Why did I have to be the one confronting the "other" woman? Why couldn't Adam be here so I could confront him to his face instead of having to embarrass myself in front of my coworkers? And why in the world was *Cherry* crying like she truly loved him, which added a whole new element to the situation?

I had assumed it was a dirty sex type of fling. That had made it much easier to be angry at her and start this showdown in the first place.

I sat for what felt like several awkward moments—but I suspect was actually only a few seconds—in a state of shock, before I bolted out of my seat and ran from the ballroom into a side hallway where I could have a little peace to gather my thoughts. By the time I made it to the quiet and secluded sanctuary, I realized I was sobbing. I hadn't thought to bring my purse with me in my big dramatic exit, so I didn't have Kleenex or a scrap of paper or anything useful to prevent streams of mascara from running down my face.

Fuck it. I was probably fired anyway. My only choice was to leave the Expo as quickly as possible, hopefully shielding my stained and swollen face from my coworkers.

I'm not an animal!

From where I stood in the hallway, I had my back to the side exit doors of the ballroom. I heard the doors open and footsteps tentatively approach me. I didn't really care who had come after me—although I assumed it was April, ready and willing to be back at it in her best friend duties. Or maybe even Gwen, ready to blast me for going totally ape-shit in front of my *High Life* superiors.

The person in question gently placed a hand on my shoulder. I turned slowly around and found none other than the home-wrecking Cherry James. As soon as I realized who it was, I shook her hand off of me, crossed my arms defiantly over my chest, and waited for her to speak since she obviously knew who I was at this point. There was nothing for me to say, so I settled for an intimidating glare instead.

It took a little while for her to get her words together. She seemed to be crying harder than I was. Like Meryl Streep, Academy Award hard. *"And the award goes to...The mistress for playing the role of the slighted and outrageously attractive, misunderstood*

170

woman in the life story of one Danielle Stark-ey." Boo! Hiss!

Cherry didn't seem to have the foresight to have brought her purse or any Kleenex with her either. She roughly wiped her leaking face across the arm of her beautiful deep-purple blazer, leaving a long string of snot that made me cringe when I looked at it.

When she spoke her voice was shaky and thick with tears. "I don't think you understand. I know how horrible this looks, but I just don't know how to explain what happened."

"Make me understand then." Even though I was crying, I was still going with my tough girl routine. I wanted to appear in control, like I had the upper hand. Although, what type of upper hand you could have when you were crying openly with your husband's mistress, I didn't know.

After a few more snot wipes onto her blazer sleeve, she continued sadly. "Well, I know this sounds horrible to even admit, but I did know Adam had a wife. I knew what I was doing was stupid, but I really had strong feelings for him. I know it's absolutely no condolence to you because what I did to you was horrible. But even though it's been more than ten months since he died, I'm totally devastated. I really loved him, which I never wanted to admit because what we were doing was so wrong. But I never thought he would die. It's just really hard for me to get over because I can't talk to anyone about it since it was cheating. When you brought all of that up today, it just caught me off guard, and I couldn't keep it together. I'm so sorry." She looked up at me with sad blue eyes reminiscent of a cuddly and lovable puppy. Dammit.

I had to admit I was pretty shocked, to say the least. I still couldn't get the idea of a knockdown, drag-out confrontation out of my head, so all of these waterworks were completely unexpected. I had clearly underestimated the depth of her relationship with Adam.

"I'm not going to tell you that it's okay," I said. "And I wish I'd never even had to find out about this. What did you think was going to happen? Were you just going to keep seeing him on the side indefinitely?"

"No, no, no, that was something I wanted to talk to him about eventually. We had only been seeing each other for about six months. I was just trying to keep it casual because I'd never been with someone who was married before. But the more time I spent with him, I knew I wanted to talk to him and tell him I couldn't keep seeing him if we didn't have a future." She stared at the floor.

Six months? Holy shit, I hadn't really thought we would be having this type of in-depth conversation. I wasn't prepared for all of these little details to start popping up, details that would only serve to torture me for many a sleepless night in the future. And the fact she wanted to have a long-term, serious relation-ship with him? This blew all of my precon-ceived notions surrounding OPERATION BOOT THE BITCH out of the water. It was much more emotionally charged and much less rife with hair pulling than I originally intend-ed.

My tears were still coming fast and strong, as if my face had sprung a leak that just couldn't be plugged. "Cherry, I can't deal with this right now. The only thing I wanted to say to you was the secret was out, and what you did to another person's relationship was inex-cusable. Right now, I don't care about all of these details, and it really doesn't matter. It'll never be resolved since Adam is dead."

I didn't quite know how to end the conver-sation. I wanted to get out of there as quickly as possible, so I concluded with, "Get over it, get on with your life, and stay out of other people's relationships."

That seemed as good of a summary as any. I turned away from her and trotted toward the exit, shutting the heavy glass doors of the Inverness on this horrible and damaging day.

I half expected her to run after me since I'd watched way too many *Lifetime* movies where the dramatic confrontation scenes extended much longer than the five minutes we spent talking. But I knew for a cold, hard fact I had nothing else to say. The interesting factor in this love triangle, if you wanted to call it that, was that the key player was dead. The mistress and I could hash it out until our faces turned blue, but all we would be doing was arguing, crying, or a combination of the two—which we'd already accomplished quite well, thank you very much.

None of this information was going to bring Adam back. I would never legitimately hear from him as to why he thought it was a good idea to cheat on me for an entire *six months* of our marriage. That was a crushing blow since we were only married for three years total. *That whittled it down to about 2 ½ years of legitimate marriage*, I calculated. All of the sudden, I was struck with such a horrible thought I almost sank down to the curb in front of the hotel until I recovered.

Oh my God, what if there had been other infidelities? What if our entire marriage was a lie? Sure, the beautiful and charming Cherry took a good six months away from Adam and me without me knowing it. But what if he had been doing it all along? How could I possibly know how long we were rightfully and honestly married when all of this horrible shit kept bursting out from beyond the grave?

I barely remembered finding my car in the vast hotel parking lot, but somehow I ended up parked in my driveway a mere fifteen minutes later. I stumbled into my house in a daze. Normally, even in my saddest moments, I would vegetate in front of reality television with only the horrible lives of other women to console me and prove my circumstances weren't that bad after all. But, sadly, even real-life TV drama wouldn't do it for me today.

I didn't know how I was going to get myself out of this one. Especially since I didn't have the satisfaction of confronting the adulterer. And now, instead of bubbling over with rage at Adam and Cherry, I just felt a deep, deep emptiness in its place. I couldn't tell yet whether or not OPERATION BOOT THE

BITCH had served its purpose in curing me. All I knew was I couldn't stop the crying, and I couldn't see an end in sight.

STAGE 3: BARGAINING

CHAPTER 9

I must have fallen asleep because I woke up two hours later on my couch with Madam curled up next to me, and my phone vibrating on the coffee table so hard I thought it was going to knock off one of my decorative votive candles—fresh rain scent, if you please.

I looked at the caller ID on my phone and was surprised to see it was April, calling for the seventh time in a row. I must have missed her other calls due to my grief-induced nap. I decided not to answer her just yet. Not because I didn't want to make up with her, because I desperately did. But I had not yet taken my own emotional temperature to see how I was doing, which would be the first question she'd ask me after that crazy scene at the hotel.

One of my biggest concerns was what I had done to my career by acting out at a corporate sponsors' luncheon in front of my boss. And the worst part of all was I wasn't even drunk! I was used to misbehaving after drinking a bit too much at an office party or two. Only to feel embarrassed the next day and wonder if I'd told my boss people around the office thought she was a lesbian or that I would sometimes take an extra-long lunch break to nap in my car.

Luckily, I had avoided any office repercussions caused by my loose lips mixed with alcohol. But now, every single thing I had done was clearly displayed in a movie montage in my mind, with some empowering music like Beyoncé's "Irreplaceable" playing in the background. Yet instead of feeling empowered, I felt even more ashamed as I put into perspective the fact my boss had been sitting next to me the entire time I aired my dirty laundry and failed at humiliating my husband's mistress in public, *after* I had lied to her about why she was there in the first place.

Oh, wow. When I connected all of the dots together, I was really in a world of hurt. Since I'd already lost my husband and potentially damaged my best—and only—friendship, my career was pretty much all I had left. I had envisioned myself being a ball-busting career woman who quickly rose to the top because she had nothing else she was passionate about.

Which wasn't necessarily a bad thing if you were the one making six figures and laughing all the way to the bank. But now I didn't think I would even be giggling softly on the way to the ATM. I had fucked up—and fucked up big time—at a work event.

My only thought was that if I somehow managed to keep my job, I was definitely going to do things differently. I knew I had been flying off the handle like crazy, with my verbal tirade on April being the prime example. I feared what further damage would be done if I didn't get my anger in check right away. I sent up a quick and meaningful prayer to God that I would one hundred thousand per cent pull it together and become a gentle, sweet, and very empathetic boss and coworker if He would simply allow me to keep my job in spite of what I had done.

I was confident in the fact God and I were quite tight. I just hoped the earthly damage I had done today wouldn't negate the weight of my very heartfelt prayer. My spirits were slightly elevated after envisioning myself truly turning my life around once Gwen forgave my crazy outburst and April and I had a tearful reunion where she told me she understood exactly what I'd been going through and was simply distraught after not talking to me for several weeks.

Yes, that was the ticket, I thought happily. I just needed to make amends with all the people I had kicked in the ass over the past several weeks, and maybe all of this nasty, mistress-related bullshit would just go away.

In fact, maybe all of my personal trauma had nothing to do with finding out Adam's secret at all. Maybe this was just the time I needed to start taking my job and my relationships more seriously—which I was more than prepared to do if I managed not to lose my job after today.

Please, please, please.

With a renewed sense of hope, I decided it was finally time to give April a jingle since she probably thought I had offed myself. This was also the perfect opportunity to make up with my long lost best friend after I had spent the past couple of weeks treating her very poorly. I was now the new Danielle hoping to turn over a new leaf and approach my life much differently. I just prayed April would forgive me for going totally crazy on her ass.

She answered the phone after only half of a ring. She was obviously standing by on suicide watch. "Oh my God, Danielle! I was so worried about you! I was literally about to leave the conference early to come bang down the door of your house, except I didn't want *both* of us to get fired in one day. Are you okay? I just can't believe all of that happened!"

I cut April off. "So does this mean I lost my job? Did Gwen already fire me?" I crossed my fingers and sent up about five thousand more quick prayers.

"Oh, I actually have no idea. I just assumed you were fired or quit or something, but I haven't heard anything about it. Now tell me exactly what happened! I know you and Cherry both ran out of room at the same time, so did you end up bumping into each other? Did she slash the tires on your car?"

"Actually, April, I really owe you an apology. I was totally horrible to you when I yelled at you a few weeks ago, and I should have apologized to you much sooner. I just hope you can forgive me. I'm really, truly sorry."

"*Pshh.* Don't even worry about that! What are friends for? I knew you'd come to your senses sooner or later, so it's all good."

Even though she was utterly stubborn, April took apologies well and very quickly. One attribute I was grateful for at this moment.

She continued on. "But really, I had no idea you had it in you. Like that bitch totally deserved it, and you pulled the rug out from under her in front of everyone at the table. If your job wasn't on the line, I'd say that must have been the greatest thing you've ever done."

"Yeah, I really need to try to get a hold of Gwen as quickly as possible," I replied. "I need to make this right before she fires me officially. Where are you? Are you still at the Expo with her?"

"Actually, I'm hiding out in the bathroom because I've been trying to stalker call you to make sure that you're still alive. I probably have to go before someone hunts me down, but I'll tell you if I hear anything at all. Do you want me to stop by after work?"

"No, I think I'm going to be fine tonight. I just need to unwind and get some sleep because this day was so stressful. Why don't you hit me up so we can go out this weekend and celebrate that I still have a job? I hope!"

She agreed and hung up, clearly relieved she didn't have to come over and untie me from my curtain rod anytime soon. Surprisingly, to the both of us, I was taking this much better than I thought I would. I knew it was all because I finally had some perspective on how I could use this to better myself instead of letting Adam's infidelity cut the legs out from under me.

Now all I had to do was get a hold of my blunt, take-no-prisoners boss and hope she had just an ounce of empathy in her to spare me my job. Since Gwen was at the Expo, I decided the best course of action would be to shoot her an e-mail. We were all addicted to our iPhones, so she should be able to respond to me within a matter of minutes as opposed to hours if I left her a voicemail.

Shakily, I typed out a quick e-mail saying how deeply sorry I was for the outburst today and how I would like to have a one-on-one meeting with her at her earliest convenience so we could iron out this indiscretion. I thought the use of the word "indiscretion" was a very nice touch. It showed my true remorse and understanding of the magnitude of what I had done. Believe it or not, I could be deep, insightful, and repentant when I wanted to be. Especially if my job was on the line.

I had to tear myself away from staring at my computer screen and tapping my nails nervously on my desk, waiting for her to e-mail me back. Instead, I thought I should do something constructive and beneficial to the world around me by giving Madam a much-needed bath.

Of course, she didn't think it was needed. She proceeded to flail around like she was dying, even though I only had her submerged in perhaps one cup of water in my kitchen sink. I decided to be even kinder to her by blowing her dry afterward with my hair dryer, which I knew was refreshing, comforting, and exactly what she needed to feel like her best self. Even though she was only a dog, I was clearly on the right track to getting over myself and becoming a contributing member of society.

After a half-hour of some hard-core dog grooming, I permitted myself to check my e-mails again, feeling both incredibly nervous and incredibly happy when I saw a response from Gwen in my inbox. The response itself was a mere three words saying, "Yes, eight a.m. Saturday."

Beads of sweat poured down my forehead, mingled with a few tears of relief, as I realized Gwen was giving me a chance to plead my case! She was notorious for firing employees who didn't meet her stringent standards. Which she would gladly do via text, e-mail, phone—you name it.

The simple fact she had given me a chance to meet with her was magnanimous and huge since she normally didn't have any tolerance for anyone other than herself. She also worked like a slave in the wee hours over the weekend—much like the ball-busting, career-driven woman I now aspired to be—so I knew she would be at the office very early Saturday morning waiting for me. Saturday was a day away, and I definitely needed the time to mentally prepare myself for this confrontation.

This was the first weekend of the rest of my life. I knew, I just knew, I would come out on top if I could show Gwen how sincerely sorry I was and also work on achieving inner peace while I was at it. This would give me the poised, serene, and simplified impression I was going for instead of the crazed, maniacal, and irate person I had been over the past several weeks. I shot April a quick text to tell her that all was well with the world (ommmm!). And then I started doing a downward dog yoga pose as the first step on my journey toward enlightenment. Although it hurt my hamstrings quite a bit, I was positive I was moving in the right direction.

CHAPTER 10

I spent the entire day Friday reading snippets of a biography of Mother Teresa online as a source of inspiration, sandwiched in between a little bit of Nicole Ritchie gossip from People.com because, hey, I was only human. I also cleaned my entire townhouse from floor to ceiling—a welcome distraction and likewise as a symbolic cleansing of my inner and outer self. As you could undoubtedly tell, I was becoming much deeper and much more in touch with my authentic core being. *Go, me.*

The only unfortunate side effect of this outer cleansing was that I found quite a few boxes of Adam's things in the very back of our closet—which I was more than petrified to open. I would have loved to tear through all of his old boxes to potentially find a few pictures of him and Cherry laughing together, sharing a glass of champagne, or skipping down the beach, which they probably did all the time. But I tried to restrain myself by thinking about what Jesus/Mother Teresa/Joan of Arc would've done in a situation like this.

Jesus probably would have smiled and lovingly shaken his head at the boxes full of memories. Mother Teresa would have recycled the cardboard to make shoes for impoverished children. Joan of Arc most likely would have burned them since people were really into burning things at the stake back then. I went with the Jesus method and happily shook my head as I returned the boxes to the storage area in the back of my closet, thinking that perhaps I would open them up at a more appropriate time and place—preferably never.

If I wanted a chance of holding on to my peaceful demeanor in time for my come-to-Jesus meeting with Gwen tomorrow, I absolutely could not dredge up the past right now. Besides, the odds were that the boxes were just full of old high school yearbooks, report cards, and movie ticket stubs that would mean nothing to me when I saw them.

After wrapping up the evening with a long and lingering bubble bath scented with ylang-ylang oil—yes, I had to go to a specialty health store just to get it since it promised to induce a sense of renewal and refreshment—I hit the hay at nine p.m. on a Friday night, if you can believe it. I wanted to look rested, refreshed, and like a competent beauty editor when I faced the Dragon first thing in the morning.

∽∾∽∾

The morning came much earlier than I hoped. Even though I was acting all confident and empowered, I was actually shaking in my boots about the upcoming meeting. I did everything in my power to push those negative thoughts aside since they were crowding my new positive being. Instead, I just thought like Jesus/Mother Teresa/Joan of Arc and focused on my impending victory of keeping my job and not becoming an unemployed, loser widow at the age of twenty-nine.

It always seemed like when you were dreading something, it came that much sooner. So, of course, I made the standard twenty minute drive to my office in about ten minutes. I found parking out front within about fifteen seconds at a free meter since it was the weekend. Just my luck, I was crazy early to my scary meeting, and I had nothing to stall or distract me. I wasted roughly three minutes putting on yet another coat of hot pink lip shimmer until I knew it was finally time for me to face the music and own up to what I had done.

The majority of the executive offices at *High Life* had large front windows made of glass, allowing all of the inner peons at their cubicles to see out to a beautiful mountain view and realize there really was life outside of their workspace. For me, these large glass windows allowed me to clearly see the piercing eyes of one Gwen Jacobs glaring at me from at least sixty feet away as I stepped out of the elevator. *Let the intimidation begin.*

I tried to maintain the peaceful and professional poise I had worked so hard on over the past twenty-four hours and walked, with what I hoped was a confident strut, directly into Gwen's large, glass enclosed office overlooking Pike's Peak.

"Good morning, Danielle," she began briskly. "Please shut the door behind you and take a seat."

I had no idea why she wanted me to shut the door. We were literally the only people in the building besides the security people on a different floor. But I figured this was all part of her POW intimidation tactics. I closed the door behind me and sat in silence, awaiting my fate.

She took what felt like several full minutes before she began her businesslike monologue. I was quite familiar with it since I had sat in as a witness on several other employees being fired or reprimanded. *Great, she brought me in here so she could fire me face-to-face.* Why didn't she just do it over the phone or in an e-mail when she had the chance?

"Danielle, since you're the one that arranged this meeting, I will let you begin."

Oops. I guess she was waiting on me. I kind of forgot I had called the meeting in the first place since it had the whole principal's office type of feel to it. I hadn't really prepared anything to say.

"Right, Gwen. I realize that my actions at the sponsors' luncheon on Thursday were completely inexcusable. I just wanted to formally apologize to you and let you know I am prepared to do everything in my power to keep my job and ensure a professional working environment."

Silence. I forged on ahead, partially due to my phobia of uncomfortable silences.

"What I basically mean is that I am very, very sorry for my strange outburst, and this job means so much to me. I can promise you an outburst like that will never happen again. I would just love it if we could put it all behind us." I smiled up at her hopefully.

She continued on with her guerrilla warfare, terror tactics by tapping her pen in rapid succession on her desk as she appeared to think about what I was saying. I, however, knew better. I also remembered this militant tapping being part of her routine, where she let her victim stew as she stalled the conversation just so that she could see them sweat. And it was definitely working on me. I tried to casually wipe off the sweat mustache my upper lip had accumulated over the past several minutes and maintain my composure.

Finally, she drew in a very deep breath and said, "Well, Danielle, I'm sure you know me quite well after working here for over a year, and you've also seen me fire more than a few people." She smirked. "Fortunately, you're not going to be fired today. But I must have you know the only reason I am letting this slide without telling you to clear your desk immediately is because of the personal obstacles you've had to face in the past year. I've never lost a spouse, but I've been through two very nasty divorces. I know that type of trauma can cause quite a bit of emotional upheaval. What I do want you to understand is that I will be watching you closely, and I will not permit any more unprofessionalism, especially in front of your superiors."

Hold the phone! Gwen had a heart? *And wasn't a lesbian*? This was news to me. It was all I could do to hold myself back from kissing her or giving her a giant hug. She had literally saved me from becoming that creepy lady who collects unemployment and never leaves her house again because her cats are her babies— overlooking the fact I hate cats.

My prayers had been answered!

I smiled in what I hoped was a restrained fashion. "Gwen, I can't tell you how much I appreciate this, and I promise I won't let you down."

Although that was a cheesy *Rudy*-inspired thing to say, I really did want to let her know how absolutely serious I was about changing my work performance and pretty much every other area of my life.

I humbly let myself out of her office—and had to keep myself from bowing prostrate before her on my way to the door. I decided one of my first steps in the right direction was to put in a few good of hours of work. Even if it happened to be a Saturday.

To clarify, this was a really big deal for my new and improved self. There was nothing I hated more than working on a weekend. I was from the firm school of thought that working hours were from Monday to Friday, eight to five, with no leeway in between now that I was a grown-up.

Of course, grown-ups still had to swallow their pride and do what they had promised to God and their boss. So I aspired to make the best impression today by starting on some of the work I had missed after I stayed at home all day yesterday. And before you think me too saintly, some of that work also included checking my clogged inbox full of eHarmony e-mails from my potential matches.

Since I had been in such a foul mood over the past several weeks, I had really let things slide when it came to maintaining my online dating reputation. I weeded through sixty eHarmony-match e-mails, and my finger ached from hitting the delete button. Apparently, I had been sent another batch full of trolls.

Seriously, was there a setting you could check on your profile to ensure all of your potential matches actually breathed oxygen and

went out into the normal light of day regular-
ly? I suspected not. I had quite a collection of
freaks waiting to match up with me.

I wasn't even trying to be egotistical or
pompous, but I felt like I was a decent-to-
somewhat-attractive person who had posted a
legitimate picture. However, my last date,
Ryan, would strongly disagree since he called
me fat and old. So was I also on the list of
trolls other people were deleting from their in-
boxes?

Normally that thought would have infuriat-
ed me, but since I had quite a bit of Mother
Theresa mojo going for me today, I just realized it was part of the circle of life. We would
all get our chance when it was the right time
for each of us.

Speaking of the right time, one of the nerdy
trolls I was about to delete actually caught my
eye, if you could believe it! He obviously was
a nerd since he worked as an accountant in
Arvada, enjoyed video games, and also loved
archaeology. Although I wasn't exactly sure
what that entailed as a full-blown hobby. Did
that mean he dug through his yard on the
weekends to find fossils? Did he travel to Isra-
el to go on archaeological digs? Either way, he
was actually pretty attractive, and he even used

a bit of sarcasm to describe himself on his profile, which I appreciated.

Besides, wasn't it kind of obvious I'd been spending too much time going for the pretty boys lately? Either they were lying cheaters or liars with an attitude problem, which was all relative. Maybe it would do me good to go the "nerd route" and see if this guy was fairly normal? His name was Ron Franklin, a confirmed nerd name that sounded like it may have belonged to his grandfather. But he seemed to have the cute nerdy appeal that was being marketed these days on every indie romantic comedy starring Michael Cera and some chick with an emo haircut.

I was now the new and improved Danielle. It would only make sense I would try to date a totally different type since my regular cookie-cutter attractive guy wasn't working out for me at all. Besides, this guy was fairly striking in his own nerdy way. Maybe he would grow on me, and we would actually have a good time together, one that didn't involve lying or yelling. There was only one way to find out.

I typed out a quick message to Ron.

Ron—Yes, I remembered to omit the "Hey."

I just wanted to drop a note to say hello, and I'd love to talk to you more, preferably not about archaeology or video games since I don't have the first clue about either one. ☺ LOL. Feel free to message me back anytime, and have a good weekend!
Danielle

Perfect! Mother Theresa or Joan of Arc couldn't have done it better. I thought sprinkling in a bit of humor was a great idea to see how Ron responded to it. I figured I would just let this potential nerd date simmer for a while to see if he replied, and I could save the long list of rejects in my inbox for later.

I tried to focus on actual work for a while as that's what I was there for. Believe it or not, I was actually able to get a surprising amount of work done since no one was in the office, and the phone wasn't ringing off the hook. In a mere two hours, I organized and edited all of my product reviews for the next upcoming issue. I gave myself a pat on the back for saving myself a couple weeks' work.

This whole goody-two-shoes, bettering-myself thing was working out quite well. I was still overwhelmed by the fact I was able to keep my job after the way I had behaved. That was something I didn't even want to think about since it caused a pit of shame to well up in my stomach. So I focused on bigger and better things. Like texting April to see what she was up to this evening so we could legitimately celebrate that I wasn't going to be dumpster diving anytime soon. *Hooray*!

CHAPTER 11

Not surprisingly, April was available to go out for a few drinks. Mainly because I emphasized to her I would be buying since I had acted like a total asshole and wanted to make it up to her. We decided to meet at the Wynkoop Brewing Company on Eighteenth. It had oh-so-delicious microbrewed beer and some naughty menu items, like beer cheese soup.

Just a side note for minute—have you seriously ever heard of anything better than *beer plus cheese plus soup*? I didn't think so.

I was right on time for our dinner/drinks meeting at eight p.m. April was around twenty minutes late, which I should've expected. No matter. My new and forgiving self didn't get all inpatient or bent out of shape about her being a few measly minutes late. I figured this was the perfect time to check my e-mails on my iPhone to see if a certain nerd had e-mailed me back. I had very low expectations. I had only e-mailed Ron a few hours earlier. Dating protocol dictates you must ignore initial contact at least for one day, preferably two.

But *nerds be glorified*! I could only assume Ron was inexperienced in the dating world. He e-mailed me back just an hour after I sent my message. I actually thought it was really cute that he wasn't all high and mighty and playing the dating game like most men do. It was very endearing that I could count on him to respond when I reached out to him. For any of the ladies out there that are familiar with the men that wait anywhere from three to seven days before they return a call just so they have the upper hand, you know how appreciative I felt.

His message read:

> *Dear Danielle,*
> *Thanks for your e-mail! Actually, not too many people know about archaeology since it is a very unpopular hobby. LOL. I'll be sure to tell you about it sometime if you're having trouble sleeping since it would bore you to death. :-) It says on your profile that you like animals? I love animals too. I actually*

*have a ferret and an iguana, which
I know are strange pet choices for
a grown man. Anyway, if you'd ever like to grab lunch, I'd be happy
to meet you. How about Tuesday?*
Ron

Sweeeet! Finally, a seemingly nice, normal, and forward guy who asked me out up
front on a date without hemming and hawing
and leading me on—I'm not sure who says
"hemming and hawing" these days, but you
know what I mean.

I'd have to ask him a few more questions
about his exotic choice in pets, but maybe he
just had a loveable eccentric streak in him. Either way, this Ron character was totally getting
the benefit of the doubt. He seemed sweet,
normal, and free from all of those stupid dating games I was so tired of. Even good old
Adam, before his sordid cheating days, was an
offender.

I had a vivid memory of meeting Adam
when I was a barmistress at the Irish Hound
Pub off of Sixth in Cherry Creek, where I
spent the majority of my evenings and weekends attempting to pay off my college loans after I graduated. Adam sauntered in looking all

kinds of dashing, confident, and very clean cut. Something I liked, since it was so rare amidst all the greasy and unwashed hippies in Colorado. He had a haircut *and* didn't have a beard or a five o'clock shadow.

Quick, ladies, get it while it's hot!

So, of course, all the other young barmaids, my coworkers, were eyeing him up and down so thoroughly it must have burned a huge hole in his fleece jacket. But I had the pleasure of elbowing them all in the face so I could be the first one to greet his table. It turned out he was meeting a few buddies for drinks after work since he already had a grown-up job—giving him yet another checkmark on the "pros" list of the many reasons why I should date this stranger.

I'd never been one to just give out my number freely, especially working in a bar where you have to be made of armor to deflect all of the douchebags that ask you for your number or leave you their own illegibly written number on a crumpled cocktail napkin each and every day. Still, this was one of the few times I wanted to get to know one of my customers much, much better.

Yet I really didn't know how to get from point A to point B. What I did do was spend a little too much time talking to Adam about our beer specials and half-price onion rings on Wednesdays, so it became overly obvious that I was trying to put myself out there.

Either Adam was totally oblivious or great at flirting because all he did was sweep his well-cut, wavy hair across his forehead, bat his hazel eyes at me, and continue on with our scintillating conversation about which New Belgium Beer went the best with the smoked pork sandwich. I voted for Sunshine Wheat, while Adam was set on the strange choice of 1554—in case you were wondering.

I finally giggled my way back behind the bar and halfheartedly served the five other customers waiting on me to pour their drinks— running back to Adam's table any chance I got to give him and his friends extra napkins, a fresh beer, and even a toothpick. Which even *I* had to admit was a really weird thing to do.

Finally, I split up his group's checks, and they all paid out their tabs. I was utterly convinced Adam would leave his number on the credit card slip. He was around so many guys it would probably have been embarrassing to ask for my number outright. When the group finally got up to leave, I collected their credit card receipts. Lo and behold, there was absolutely—*nothing*!—left for me other than a few decent tips. Seriously, wasn't I flirting my ass off? Didn't I bat my eyes at him until they were dry and aching? Didn't I give him a *toothpick*?

It was obvious this guy just wasn't into me. I was even more embarrassed about the fact I had completely misread what I thought was some hard-core flirting. I returned to my place behind the bar, where I wiped down the sticky bar-top with a dirty rag, as was my lot in life. It was probably because I was so downtrodden and full of self-pity that I didn't see Adam sneak back in after his friends left to approach the bar and ask me for my number.

Score!

I was elated this one-in-a-million hot guy wanted my number as opposed to all of the perverts at the bar who normally hit on me. Over the next few days, I was on the edge of my seat waiting for his call.

But, of course, you know how the story goes. Even though I ended up marrying the guy, he called me for the first time to ask me out for drinks *three full weeks later*! Can you believe that shit?

I teased him about it later on in our marriage. His excuse was to flatter me by telling me he was so into me he didn't want to come on too strong. I don't know what it is about most guys' genetic codes. They would rather err in the opposite direction and convince you they hate you before they ask you out on a first date.

Just as I was about to type a quick e-mail back to Ron to set up our first lunch date—since he was one of the good guys who managed to communicate on time—April rushed into the brewery in a swirl of citrusy perfume, apologizing profusely for being late. She claimed she had gotten halfway here without her ID and had to turn around and go get it. That was just one more typical April story as to why she was always late—her cat got out, she had a flat tire, her watch was twenty minutes slow, etc. etc. etc. Believe me, I had heard them all. Yet these days, I was much more forgiving, especially after the way I had berated her a few weeks earlier.

We got down to business right away and ordered some delicious microbrewed beers paired with more than a few appetizers to get us started Of course, April ordered more food than usual since I was the one paying, but I gently reminded myself she deserved every morsel of food I bought her tonight as I was the one who had humiliated her publicly. I tried to bring up the subject again—to make sure we were all good—but she quickly waved off my concerns.

"No, I already told you. That is *so* water under the bridge. You don't need to apologize to me again. What I really want to know is exactly what happened between you and Cherry! Like, did you know what you were going to say to her in advance, or was that all improv?" Her eyes were shining with the excitement of it all.

"Actually, I had no clue what I was going to say, and I didn't get the chance to tell you about this, but I bumped into her in the restroom beforehand. We were both touching up our makeup, and I didn't even realize it was her until she said her name when she answered her phone. I was so shell-shocked I didn't have time to say a single word to her. I think that's why I went so crazy when I brought up all that stuff about Adam at lunch."

I shoved about five cheesy fries into my mouth as I waited for April to reply.

She had the same idea and stuffed her face to the max while I was talking, so we both sat there in silence until we chewed enough food we could speak. April got there first.

"Yeah, that was crazy! I thought you were maybe just going to introduce yourself so she could recognize your name, but you went out there with guns blazing and didn't even give her a chance! I have to say I really admire this new gutsy, ballsy side of you where you don't let anyone walk over you anymore. If I were a guy," she said with a wink. "I'd think it was pretty hot."

"Um, ew. I don't know if I should be offended that you're hitting on me or take it as a compliment. Anyway, we bumped into each other, or rather, she came out and talked to me after I stormed out, and I just told her to move on with her life and leave me alone. There's really nothing that can be said since Adam's dead. But I do think it was a good idea to get it all out, even though I was barely able to keep my job after all that craziness."

"Oh, yeah! How did Gwen take it all? I'm not going to lie—I really thought you were out of a job for sure. I didn't want to tell you over the weekend, but the word got around a little bit about your lunch confrontation, and all of the other editors were saying you'd be fired for sure. I didn't want you to kill yourself or anything, so I just waited to tell you until after you'd heard back from Gwen. Which is why we're here, celebrating," she concluded, making a "cheers" gesture with a handful of french fries.

"You can say that again. I probably would have flipped out if I'd gotten fired, but I'm totally pulling it together and turning over a new leaf, like no drama, no anger, and no public outbursts."

"We'll see how that goes," she muttered under her breath.

I caught myself before I shot her a dirty look. "And—onto bigger and better news, I think I have a legitimately good date lined up. I have to admit he looked a little bit nerdy at first glance. I almost deleted him, but I think it's time I break the mold and actually try to date someone normal instead of a pretty boy with a bad attitude."

"I hear you," she replied through a mouthful of food. "I've only had, like, three online dates, and they all were either totally weird and unfit for society or trying to grope me before we'd even ordered our entrées."

I smiled proudly. "Yeah, I think this new guy may be a good one. He e-mailed me back an hour later, which is totally against 'guy code.' I think we're going to go to lunch on Tuesday."

April's eyebrows rose, but she continued to eat with full force. We both knew it was a cold day in hell when a guy called you back the same day. Let alone within an hour. We spent the rest of the meal trashing all the said guys from our past who had difficulty using the phone and especially communicating in person, until we had had so much beer and greasy bar food—beer cheese soup!—we were barely able to roll out the door and make it home in one piece.

As soon as I was home, I sent Ron a quick e-mail telling him I would absolutely love to meet him for lunch on Tuesday. I didn't want him to think I'd blown him off since he was so quick to reply to my message in the first place.

I decided to run myself another ylang-ylang bath to soothe all my senses. The perfect ending to a Saturday night. I still had gainful employment, thank the Lord.

As I was relaxing in a wonderfully steamy and intoxicating bath, trying to release all of my stress over the past several days, I heard my phone buzz from the other room. Since I was all hopped up on the pre-dating jitters I normally got when there was a new candidate in the picture—coupled with a pretty strong beer buzz from the brewery—I jumped out of the tub, sopping wet, and left a trail of water behind me as I trotted over to my phone to see who sent me a message.

Lo and behold, Ron had already e-mailed me back within a mere twenty minutes! I decided to shrug off the fact that maybe he was a creepy nerd, sitting by the computer, as I had initially suspected. No, he was part of the new breed of mature men on the planet I had yet to meet who were more than obliged to respond to a call, text, or e-mail whenever they received it.

Who made all of these crazy dating rules anyway? It was entirely refreshing that someone was willing to reply to a message as soon as they read it. If I were to fault Ron for responding to my e-mail so promptly, I would be the one perpetuating the stereotype of guys never calling back in the first place. Ron's e-mail was short and sweet. He asked me to meet him at a downtown restaurant called Zengo's close to the highway. From his description, it was supposed to be a Latin-Asian fusion restaurant, which I had never heard of before. But I definitely liked a good enchilada and a good piece of sushi—though not necessarily on the same plate—so I was game.

Living by a new set of rules these days, I returned Ron's e-mail, leaving myself at risk for looking like a desperate shut-in who spent all of her time on the computer on a Saturday night. So be it. I confirmed our date and told him I couldn't wait. I would be there with bells on. Admittedly, that last part was a little weird and the result of the many beers I'd had earlier in the evening. But I thought it would pass as whimsical and cute. Hopefully. Or else inebriated and loose-lipped.

I couldn't decide.

CHAPTER 12

The few days before the big nerd-date at Zengo's seemed to magically fly by. It was all work, work, work for me. The new and improved version of Danielle definitely had a passion for her job. I wanted to keep my nose to the grindstone and prevent any more work related outbursts or casualties. Things with April and I were also going well after I bought her that truckload of food Saturday night to win back her favor.

We spent our lunch break on Monday plotting exactly what I was going to wear, say, think, and do on my lunch date the following day.

One thing I knew was I wanted to put the ball in Ron's court. I'd already had two botched dates under my belt, so I was trying to look at my dating life with a sense of humility and open-mindedness. After all, I could have been the one who caused much of the conflict on those dates, given my recent bouts of hostility. This time, I would be demure, relaxed, and easy going and give Ron a chance to get to know the true me. And if he wanted to eat a piece of sushi rolled up in an enchilada and smothered with salsa, that was fine, too.

Tuesday morning brought with it quite a few butterflies rumbling in my stomach. I wasn't exactly sure what I was so nervous about. Maybe it was because this geeky Ron was a whole different animal. I mean, if he wasn't going to play games with me, then how were we going to have a proper date? As horrible as it was, I'd only had experience in the dating world with guys who didn't call, didn't tell you outright they were into you, and you only found out they were serious about you when they proposed. *Ahem, Adam.*

I think this date with Ron made me even more nervous because I didn't know exactly what we were going to talk about—if we weren't going to be coy, flirty, or asking "first date" questions. Ferrets and iguanas, perhaps?

I arrived at Zengo's at twelve-thirty p.m. on the nose, and—surprise, surprise—Ron was already there, waiting for me at a table. I knew it was him because I asked the hostess if there was a Ron waiting, and she brought me directly to him, commenting along the way that she thought it was adorable we were on our first date. But despite Ron oversharing information with the restaurant hostess, I still had a great feeling going into this lunch date.

I relaxed immediately when I saw Ron. He looked exactly like his profile picture, thank the Lord above. I was more than well acquainted by now with all of the bait and switch maneuvers with profile pictures—much tricking someone into going on a date with you before revealing your actual face. *Gasp*! Luckily, Ron was of medium height, looked to be in good shape, and had short dark hair that perfectly complemented his dark brown eyes. So far, so good. Now let's see if he had a personality.

Ron stood up and eagerly shook my hand. I looked down and saw he was wearing a full-fledged business suit, which was more than awkward, seeing as I was wearing a pair of skinny jeans, a graphic T-shirt shredded to the point of being fashionable, and bright yellow ballet flats.

Since *High Life* was a hot and upcoming magazine, any type of trendiness was encouraged. I wasn't necessarily limited to wearing a vesty business pantsuit day in and day out.

Although Ron greeted me as if he were a vacuum cleaner salesman going door-to-door, he immediately put me at ease with his friendly smile. "Danielle! It's so great to meet you! Thanks for coming."

"You, too!" I sat down and made myself comfortable at our corner booth in the back of the restaurant. "So, I see you have to dress up for your job as an accountant, huh?" I joked, trying to break the ice.

"Oh, this?" Ron looked down at his funeral attire. "Actually, our office is normally business casual. I just wore this suit because I wanted to make a great first impression for our date."

Wow, how endearing. Still, this guy was much more clueless than I had anticipated. I forged on with the conversation, asking Ron more about his strange taste in hobbies, like how he got interested in archaeology in the first place. I sandwiched my many amicable questions between several strong glasses of sangria. This helped to relax me, so I suddenly felt I was the life of the party. Especially compared to straight-laced and buttoned-up Ron.

Don't get me wrong. He was definitely cute—in his own way. But this was one of the first dates I had been on where I didn't struggle with being intimidated or worrying I was making a bad impression.

It was glaringly obvious Ron had little practice with women. He seemed to be staring at me adoringly and vehemently agreeing with every single thing I said. I think if I'd told him I hated the homeless in Denver and thought they all should be carted off to a ranch in South Texas, he would have agreed that was the best idea he'd heard all day. That's how much he was hanging on my every word.

The few drinks I'd had, coupled with the fact Ron was practically worshiping me, made me bolder, funnier, and wittier than ever— least from my point of view. Normally, my first dates had a few strange halts, stops, and starts, where you look at the other person during an awkward silence and then nervously laugh together and both try to speak at once.

Nope, not this time.

I was navigating the conversation like an experienced sea captain. Ron was simply a member of my crew, along for the ride. It got to the point where I stopped asking him about his life altogether—because, honestly, you can only really talk so much about archaeology— and moved on to a highlights reel of my best years in high school, college, and to date.

I was wrapping up my self-obsessed montage with a *hi-lar-ious* story about how I had recently gotten into a fight with a cashier at a bakery near my house—she was giving me attitude about being out of my favorite type of muffin when I could *clearly* see half a dozen in the display case.

Suddenly, Ron interrupted me mid-sentence. "Would you like to go out again?"

Hmm, very flattering. But had all tact gone out the window? I guess I could have been talking about myself too much, but he just seemed so riveted. "Yes, absolutely. When would you like to do it?"

Being used to all the flighty and coy men I had dated in the past, I was sure Ron would want to see me in a week or two, if I was lucky. Silly me,

"How about tomorrow night?"

Whoa there, buddy. *Give a girl a chance to breathe.* Since I didn't have a reason as to why I couldn't go out tomorrow, I agreed to meet him at a cute little hole-in-the-wall Italian restaurant called Bella Bistro near his house in Arvada. I figured I had spent so long in past dating relationships—Adam included—wasting time trying to show the other person I wasn't interested in them so they wouldn't think I was coming on too strong, when all I really wanted to do was spend a few good evenings with the person to see if they were worth my time. Of course, it would normally turn out that by the time I discovered my date was psycho, boring, or had a creepy love for cats, I'd already been seeing them for two or three months since I had to spread out our dates so I wouldn't look desperate. Stupid, if you ask me.

Maybe this style of in-your-face dating was exactly what I needed. I could microwave any potential relationship to see if it was worth hanging onto for the future. With that thought in mind, I was actually looking forward to seeing Ron again within roughly twenty-four hours. I thought our lunch meeting had gone exceptionally well for a first date with someone I'd met online. Granted, I'd found out very little about Ron, other than where he worked and the fact he got into archaeology after an especially riveting field trip in the fourth grade. But I knew our next date would give us a chance to dig even deeper. I gave Ron a quick and polite kiss on the cheek and headed back to my office with ten minutes to spare.

Yes, this was truly the way I needed to approach dating from now on. I absolutely loved my new and improved self—calm, cool, collected, and willing to take risks with a nerdy stranger. Instead of feeling like Ron was socially awkward and didn't have a clue, I was able to see deeper and appreciate the fact he was unencumbered by the dating rules society put in place. He was simply sweet and endearing, and he was willing to show someone his true feelings right away. What a rare find.

This was something I was going to have to discuss with April in detail when I got back to the office. I sent her a quick text to call a fake meeting so we could talk about my date and told her to schedule it into my afternoon appointments so I would have a good twenty minutes blocked out to go over the play-by-play and obsess about how tomorrow night was going to go. You know, the usual.

She texted me back within three seconds, showing not only what a good friend she was, but also that she wasn't working very hard in my absence. She confirmed our "debriefing" was on for one forty-five sharp.

CHAPTER 13

Behind the closed doors of my office, April shrieked in disbelief. "So you're telling me he just flat out interrupted you and asked you out tomorrow night? Is he, like, a total freak that's desperate for a woman?"

"No, I just think he doesn't have a lot of dating experience, but in a good way. He's willing to say exactly what he means. And he doesn't seem to have any of those crazy dating rules ingrained in his mind. Which is the only explanation for him asking me out a mere day later. Maybe I've just found myself a whole new breed of man that actually says what he does and does what he says." Even I couldn't follow that profound train of thought, but it sounded good.

"No, Danielle. Sorry to break it to you, but I think this guy is either a stage four clinger, or else he is a total nerd who has no idea what he's doing when it comes to dating, which will not serve you well in the end."

We agreed to disagree since I was absolutely sure this evolved type of guy was perfect for my new persona as I made subtle, yet meaningful, changes in my life. Speaking of which, I needed to get back on task. I had to take care of a few follow-up calls to a skin care rep who was selling Inch Loss Cellulite Cream, which we hoped to feature in our spring lineup in the magazine. This was a company Gwen had referred me to herself, and I wanted to make sure I got their go-ahead to feature their product in one of our spring issues—not to mention the fact I wanted to slather a little bit of this magic cream on my backside to see if it actually worked. Two birds, one stone.

I had no luck getting a hold of the magic cellulite cream company, but I made sure to leave numerous voicemails with their receptionist and send a few e-mails to the distribution rep just to cover all my bases. Since I was skating on thin ice with Gwen, I wanted to make certain I did exactly what she commanded and more.

My e-mail alert suddenly flashed that I had received an e-mail from Gwen wanting to talk to me about an urgent matter in her office at the end of the day. Normally, this type of e-mail wouldn't even faze me since Gwen thought anything and everything on her agenda was urgent. But ever since she witnessed my unfortunate meltdown at the Expo, I had been on the lookout for something to go wrong, causing me to finally lose my job. I felt like I was working on borrowed time until I could prove to her I was an amazing and completely brand-new person, and I didn't know just how secure my job was.

I managed to sweat it out for the next few hours, but as I wrapped up my work day, I was utterly convinced this was my last day in my beautiful office overlooking Pike's Peak. *Goodbye, Danielle Starkey, successful beauty editor of High Life magazine. It was nice knowing you. We definitely had some good times together, which I will make sure to re-member fondly when you are laying in your townhome in a pool of your own vomit after drinking yourself into a stupor on lemon drop martinis on a Monday morning.* Yes, that sounded about right.

I gathered up my laptop, purse, and a few extra folders—just to seem professional and hardworking—and headed down the hallway as a *Dead Woman Walking*. Sean Penn ain't got nothin' on me!

Making my way to Gwen's glorious glass office, two doors down from my own, I knocked meekly on her beautiful mahogany door with a gold nameplate that read "Gwen Jacobs, Editor in Chief." Her receptionist was already gone for the day. *Lucky girl*, I thought bitterly. Through the door, I heard Gwen bark for me to come in, which I reluctantly did.

Oddly enough, Gwen looked positively delighted to see me—which caught me so off guard, I didn't notice the person sitting in one of the two plush chairs in front of Gwen's desk.

"Danielle!" Gwen exclaimed. "I'm so glad you finally made it! And, of course, you know Cherry James from the Expo, correct?"

Cherry turned to face me and gave a little wave. Her soft, golden blonde hair framed her face in delicate waves. She looked even more beautiful than the first time I'd met her during my verbal assault at the Expo.

What the hell was going on here? Was this some sort of cruel joke? Oh my God, what if Gwen was planning to publicly fire me in front of Cherry, thinking it the ultimate punishment? I knew she was cold-hearted and ball-busting, but I never thought she would be so evil as to plot this cunning of a revenge strategy to kick someone when she was down. What could I have possibly done to deserve this?

"Okay, ladies," Gwen continued happily, obviously delighted to be firing me in such a manner. "I know we didn't necessarily get started on the right foot." She paused to laugh at her own joke. "Danielle, I called you in here today since you were the one who recommended Cherry's work as a graphic designer to us in the first place. I've had the opportunity to look over her portfolio, and I have to say I'm greatly impressed. I truly believe Cherry has the fresh outlook we need to create a whole new face for *High Life* online. Which is why I've decided to contract her through her company for a year as our lead graphic designer for the upcoming online magazine launch."

This was great. Just great. Not only was I going to be fired and humiliated publicly in front of my husband's mistress, but my boss was basically hiring *her* right in front of me just to rub it in my face. Gwen should get an award for the cruelest firing scenario to date. I had never seen anything quite like this. In a sense, I admired her attention to detail, but I also knew this was a moment that would haunt me for the rest of my life. It was possibly the worst thing I could have imagined happening. Cherry wins, yet again.

I tuned back into the conversation as Gwen addressed me. "And since we are going to have a weekly beauty product featured for all our online readers, as well as a new beauty blog and Q&A section, I thought it would be ideal if you helped coordinate Cherry's portion of the project, Danielle. Of course, she'll be working mainly with the IT department for the programming aspect of the website itself, but she'll need quite a bit of your input for our new Featured Product Section, as well as the beauty blog we're designing."

I tried to regain my composure as I realized what Gwen was saying. The upside to the situation was that I was keeping my job, which was all I could ask. But I would be working side-by-side with Cherry, which I didn't think was ethical—not to mention the least bit beneficial to my newfound sanity! What the hell was I going to do?

I heard my own voice replying in what could only be described as an out of body experience. "Excellent! I'm very excited to be launching the new beauty section of the website, and I'll be more than happy to collaborate with Cherry to make sure it's a hit with our readers." I looked at Cherry, and she seemed just as overwhelmed—albeit more attractive—as I was. The only comfort I had in the midst of this shit storm was that Cherry had obviously been tricked into this scenario, too. Yet there was nothing either of us could do about it since we were sitting face-to-face with the Dragon herself. So we both agreed to work together for the next year.

I had no idea if my new, cool-as-a-cucumber personality could handle this. Especially since I had hoped to never lay eyes on Cherry again. Except for when she haunted me in my dreams, looking absolutely beautiful in a low-cut, black cocktail dress, when she showed up unannounced at Adam's funeral and threw herself on top of his coffin, crying dramatically.

Now I would have to experience her in the flesh at least several times a month in meetings, and I'd probably have to talk to her on the phone and e-mail her weekly. I felt numb at the thought of having to get to know this woman even more than I already did. Particularly since she seemed overly friendly. A cover for her slutty mistress tendencies?

"After talking to her company, Cherry has agreed to work here in our extra office on Thursdays and Fridays since this is such a big project for their firm." Gwen smiled triumphantly. "Danielle, this means you'll be spending two days each week with her, helping to collaborate and iron out all the details for the magazine launch. You can keep her informed on our *High Life* vision and spirit."

Wow. As it turned out, Gwen wasn't necessarily the devious boss I'd thought she was, but she was definitely a closet masochist who wanted to make me pay for my mistakes. Publicly. You'd better believe I had learned my lesson about never acting out in public again, since I was now forced to spend eternity working side-by-side with "The Mistress." Perfect, just fucking perfect.

We wrapped up our meeting in record time, as Cherry and I had very little to say about the matter. Not surprisingly, we both feigned delight and excitement about embarking on this new project together, but I could only assume she felt just as sick to her stomach as I did.

Walking down to my car like a zombie, I managed to send April a quick "SOS" text before I drove off into the crisp September evening.

Luckily, April and I had devised a system for such emergencies. An SOS text would signify that the recipient had to get to the sender's house as quickly as possible, or she may have a mess on her hands. I'd only had to use this SOS text signal three other times in our friendship. The first was when I'd gotten my period as a hostess at work and had no feminine supplies, so April hightailed it to the restaurant and brought a few backups for me. The second was when I'd gotten engaged to Adam—which was a complete and utter surprise—and wanted April to get her ass over to my apartment so I could tell her my good news face-to-face while showing off my sparkling engagement rock.

The last and most unfortunate use of the SOS signal was when Adam died, which had definitely put a damper on SOS-texting ever since. So, today, I was somewhat happy to be able to use the old code without having the excuse of a spouse dying or anything quite as morbid. Although at this moment in time, I almost felt that having to work with Cherry for the next year was a fate much worse than death.

Since I knew April had left work about an hour before me and planned to go home and catch up on some *Weeds* she had DVR'ed, I was fairly confident she could get to my house within a half-hour. And I was right. She showed up on my doorstep a mere thirty minutes later, with not one, but two bottles of wine.

"Hey, boozehound," I quipped as I let her in the door. She looked positively scared out of her mind, so I quickly reassured her. "Don't worry, nobody's died this time."

"Either way, I figured we'd at least need a bottle each, so I came fully prepared."

She had never been one to waste time and opened a bottle of Pinot Noir before I even had the chance to get out my beautiful red-bubble wine glasses. I was afraid she was going to start drinking out of the bottle if I didn't start talking soon, so I passed her the wine glasses and spilled the beans.

As I wove the whole sordid tale of the project both Cherry and I would be working on together, April sucked in her breath until I thought she was going to vacuum all the oxygen out of the room.

"April, you just need to breathe. You look way more stressed out than I do. Take a few drinks of wine at least."

She mutely did as I said, and I went on with my story. "So I have absolutely no idea what I'm going to do. There's no way I can make another mistake—since I've already screwed up beyond belief—and I don't think I can turn down working on this project. Not if I want to keep my job. I guess I'm just going to have to suck it up and somehow get along with someone who's seen Adam naked," I wailed as I clutched my glass of wine for support. "But I really have no clue how I'm going to do that!"

"Okay, there's got to be a way around this. Like isn't this a conflict of business and pleasure? I mean, not pleasure for you, but the fact she's pleasured your husband? Isn't it illegal for the two of you to work together?"

"No, I really don't think so. It's not like she slept with someone at her own job—which would have been way better for me. I think it's Gwen's call as to whether this is unethical or not. And it's clear she's getting some sick pleasure out of throwing us together. I think this is a test to see if I'll freak out and give her a good excuse to fire me."

April nodded sagely in agreement. "Yup, she's totally trying to bait you to see if you'll go crazy on The Mistress. Although I have no idea why she has it in for you. Maybe you just embarrassed her too much at the luncheon."

"Well, either way, I'm not going to let this get the best of me. If this is a clever test, then I'm going to do everything in my power to pass it. If anyone crashes and burns, it will be Cherry, not me."

With that little bit of resolve to calm me down, I sat back. We finished a bottle of wine a piece and watched reruns of *Dancing with the Stars*. If there was anything that could make me feel better about my own depressing life, it was watching washed up celebrities dance together in a competition. Pure gold.

CHAPTER 14

The next day at work passed fairly normally. It was a Wednesday, and I didn't have the pleasure of working with my nemesis until Thursday and Friday. I treasured my last twenty-four hours of sanity before I had to handle this drama, head-to-head, in my very own office. Fortunately, I did have an exciting nerd date to look forward to.

The more I thought about seeing Ron for the second time, the more it felt right. Yes, he may have dressed up as a Jehovah's Witness for our first date in order to impress me, which was somewhat strange. Still, he did seem to hang on to my every word and look at me with admiration—something I could use a little more of in my daily life. Especially with all of the potential work conflict I was facing.

I vowed to focus more on Ron on our upcoming date so I could find out about where he grew up, where he went to high school, and what his family was like. The works. It seemed a little odd I hadn't taken the time to find out all this information the first time I met him. But our conversation seemed to be flowing so well, and I was coming up with story after story, so it was difficult to stop and ask him the 411 about his upbringing.

Getting off work at a reasonable hour, I made it home by six p.m. Which meant I could shower leisurely, air-dry my hair, try on ten different outfits, and do my makeup two or three times before I had to leave to meet Ron. . Call me neurotic, but practice truly makes perfect. I absolutely loved considering numerous options before I decided on my final look.

I ultimately went with a short, black, ruffled skirt with a tucked-in beaded top and knee-length flat boots. I paired this with long, silver chandelier earrings, which I thought gave me the perfect balance of casual/chic, ideal for a second date at a cute Italian restaurant. I would knock Ron's socks off—as long as they weren't held up by those old man sock-suspender contraptions.

I arrived at Bella Bistro at exactly seven forty-five as agreed, since I was never one for being late. Seriously, it drove me up the wall when people weren't on time. How much effort does it take to leave the house X amount of minutes early to get from point A to point B?

April's constant tardiness had also done quite a bit to encourage me to be constantly punctual. I always tried to make it to my next engagement at the exact moment I was due. So far, the rest of society hadn't quite caught on to the virtue of punctuality, so I usually sat around for five or ten minutes by myself, waiting for my friend/date/sister/ doctor to arrive. Tonight, however, Ron had beaten me to the punch again. He was already sitting at a two-person table in the back corner of the restaurant.

What time had this guy gotten here in order to reserve a table? No matter. I was just happy to see him waiting for me with a huge smile on his face. I was even more pleasantly surprised when he handed me a single red rose. Granted, it was a little cheesy and *Bachelor*-inspired to give someone a single rose on a date. I was normally the type of girl who appreciated originality, like a bouquet of daisies, but I had promised myself I was going to be open-minded and not mercilessly picky any longer. The new Danielle was in the house! If a well-meaning nerd wanted to give me a single red rose, I would gladly accept it, while truly valuing his gentlemanly intentions.

We ordered our entrées—gnocchi and pasta primavera, respectively. Then I started firing off questions about where he had grown up, if he had any siblings, and if he was close to his family—saving the bigger dating history questions for later.

As it turned out, he grew up in Idaho, in a small town outside of Boise. He had a robust family of five brothers and sisters, still living there and running the family feed and grain supply company. How charming.

"So how'd you end up in Denver?" I asked. "What made you want to get away from working for the family biz for the rest of your life?"

"Well, actually, I've always loved numbers, and believe it or not, one of the best accounting programs is at CU in Boulder. My parents always thought I would come back and take care of the books for their business. But I was offered a job in Arvada right out of college, which I didn't want to pass up. I still see my family on holidays, but it was time for me to branch out. I'd grown up pretty sheltered," he added with a grin.

I smiled in return. "Oh, really? I couldn't tell."

"Yeah, you'd never know it to look at me, but we actually didn't have a television until I was fifteen. And by that point, I really wasn't all that interested. Which is probably why I have all these strange hobbies, like archaeology, astronomy, and leaf collecting."

Leaf collecting? That was a new one. I took a good, hard, look at Ron. It was quite obvious that being sheltered was an understatement. He had again shown up for our date wearing dress trousers, a tucked-in dress shirt, and a tie. Luckily, he had gone without the formal suit jacket this time, but he still looked like he was ready for a church dance, a barn raising, or something of that nature. I didn't know what it was, exactly, that made his outfit look so much different than what other men normally wore on a date. Maybe it was because his dress shirt seemed a little too tight, with cuffs that were noticeably too short, like something he wore for his college graduation, several years ago.

"I like your tie," I said because I couldn't think of anything else to say.

"Really?" He beamed at me. "Actually, I got these clothes five years ago for my younger sister's wedding, but I haven't had the opportunity to wear them again until now."

I'd hit the nail on the head with that one. I wasn't sure what, but there was something just a little bit different about Ron. I had yet to decide whether or not it was a good thing. Yes, he had all of the qualities I looked for in a man, like calling on time, holding open the door for me, and always paying for a date. In fact, I didn't even have to wonder or fret whether I would see him again since he'd already asked me to go to a movie on Saturday at the very beginning of our meal.

That forwardness seemed like something I'd always wanted in a guy. But there was also very little sizzle or chemistry. The thrill of the chase was pretty much shot. In fact, he was treating me as if we were already an old married couple, where it was a given we would want to go to a movie on a hot and wild Saturday night.

Of course, I agreed to the movie right off because, as I already said, I wanted to microwave our potential relationship to see if anything was there. If I could spend as much time with Ron as possible, I could get rid of him much more quickly if it turned out we weren't compatible. Perhaps this was an irrational approach to dating, but I'd had so many bad experiences, I was willing to try just about anything. I had also vowed to be open-minded and accepting, so I felt it was only right to give him a few more chances.

Besides, the other interesting thing about our dates thus far was the fact we hadn't even brushed hands, let alone kissed. Most guys I had gone out with in the past definitely wanted a good night kiss on the first date. If not a little more. Ron, on the other hand, seemed to jump back in surprise if I even put my arm near him when reaching for a fork. I had no clue whatsoever if we even had any physical chemistry. My thinking was that we just needed a few good make out sessions to establish a physical connection. That had always seemed to work for me, starting from the eighth grade on.

Our second date ended quite pleasantly with me finally caving in and telling story after story about myself for the second half of the meal. The truth was Ron and I didn't have very much in common. He seemed more than happy to turn the floor over to me. Since he fed my ego with all of his adoration, I gladly obliged him and put on a show, expounding on my life, while he eagerly ate it up.

Anyway, having everything in common was not only overrated, it was also unrealistic. Hadn't Adam and I always prided ourselves on our shared interests, like obsessing over The Killers, playing poker, going hiking, and taking salsa dancing lessons? All of our friends were always jealous about how we did everything together. And you can see just how far that got us. In fact, I was sure my next step should be dating someone completely opposite from me, since opposites attracted so well. No more of this matchy-matchy, we're-best-friends bullshit. It was time to grow up and join the real world by finding someone who was sincere and didn't lie to me. No matter how little I cared about archaeology or leaf collecting.

Ron behaved like a perfect gentleman and walked me to my car after the meal. I was sure this was when the first kiss was going to happen. Even if it was just a peck on the lips, I really didn't mind. I just wanted to see if I was somewhat physically attracted to him.

Instead, he gave me a very chaste hug. I tried to hold on for a little longer to give him the chance to make a move since he seemed to be very shy. Don't all men work the same way? Just because you're shy doesn't necessarily mean you're a prude. I was pretty sure that when given the green light, almost any red blooded man would be happy to make a move. *Right?*

Wrong.

Ron only hugged me warmly for the few extra minutes, as if I was his grandmother, and then broke free. "I had a really great time, Danielle, and I can't wait to see you on Saturday. I'll e-mail you a few movie choices so we can decide what we want to see. Bye."

And with that, he jumped into his Ford Focus and screeched out of his parking space.

I, too, climbed into my car and drove home, hoping to at least catch part of *Top Chef* since it was only nine o'clock. I had assumed Ron was made up of the complex DNA that most other men were, and he would want to go out for drinks after dinner, invite me back to his house, and make me put my foot down, saying that I had to get up early in the morning. But, no. Here I was, driving alone back to my own townhouse in Cherry Creek after ending our date at a fairly reasonable hour, with only a movie to look forward to this weekend.

Was it something I did or said?

I was mystified. I'd never dealt with a man like this before. The normal gender roles I was used to involved being a woman who tried to act respectable and modest, until she decided she'd resisted long enough, and it was okay to jump in the sack. As for guys, they were supposed to be always wanting more, yet restraining themselves out of respect for the invisible boundaries already set in place.

In these situations, both players knew exactly what was going on. But they continued to play the game because that was just the way it was. As a woman, I had never had to deal with a guy who wasn't pursuing me sexually, at least a little bit, whether it was the checker at the grocery store looking down my shirt when I reached into my purse for my credit card or a guy pressuring me to come home with him on our second date. I didn't necessarily want to be sexually *assaulted* by Ron, but why wasn't he treating me any different than he would his sister?

Still, I had our next date to figure out this dilemma, and I was sure that even the shyest and most prudish guy would become uninhibited in a dark movie theater. I mean, wasn't that exactly why high schoolers went to the movies every weekend? So they could feel each other up without getting in trouble with their parents? Yes, perhaps that was why Ron suggested a movie in the first place. He was shy and wanted to grope me in the anonymity

of a dark theater—which was perfectly ac-
ceptable to me.

To say the least, he was a mystery—unless
he was gay and planning to use me as his
beard.

CHAPTER 15

I awoke the next morning with a pounding in my head. I initially thought it was a hangover, although I'd only had two glasses of wine at dinner. Then I remembered my headache was due to the fact I had woken up at hour intervals throughout the night, worrying about what I was going to do when I was forced to work side-by-side with Cherry.

I'd also bitten off all of the fingernails on my right hand—but not my left— and now resembled some kind of deranged wolverine with retractable claws on only one hand.

I could barely eat a single thing for breakfast as I was so stressed out about what I was going to say to Cherry. I also worried that maybe she would want to talk casually about her affair—like we were girlfriends dishing the dirt and gossiping. Both of those options horrified me. I didn't think I had it in me to deal with this for a whole year. Still, my only other alternative was to get a whole new job, which I definitely wasn't willing to do. My career was all I had left at this point.

If I wanted to be the ball-busting, career-driven woman I aspired to be, I couldn't let a small thing like working with my husband's mistress put a wrench in my plans. I would just have to treat her like any other coworker—fair, friendly, and aloof. With my main emphasis being on aloof.

We were two professional women, so we should be able to work together without bringing our personal lives into the mix. I hoped.

I walked into my office looking much brighter and more chipper than I actually felt, even though I was on edge, anticipating Cherry jumping out from behind every corner. I gave April an overly cheerful little wave, to which she returned a look of disgust. Since I had never acted that peppy or exuberant before, she was obviously on to me.

I knew Cherry would be in the far corner office at the end of the hall, the one that sat empty after the magazine let a few people go because of the economy. Of course, that was before I'd gotten my cushy beauty editor position as one of the new hires when the economy started to bounce back in the past few years.

I planted myself firmly behind my desk, which was much larger than I ever remembered it being. It was five minutes before eight o'clock and Cherry was probably already sitting behind her perky little desk, powdering her nose, and dreaming about the next married man she was going to seduce.

Last night before bed, I had done a few extra, strengthening yoga headstands which were supposed to increase blood flow to my brain so I could think more clearly. Maybe I was imagining it, but I did feel much more alert. Like an animal that could see in the dark and smell fear, I was ready for any sign of attack.

Of course, I spent the past several weeks making myself over on the inside, so I also had the saintly resolve to keep my bad attitude in check and work peacefully side-by-side with The Mistress—oops, the name-calling was a habit I needed to break right away, or I would probably say it to her face and be fired for sure.

Cherry, Cherry, Cherry, Cherry, I mumbled, making sure I had her name fully memorized and at the tip of my tongue for our meet-and-greet this morning. I must have been mumbling somewhat audibly because I didn't hear anyone step into the room and was alarmed when my visitor cleared her throat.

Yes, predictably, Cherry stood before me. Hopefully, she hadn't heard me, or she would think I was even more obsessed and deranged than the impression I had given her on our first meeting.

What a sitcom I was living in.

"Good morning," I called enthusiastically, although she was only five feet away from me. I got up from behind my desk and approached her, not sure if I should give her a hug or a handshake, so I went with the awkward side hug. We were definitely off to a rocky start if I thought the best way to greet my new coworker/husband's-girl-on-the-side was with the open-faced hug we were always instructed to use with the boys at church so our breasts wouldn't rub against their chests and cause an erection. No danger of that here.

Cherry looked visibly uncomfortable. I couldn't blame her.

"Yes, good morning," she replied stiffly. "I was supposed to report to you first thing so you could tell me what I needed to do to get started on designing the homepage and beauty blog section of the website."

"Right, right." I shuffled back behind my desk and tried once again to look important and confident. I suspected I failed miserably since my hands were shaking like I was a drug addict in desperate need of a fix. "I printed out a few samples of websites that I absolutely love," I said. "And I made notes on them about possible design changes based on the existing layout of our magazine. I also clipped a few pages from our beauty-product-features section from the last few issues so you could get an idea of the font, color, and style that our readers are used to."

Not bad for someone who spent all night eating her fingernails instead of sleeping.

Cherry silently, took all the papers I shoved at her and hugged them to her chest as if they were a shield.

Again, I couldn't blame her. I was pretty psychotic the first time our paths had crossed.

She was about to step out of the room when she turned back to face me. "I don't know if I should even say this, but I really don't want things to be weird between us. I don't think I can say, 'sorry' enough, so I just hope you know that I plan to work professionally and respectfully with you on this project," she concluded with a weak smile.

"Sure thing! Just e-mail me or IM me if you have any questions about my notes, or you know, you can just come right on down the hall because we're in the same office after all, so it's totally convenient." I almost had to clap both hands over my mouth to keep from spewing out any more verbal diarrhea.

Sure thing? *Sure thing?* Why was I acting like she was a neighbor asking to borrow a cup of sugar? What the *hell* was wrong with me? I needed to get a handle on myself and dial down my overly cheery persona before someone got hurt.

Cherry nodded, turned, and trotted out of the room on her immensely tall high heels, click-clacking her way down the hallway. I hoped I could keep my interactions with her to a minimum so I wouldn't act either totally irate and off-the-handle or overly June-Cleaver every time I saw her.

Please, God, couldn't there be a happy medium?

April sent me a quick IM, asking what the hell was wrong with me. Apparently, she had the amazing ability to hear everything I said through the thin window that separated my office from her front-receptionist desk. Something I made a mental note of for a later date when I might have need for a private conversation.

I responded by telling her this was the new and improved me, and would she mind grabbing me a muffin next time she was in the break room, thanks so much.

Always use food to deflect from what's really going on. Yes, I was on the right track.

I buckled down under my immense workload, consumed with preparation for our new online magazine launch since it was going to be primarily beauty centered. On top of having to deal with The Mistress as My New Coworker, I also needed to make sure I crossed all of my t's and dotted all of my i's, so to speak, so that I left no room for errors which could potentially get me fired in the near future.

My neck was in the guillotine, but if I could somehow remain friendly with my scumbag husband's sickeningly-adorable side dish—and create a successfully launched website in a matter of a few months—life would be just peachy. It couldn't be *that* difficult. Could it?

To distract myself, I took a half hour out of my workday to answer a few personal e-mails, check out Facebook, see who showed their crotch on People.com, and finally answer an e-mail from Ron that had been rotting in my in-box since the evening before. Yes, you guessed it. Ron e-mailed me directly after our date the previous evening to tell me what a wonderful time he'd had and how much he looked forward to seeing me on Saturday, a mere forty-eight hours away.

I simply did not *get* this guy. He Talked The Talk via e-mail, but when we were in person, it was like having lunch with an insurance salesman—except *he* would probably flirt with me. I tried to remind myself dating someone totally opposite from me was all for the greater good. I was transforming myself and making important life changes. Perhaps, it would be like a delightful Drew Barrymore romantic comedy, where I would suddenly discover I had something in common with a random stranger, my eyes would get all starry, upbeat "indie pop" would play in the background, and I'd fall in love.

That would be ideal. But I didn't see my-self suddenly developing a passion for leaves, ferrets, or fossils in the near future. I sent Ron a quick e-mail back telling him pretty much the same thing. That I had a great time. That I was looking forward to Saturday. Yada-yada-

yada. As they said on Seinfeld, *'But you yada yada'd over the best part. No, I mentioned the bisque.'*

I also decided it was time to summon my sister from out of the woodwork. I hadn't seen her in a good three or four weeks. Not surprising, she was hardly up-to-date on any of my confrontation drama. I thought this would definitely give her some fun fodder to talk about since she was locked into the world of caring for a five-year-old. Anything besides Dora the Explorer—or whatever kids watched these days—kept her on the edge of her seat.

Yes, that was exactly what I needed. The perspective of an outsider who wasn't myself or April—the blind leading the blind, as we always said—to reaffirm that Ron was an excellent and outstanding choice as a date, and that the chemistry would come eventually. I sent my sister an e-mail asking her if she wanted to do dinner tonight or tomorrow night as I was all kinds of booked up with my big movie date on Saturday. Since I sent her the message through Facebook, I knew she would hit me back within five minutes. She always had her phone attached to her hip, vibrating constantly with Facebook updates.

And, boy, was I right. A mere two minutes later—the time it took to type out a reply—Lacey told me with many, many exclamation points that she'd absolutely love to have dinner with me tonight. Bryan was taking Jackson to karate, and she had the night to herself. The timing simply couldn't BE more PERFECT!!!!!!!—Lacey's words, not mine.

I told her I would meet her at the Outback near her house in Thornton because that's what suburban moms do, you see. You spend time frequenting chain restaurants and drinking moderately priced margaritas while your children attend a variety of classes to better themselves. I was flattered to be a part of the action.

I said I'd see her around seven p.m., which would give me enough time to lie low at home and beat the horrendous traffic on I-25. It was also early enough to give Lacey time to get a good buzz on before she had to sober up and drive the three blocks home. Her life was so tough.

The rest of the afternoon went by in a whirlwind. I communicated with Cherry primarily through e-mail, though I had a strange run in with her at the coffee pot in the break room. We both approached the coffee machine at the same time and then laughed and did it again and then laughed and made gestures like, "No, you go first"—all without uttering a word. By the time Cherry's one-year contract was up, I would be an expert mime, ready to make my big break into show business.

After the song and dance routine in the break room, I was, thankfully, able to avoid her for the remainder of the afternoon while we toiled on our separate portions of the project. As the day drew to a close, I got caught on the phone with one of the product chemists for the Inch Loss Cellulite Cream. He was trying to explain to me in detail the importance of using the CoffeeBerry Extract—patent pending—in their product to shrink and flush water from the pocketed, cottage-cheesy areas of the body.

I couldn't seem to get a word in edgewise. All I needed was a simple quote for our product feature. Something along the lines of "Inch Loss Cellulite Cream is designed to visibly lift and reduce inches with the use of the patent pending CoffeeBerry extract directly from the organic coffee plantations of Mexico, as confirmed by leading product chemist Grant DeGraw." But Mr. DeGraw didn't seem to care about that one bit. He went on and on and on about the exact process that was used to extract said CoffeeBerry Extract, which all sounded pretty redundant to me.

As the clock neared six p.m., I feared I'd be late for margaritas in suburbia with my sister and politely cut off the passionate product chemist.

"I'm so sorry, Mr. DeGraw, but I'm going to have to wrap up this call. I have another skin care distributor on hold. Thank you so much for your time. I think I got the quote I needed."

Although that was a total lie, it served its purpose. I was positive even Mother Theresa bent the truth from time to time if she happened to be dealing with a pesky impoverished child that just wouldn't leave her alone so she could go out to dinner with her friends. We've all got to eat, right?

I gathered my faux leather bomber jacket—very hip this season—and made my way out of my office without bumping into any mistresses, best friends, or evil bosses wanting to ask me questions about how the project was going. Thank God. I just needed to make it to Outback in one piece, and fast, so I could vent to my compassionate and people-deprived sister.

What I truly appreciated about Lacey was that she was an excellent listener—evidenced by the fact I had literally seen her listen with undivided attention to her son speaking in gibberish for several minutes straight, which she later told me was him reciting the alphabet he had created in a goblin language.

We had a creative genius on our hands, ladies and gentlemen.

Still, I firmly believed that Lacey's ability to listen to fabricated goblin alphabets also made her an amazing choice for laying all of my problems out on the table and seeking her advice.

The only glitch in the plan was that she often compared my problems to episodes of *Sex and the City* since there seemed to be one for every circumstance life could present a young, single lady in any city—which I guess was the whole idea.

Still, it was infuriating to have her describe Adam as being just like "Mr. Big," when I didn't think he wanted to commit early on in our relationship. Or telling me the foreign exchange student I dated in college was "just like when "Carrie" dated the Russian and moved to Paris—even though the foreign exchange student happened to be from Hungary. But I guess that's just splitting hairs.

I pulled into the Outback parking lot and went on an animalistic hunt for a parking space that ended with me facing off with a suburban mom—with very large hair—in a Range Rover. I was able to zip in front of her and score a parking space near the front door. I only hoped the aggressive looking soccer mom wouldn't be sitting near us with her three children since there would probably be a scene. The only area of my life my personality makeover had not yet affected was my driving. I was a horrible, self-centered, and very rude driver. And I didn't see that changing anytime soon.

I had always gotten terribly offended when Adam told me he didn't like my driving. I was the one who had never been in an accident, while he had been in *four*. Granted, I got into near-accident situations several times per day. But they had yet to end in a collision. Adam, on the other hand, had had two or three fender benders and the added offense of backing into a school bus in high school. So he was the one with the bad driving record, not me. That was just further evidence for my case as to why I was a perfectly good driver, albeit a little—okay, *a lot*—aggressive.

Luckily, I rushed into Outback yards ahead of the sour-faced soccer mom and her large brood of children.

I saw Lacey waiting for me at a small bar table, since all restaurants in Colorado were now non-smoking. Yes, Lacey was the type of mom that always complained about smoking, even if she was without her son, simply because she "hated the smell" and "could never get it out of her hair." I was on the other side of the argument since I was a big fan of having a casual cigarette or two—especially after drinking. I truly missed the freedom of being able to publicly poison myself when out drinking at a bar. Isn't this *America*?

Giving Lacey a quick hug hello, I settled back in my seat and ordered a tall Blue Moon from our friendly server. I didn't know what it was about chain restaurants, but all the servers were so darn friendly it made me feel guilty for how I acted during my years as a waitress. Someone had once told me a rumor that you were likely to make better tips if you were in a bad mood. I took that to heart and always treated my customers with a frosty attitude to see if maybe they would reach a little bit deeper into their wallets.

"So, how have you been?" I began. "I feel like I haven't seen you in forever. I thought I was going to have to wait till Thanksgiving or something, even though I wouldn't be sober enough to talk to you then."

Our dysfunctional-family Thanksgivings were always an excuse to drink heavily. Our parents were both divorced and remarried, as was the norm these days. My dad and my stepmother Carla lived here in Denver, although we hardly saw them since they had a three-year-old and a two-year-old—aunt and uncle to my sister's son Jackson, though he was a good two years older than them.

My mom and her husband Kyle lived in Colorado Springs, just an hour south of Denver. Even though it was oh-so-close, it was definitely far enough I only wanted to travel down there for holidays or very, very special occasions. My mom and I would sometimes meet in the middle for lunch in Castle Rock, but come to think of it, I hadn't seen her in several months either. I'd been crazy busy with work, scheming, and now making over my life. I made a mental note to call her for lunch sometime this week.

Lacey replied to my casual question like an overly eager puppy dog, "Goood!!!"Even her speech seemed to have several exclamation points and extra vowels because she was always so, so excited.

"We're redoing Jackson's room, and it's totally adorable," she said. "You have to come see it when we're done! It was always decorated as his baby room with cute little bears, but now he's all into alligators for some reason, so we have it done up as a swamp with an alligator mural and huge alligator stuffed animals!"

Sounded creepy to me. But at least it was an improvement upon the goblin fetish. I smiled. "Absolutely, I'd love to come see it. How's Jackson doing?"

"Oh!!! So great! Thanks for asking! He moved up the next belt in karate, although I have no idea what color it is now, but he's really, really excited about it! In fact, I feel a little bad for missing his class tonight, but Bryan absolutely insisted we have a sister night since I haven't talked to you in for-EV-er!!" That was literally how she said it. "So what's new with you?" she asked. "How's everything with work?"

"Well, I have a lot to catch you up on. I think I told you last time about Adam's big indiscretion. I tried to let it go, but I finally decided to Google her."

I let this sink in for a moment for emphasis. Lacey's eyes were bright with anticipation. She nodded six times in a row as a gesture for me to continue.

"So, I ended up finding this woman, and I invited her to our fall Fashion and Beauty Expo. She actually sat at my table at the luncheon, which I planned out in advance. I didn't really know what I was going to say to her, but I ended up confronting her in front of everyone about planning a vacation with my husband, and then I fled the room, crying, so it was overall extremely embarrassing."

Lacey looked pleased with all of the drama but not overly surprised. "Go on."

I shot her a sideways look. "So I was really worried about whether or not I was going to keep my job. I ended up begging my boss, and she told me I was on my final warning so I had to behave. So I've pretty much been working like a dog and trying to act perfect, and then this week I found out my boss went ahead and hired Cherry to work on a big project with us anyway. So now I have to work with her side-by-side."

Lacey didn't look at all impressed by my story, and I was wondering if she was even listening. "Did you hear what I said? Isn't that totally crazy?"

She didn't miss a beat, "Yes, that's really interesting. So what's it like working with her? Is she crazy? Are you guys getting along?"

I stopped her. "Wait. Why don't you have more of a reaction? This is actually a really big deal, but you're acting like we're talking about whether or not we liked *Avatar* or something."

She blushed and looked down at the table, "Okay, I have something to confess. I didn't think you were going to find her, so I did a little bit of snooping myself. I just wanted to see what she looked like, and if she was a totally awful person, and especially why Adam felt like he needed to get some on the side. So I went up to Cherry's office after I found her LinkedIn profile, and I made a fake appointment with her to see if she could help me design a creative writing blog I could use as a stay-at-home mom, or something like that. I can't remember what I said exactly."

"Are you kidding me? You mean you'd already met Cherry before I even Googled her, invited her to the Expo, and made a total fool out of myself? What the *fuck* is wrong with you? Why didn't you tell me right away?"

She was visibly offended at my language since she now thought the "s-word" was "shut up" when it came to dealing with Jackson. "I don't know. After I went in and met with her, she actually seemed really sweet, and it's not like I asked her flat out why she slept with Adam. I didn't have any dirt to report back to you, so I just decided to butt out."

"Yeah, you could've done that before you even met with her, and I'd have been much better off. I can't believe you didn't even tell me! You seriously could've saved me so much trouble and embarrassment, not to mention almost losing my job. Do you know that?"

I glared at her. She was always the guilt-grabber in our family, so I knew all I had to do was point the finger at her to make her buckle. I actually did point my finger at her, and she winced.

"Danielle, seriously, I'm really, really sorry. That wasn't my business at all, and I should have stayed out of it or at least told you what I was doing." "She looked absolutely distraught. "Do you forgive me?"

I let out a long sigh. At least someone was apologizing to me, even though I would have much preferred Adam on his hands and knees begging for my forgiveness. But who was I to hold something like this against my sister? It's not like she meant to hurt me. She was actually trying to do me a favor, even if it was a poorly planned one. "Yeah, I guess I understand. But you have to promise to tell me next time you stalk anyone in my life."

She bobbed her head enthusiastically, obviously happy I had forgiven her.

"Now, on to bigger and better things," I said. "I'm dating someone. Or did you already know that too?"

Lacey looked overjoyed and a little bit relieved I had dropped the subject of her meeting Cherry so quickly. "Wow!!! That's really amazing! Is it serious? Where'd you meet this guy? You have to tell me all about it!"

I signaled to the waiter for another tall Blue Moon and launched into the nitty-gritty of my not-so-sordid love affair and how we had date after date lined up until the next millennium.

Then I fired question after question at her. "So does this make any type of sense to you at all? Was that how Bryan was when you met him? Is this what it's like to have a real and long-lasting relationship with someone who isn't going to die and cheat on you—not in that order, of course?"

She took a few seconds and chewed thoughtfully on the straw of her margarita. "Um, actually...Bryan was all over me on our second date. It was a double date with one of his frat brothers, and I had to constantly slap his hand to stop him from feeling me up in front of the other couple. But overall, it sounds like Ron is a really sweet guy."

"I think I need to give Ron a chance. I'm just a little confused because he acts pretty opposite from anyone I've ever dated. I was wondering if maybe it was something wrong with me, but then why would he keep asking me out again? I really don't think he's gay, but maybe he's shy and needs a little bit of encouragement. My main objective here is that I'm trying new things since I had such a horrible experience with Adam. So I guess I'll just have to give it another few dates to see if he warms up to me."

Lacey agreed wholeheartedly. Or could she still be trying to pacify me because of her bad behavior? I would never know. However, this reaffirmed for me the whole Ron dating situation wasn't as strange as it seemed to me. Just because some guy wasn't trying to get in my pants on the second or even third date, didn't mean I wasn't attractive. That sounded like something I should have embroidered on a pillow and placed directly on my couch for all the world to see. But, seriously, this potential dating relationship was probably not as odd as I made it out to be. Every man puts the moves on in his own way, and Ron was probably just a late bloomer—although I didn't know how late he could possibly bloom since he was already thirty.

With my renewed sense of determination to give Ron another chance, I happily—and generously—paid for our tab and picked up Lacey's drinks. She thanked me and thanked me and thanked me *again*. Although I knew she was really only showering me with thanks because I had forgiven her for stalking The Mistress behind my back. But I took it all in stride.

We parted for the evening at the very late hour of eight-thirty p.m. Lacey needed to get home to put Jackson in bed and wash his karate uniform for the weekend. Although I didn't have anything quite as exciting waiting for me at home, I figured I may as well give Madam a good brushing and perhaps catch up on the *Jersey Shore* marathon. There's nothing like a little orange-tinted drama in someone else's life to make you feel better about your own, I always said.

Yet another saying that would be perfect for my embroidered pillow collection.

CHAPTER 16

efore I knew it, Saturday evening was staring at me straight in the face. And by that I meant dependable old Ron was ringing the doorbell of my townhouse as I scrambled to find my other green sequined shoe that perfectly matched my faux crocodile clutch and my backless, high-necked silver jersey top.

Yes, I was dressed to kill, even if we were only going to a movie—with a historical theme at that. Still, I thought that a Western like *True Grit* would be potentially romantic for a movie date—nothing like rough and tough cowboys to get that testosterone pumping. I made sure to dress to the nines to provide a little eye candy for the chaste and disciplined Ron. *This ought to get his pulse going*, I thought as I rushed to answer the door.

Lo and behold, there stood Ron shivering on my doorstep with a single red rose in his hand. Hmm, what was with the single romantic flower as a love token? Had he been taking his dating cues from Zorro? Instead of placing the long stemmed rose in my teeth and dancing the tango as I had an impulse to do, I thanked Ron profusely, kissed him on the cheek, leaving a giant pink lip print there on purpose, and busied myself with finding a vase to put the flower in so it wouldn't die between now and the end of the movie.

In the hall mirror, I saw him blushing furiously and trying to scrub off my juicy lip print. I caught his eye and gave him a little wink. Instead of responding to me, or even acknowledging my flirtation, he grabbed one of my coats from the hook near my door and tried to force my arms into it in a businesslike manner.

"Um, actually, I wasn't going to wear a coat tonight." I smiled sexily as I sidestepped him holding out a large ski jacket for me.

"You weren't? It's pretty cold outside, and I heard on the radio that the humidity is up to forty per cent, so it feels much colder than it actually is. I think it would be best if you took a coat."

Thanks, Grandpa. "No, no, I promise you, I'll be fine. This top is a lot warmer than it looks, believe it or not." I laughed merrily as I grabbed my alligator clutch and keys, and we headed out the door.

Ron was driving, and the radio in his car startled me by blasting NPR at top volume when he turned the keys in the ignition. He looked embarrassed and made a mumbly comment about loving to listen to talk radio while he quickly turned down the volume. The conversation in the car on the way to the movie was minimal since we were listening to some type of Dr. Laura style call-in program where callers were given counsel on marrying someone of a different religion, whether or not it was okay for a woman to make more money than her spouse, and how many children a couple should expect to have by the time they are thirty. *Snooze*!

"Why are all these people so obsessed with having children, anyway? Most of the couples I know who got knocked up by accident, or on purpose to keep their relationship together, ended up hating each other a few years later," I mused.

Ron stared at me as if I were speaking in tongues. "What? You don't think it's a good idea to have children?"

"All I'm saying is that children shouldn't be in the forefront of your relationship planning. If you end up having a child, that's great, but I don't see what all the fuss is about. People make way too big of a deal about having kids, and if I see one more wrinkly baby photo on Facebook, I'm going to puke." I laughed at my own cleverness.

My wit and humor were met with a silence that lasted several minutes. Finally I said, "Why? Do you want children?"

Ron visibly relaxed and his face lit up in a smile. "Yes, definitely! I'm a really big family person. I just wish I'd already met the right person so I could have children by now. Ideally, I'd love to have four or five, but nowadays, I know most women are only comfortable with having two or three, which would work great for me. What about you?"

Four or five? I knew he'd been sheltered, but was this guy Amish? I shook my head and answered his question. "Sure, I can see children in my future, I guess. For me, I think one would be perfect, but nowadays, all of these celebrities are adopting or using surrogates at any age, so I don't see any type of rush. Besides, I'm not sure how I feel about the whole not drinking for nine months thing. That seems like more of a punishment than a blessing."

I could have sworn he rolled his eyes, but I couldn't tell for sure because the car was almost pitch black since it was eight o'clock at night. There was no light, give or take the odd streetlight flashing as we drove past. We lapsed back into a slightly uncomfortable silence. Fortunately, we were within a few blocks of the movie theater in the Cherry Creek mall.

He was the perfect gentleman and bought my tickets and snacks. He also offered to let me wear his large tweed pea coat when I became freezing cold during the previews. That could have been an "I told you so" moment for any other guy, but Ron handled it with humility and didn't hold it over my head that I had insisted on not bringing a jacket in the first place.

As the theater darkened for the start of the movie, I waited for that telltale moment where your date grabs your hand for the first time. I waited. And waited. And *waited*. By the time the little girl had turned into an old woman with only one arm—spoiler alert!—Ron still had both of his healthy and capable arms crossed over his chest so that even our elbows weren't touching on the armrest. If I hadn't known better, I would have thought he was deliberately trying to avoid human contact, since he had the perfect opportunity to touch and grope me as he pleased here in the comfortable darkness of the movie theater.

I didn't think I had done anything wrong in this situation. I had accomplished the whole checklist—sexy clothes, tall high heels, overly glossy lips, flirtatious conversation, refusing to wear a coat so I could borrow his, and sitting in a dark movie theater, inviting him to cop a feel. I had tried everything in my limited bag of tricks and failed miserably.

In the car, I made the grave mistake of trying to change the radio to something a little more upbeat, like Bon Jovi, who I thought was an ultimate crowd-pleaser. I mean, if you don't like Bon Jovi, then what does that say about your character? As I reached for the stereo knob, Ron put his hand over mine.

At last! He's going to make his move. Maybe he was just waiting for the car ride to try something a little bit romantic.

But, no, I was definitely wrong on that one. Placing his hand firmly over mine, he pried it off of the knob, moved it back to my lap, and patted it gently—as if I was a small child that had tried to pull his hair with sticky fingers.

Son of a bitch! What did a girl have to do to get a little affection around here, anyway?

He carefully pulled his car up in front of my townhome, not even bothering to pull into the extra space in the driveway. With that gesture alone, I knew this was going to be a short drop-off, and I shouldn't even waste my breath asking him to come in. Suddenly, I decided this was a now-or-never moment. I was going to have to put myself out there to see if he was absolutely repulsed by me or by women altogether. So I leaned in for a kiss.

I have to qualify this by saying I had absolutely never, ever made the first move. Not because I was so amazingly attractive and thought myself to be above every man on the planet, but because most guys didn't have a problem going for the first kiss after a drink or two. So it usually happened naturally. I'd never found myself in a situation where I *had* to make the first move. This was entirely foreign to me.

It was obvious Ron was shy and needed a nudge in the right direction. If a dark movie theater wouldn't do it, then I had to be direct and plant a kiss on him myself. Besides, we were two people in a tiny vehicle. He had nowhere to run or even turn to deflect me.

"I had a great time tonight. Great movie choice," I said generically as I slowly leaned toward his face. His face didn't seem to be backing away from mine. That was a good sign. But it also didn't seem to be moving any closer. I had a vivid flashback, within that split second, of the movie *Hitch* where Will Smith coaches Kevin James to move in ninety per cent, and the girl would move in ten per cent to seal the kiss. Ron obviously hadn't been briefed on this maneuver and was giving me nothing.

Damn. I moved in the rest of the ten per cent and finally touched my lips to his. They didn't part or budge in the least. What could have been a nice, sweet goodnight kiss with a little bit of tongue turned into a chaste church kiss I would have been comfortable giving to my brother. Fucking fantastic. I again thanked Ron—and his lips of steel—for a lovely evening and headed dejectedly back into my house.

Just as I reached my door, Ron honked his horn to get my attention. He rolled down the window and called out to me. I perked up immediately. Maybe he wanted to do the romantic thing and run after me to give me the knee-buckling kiss he had been too nervous to give me the first time around. Excited, I trotted back to his car window.

"I forgot to ask," he said. "What are you doing next Tuesday?"

$$\mathcal{C}\mathcal{O}\mathcal{C}\mathcal{O}$$

I spent the next few hours of my evening sitting on my couch, forlornly contemplating my dating relationships. Or lack thereof. I was also absentmindedly dipping my finger into my wine and running it slowly around the rim of my wine glass, creating a surprisingly soothing high-pitched noise to drown out the majority of my insane thoughts.

Quite a lively Saturday night, if you ask me.

I wasn't sure what made Ron tick, and I truly didn't know what I could do at this point to find out. He was the perfect gentleman at all times. He was perhaps the most prompt, punctual, and courteous guy I had ever gone out with, Adam included. My impression up until this point was that most men were missing the chip in their brain that dictated organization, planning, and setting up dates weeks in advance. Which actually made it all the more fun waiting for a guy to call to see if he was really going to ask you out.

Ron worked on a completely different cylinder. He seemed happy to schedule all of our dates as if they were his monthly dental appointments. However, the physical aspect and the chemistry weren't just lacking, they simply weren't there. Besides embarrassing myself by aggressively forcing a kiss on him tonight, I didn't know what I could do to stir the pot and create some sexual attraction.

I had really pulled out all the stops. I'd never, ever initiated a first kiss with a guy before, even when I was totally smitten with Clayton Hall in the fifth grade and was encouraged by all of my little girlfriends to walk up to him at recess and kiss him. What a horrible experience that would have been. For some reason, I had never thought it was the girl's role to initiate the first kiss. So it really said a lot that I had stepped outside myself and decided to go for it tonight.

And what was I rewarded with? An unmemorable kiss I could have gotten from my grandmother or an overly friendly European. I had nothing to show for my boldness this evening, except yet another date with Ron lined up for Tuesday of this week, since I said yes.

I wasn't sure *why* I'd said yes. I was frozen in the moment and anticipating he was going to kiss me again or declare his undying love for me. So I had nodded my head mutely when he asked about Tuesday night. He told me he'd call me then sped away, leaving me in his dust, so I didn't know what this promising Tuesday night held in store. If things continued on the same level, then it would probably be bingo, shuffleboard, or some other activity popular with the retirement homes these days.

I didn't know how much longer I should hang on to this "keeper," since our relationship seemed to have stalled before it even started. I had done everything in my power to become the Mother Teresa of dating and had definitely given Ron more than one chance to prove himself. Any other man with a beating pulse and a healthy dose of testosterone would have tried to sleep with me by this point. While I was happy Ron wasn't pressuring me, it seemed a little strange he didn't even want to take me by the arm or give me a quick kiss goodnight.

He had all of the "goods" on paper—qualities that made me want to continue seeing him because I thought he'd be good for me.

But it also seemed like a warning sign that I was approaching our potential relationship as a necessary dose of medicine. Hmm...

Just as I was about to send him an e-mail to cancel our date on Tuesday—giving myself more time to think our situation over—my phone vibrated with a call from an unknown number.

For some reason, quite a few local students confused my phone number for the student clinic at DU. I would get people calling from time to time, trying to book an appointment or asking whether or not we gave out free condoms. I had half a mind to start asking the students to come help themselves to my own supply of condoms that was no longer being used. But I was pretty sure they had expired by this point. I let my phone roll over to voicemail so the sick student seeking medical help could hear my recording, realize they had called the wrong number, and leave me alone with my vexing thoughts.

A few seconds later, my phone pinged loudly with a voicemail alert. This was pretty strange. Any student with a wrong number normally hung up as soon as my voicemail came on. Who could be leaving me a message this late on a Saturday night? As I listened to the new voicemail, my hands shook so uncontrollably I literally had to use both of them to hold my phone to my ear.

The message was from Adam's only sister, Amber. I hadn't spoken to Amber since a few months after Adam's death when his family would call me up periodically to make certain I hadn't offed myself or starved myself from depression mixed with an inability to leave the house and buy more groceries. Adam's family was exceptionally kind to me after his death. This had been difficult for me to deal with since they were also coping with the loss of their son and brother.

Amber was eight years younger than Adam, and although there was a significant age gap between Amber and me, I'd always been close to her and thought of her like a younger sister. After all, I was the youngest in my family and had never before had the pleasure of being seen by a sibling as wise and cool. Instead, I was always the annoying younger sister following Lacey around and begging to hang out with her.

When I met Adam at the age of twenty-four, Amber was only sixteen and still a few years away from her high school graduation. As Adam and I started spending more and more time together, I wanted to put my best foot forward to make a great impression, so I helped teach Amber to drive and study for her license, I gave her a bit of dating advice, when appropriate, and also helped her buy her prom dress. It was more than flattering that Amber asked me to be a part of all of these special moments as opposed to her totally capable and very sweet mother, which only made our relationship that much closer.

Still, after Adam died, it was awkward spending time with Amber to say the least. She was twenty-one by that time and we were both grieving. She didn't really have time to tend to her brother's widow and leave casserole after casserole on my doorstep until I was ready to come out of my house. And I didn't blame her. We drifted apart as anyone would expect since we were no longer tied by having Adam as a shared family member.

Since I hadn't spoken to her in roughly a year, it was a shock to hear her voice. Her message was even more surprising: "Hey, Danielle, it's Amber, your old sister-in-law. Well, not exactly old, but you know what I mean." She laughed nervously. "I've been meaning to get back in touch with you, and I'm so sorry we haven't talked in months. I hope you're doing well. My mom said you went back to your job. That's great. I actually had some big news I wanted to tell you, which was why I'd hoped you would pick up the phone. But since it's a Saturday night, I can't really blame you."

She cleared her throat. "I'm engaged! I think you met Shawn before Adam passed away. He proposed to me last night, and I wanted to tell you my good news! I know that this may be difficult for you, but I still feel like you're my family, and I'd love for you to be a part of the wedding. Call me back please."

Holy shit! I wouldn't have thought think Amber's message would have such an impact on me, but hearing her voice was like hearing a ghost. It had been much easier to shut out Adam's entire family after he died, and that meant my relationship with Amber went, too. Pain is pain. And no matter how much I'd enjoyed spending time with her when Adam and I were married, seeing her after the fact was just too hard.

My hands still shook as I brought my wine glass to my lips, inevitably spilling a few drops of red wine on my silver jersey top in the process. Just perfect. Not only had I had a horrible date, met with some seriously strange news, but I'd probably just ruined my new top. Not like it mattered. If I had any future with Ron, I'd likely be spending my weekends shuffling around the house in a muumuu. Goodbye, high heels, goodbye, backless tops, and *hello*, orthopedic support hose.

I couldn't bring myself to call Amber back just yet. Especially since I didn't have an answer for her about whether or not I could be in her wedding. It was sweet that she still considered me her sister, but how could I face her family with a big elephant in the room? I sucked in my breath, choking on wine, as I realized another huge factor in the equation. Adam's family had no clue he was a cheating slut, and I didn't think I could face them with that big of a secret.

I decided I'd have to be the grown-up here. I would call Amber back, tell her I didn't think it was a good idea for me to come to her wedding, and also give her my heartfelt congratulations. With trembling hands, I hit redial on my phone and waited for Amber to pick up. I silently prayed she wouldn't, so I could leave her a non-confrontational voicemail. But no such luck. She appeared to be waiting by her phone for my call and answered on the second ring.

"Danielle! How are you? I'm so happy you called back. I haven't talked to you in forever!"

I let out a low sigh I hoped she couldn't hear. "Yeah, it's really great to hear from you too. I'm doing pretty well. Congratulations on your engagement. That's so exciting! How did he propose?"

I let Amber do the normal girl stuff of rambling on and on about how Shawn took her hiking up near Boulder with a gorgeous picnic of wine and cheese and then waited until sunset to get down on one knee and propose. How romantic. She talked excitedly about all of the little wedding details she was already thinking about, and she told me their wedding was planned for March, a mere five months away as it was now early October.

"Wow, that's pretty soon! Do you think you're going to have enough time to plan?"

Not like I was one to talk. When Adam proposed to me on that wonderful Christmas Eve night, we decided to get married in February because we just couldn't wait. Our wedding was small with only forty people. That way, we could blow the modest wedding budget from our parents on an elaborate reception with an open bar, ensuring every single guest who attended was literally stumbling out the door at the end—if they hadn't thrown up their drinks already.

Now that's a wedding!

"We're just really excited and didn't want to have to wait until summer," she said. "And we're going to save a ton of money getting married off-season. But what I really wanted to ask you was if you'd consider being my maid of honor. I know it may be a lot to ask, but I've always thought of you as my big sister. It would mean so much to me if you were a part of the wedding."

I took a moment to compose myself before I answered and burst her wedding bubble. I must've spilled more wine on my new top because a huge wet spot on had developed my chest. As I started to dab at the wet spot with a napkin, I saw that it wasn't even red. It couldn't have been wine. Suddenly, I realized a flood of tears was pouring down my cheeks, running down my chest, and pooling directly in the center of my shirt. I hadn't even known I was crying because I was doing so silently— as if someone had opened up floodgates inside my face and hadn't even told me about it.

"Are you still there, Dani?" she asked anxiously.

"Yes, yes, sorry about that. I just spilled something on my top and was trying to clean it up. Listen, Amber," I began. "That really means a lot to me. I've always thought of you as my younger sister too, but I just don't know if it's a good idea for me to do this right now. I hope you can understand."

"Oh."

She was obviously disappointed by my reaction. She'd probably hoped we would spend hours on the phone giggling and planning her wedding. Abruptly ending the call, she wished me well and said we should get together for lunch soon, which we both knew wouldn't happen.

And still the crying didn't stop.

I had cried over breakups, getting reprimanded at work, and especially Adam's death. But nothing like *this* before. These tears weren't the heaving sobs you often see on *Lifetime* movies. It was more like my body was purging me of all of the stress and sadness I'd been holding in for the past year. The weird part was I didn't even feel like I was crying. If my shirt hadn't gotten wet from my tears, I probably wouldn't have even noticed. I was fully functional but crying nonstop. I could have watched a movie, typed out a few e-mails, or even taken a shower without interruption, except for the flood of tears that continued to pour down my face.

This went on for the next forty-five minutes until I decided the best thing for me to do was just to go to bed and put myself out of my misery. I was slightly concerned I would drown or choke on my tears while I was sleeping, but I figured that would be poetic justice. If that was the way I was meant to go, so be it.

STAGE 4: DEPRESSION

CHAPTER 17

I woke up with a start and peeled my damp face off of my even damper pillow. What had happened to me last night? For a second I thought I was having a college flashback and I'd been lying in bed in a pool of my own vomit—which believe it or not, had happened more than a few times in the past. But no, my pillow hadn't been puked on. It was completely saturated with my tears.

This sounded even more pathetic when I put all of the pieces together. What kind of a woman cries herself to sleep all night over something as trivial as being invited to be in a wedding? And the wedding of an ex-sister-in-law she was close to, no less?

This should have been a circumstance I was able to handle in stride. Adam had been dead for over a year. But hearing Amber's voice again was far too much to deal with. It brought me back to the horrible night I had met her at the hospital after Adam's car accident.

I was called by the police at eleven p.m. I was in bed, and Adam was out with a few friends from work for a business-type celebration I had been unable to attend because I'd been working too late. We hadn't seen each other since seven in the morning, but we exchanged a few texts, with Adam saying he'd be home soon and he loved me, and me saying he'd better and I loved him too.

The ringing of our home phone woke me up with a start. I had drifted off to sleep reading a book in bed and was confused and disoriented since hardly anyone ever called on our landline, except for the phone company to make sure the phone was working. Our home line was given out to family members strictly for emergencies—which happened to be what the call was about this time. It was a police officer asking me to come to the hospital immediately regarding my husband. But they couldn't give me any more information than that.

What the fuck, right? I'd always seen scenes like that on TV or in the movies where the anxious wife is told to come to the ER right away and she would be given further information when she got there. I thought it added a great deal of depth and suspense to the *Lifetime* movie of the week when that happened. But when it was happening to me, it was excruciating. I mean, why couldn't they just tell me my husband was injured or dead before I drove all the way to the hospital so I'd at least have time to prepare myself?

But instead, I found myself trying to start my car with shaking hands and calling Amber over and over on my short drive there, trying to tell her to meet me at the hospital. She didn't answer at first. She was studying for a test and screening my calls, she told me later, but she finally decided to pick up after my fifth or sixth try. I begged her to meet me as quickly as possible and not to bring her parents with her. I foolishly didn't want to alarm them if nothing was actually wrong. I would have felt silly waking up Adam's parents and forcing them to get dressed and come to the hospital if he only had a broken leg or something like that.

At his funeral, I felt even "sillier" that I hadn't urged his parents to get to the hospital right away so that they could potentially say goodbye to their son one last time. But how was I to know his situation was urgent? That's just another reason why they need to tell you exactly why you're being called to the hospital before you get there. Otherwise, maybe you won't think it's a "good idea" to tell important family members their son is dying before he actually passes away.

Thanks a lot.

Amber and I sat together for hours in the hospital waiting room while we prayed for Adam to wake up from the accident. Amber was positively distraught and anxious to call her parents. I kept telling her it wasn't even a big deal, and there was no reason to wake them up just yet. It wasn't until the doctor came out with a grim-looking face that I knew he was delivering very bad news. Just like on *Grey's Anatomy*.

Later, I tortured myself about not calling his parents sooner. Hadn't I watched enough primetime television to know that if they tell you to get the hospital right away it was a legitimate emergency? In the future, I was much wiser and better at making that type of decision. I could easily see the error of my ways. Adam's parents were incredibly nice about the whole situation. They soothed me and comforted me by telling me they would have done the same thing if they were in my shoes. But how could I ever know that?

As incredibly angry as I was with Adam for being a lying cheater, the memory of his death made my face leak all over again. Wouldn't this crying ever stop? I didn't have the energy to get out of bed this morning. I rested my head back onto my very wet pillow and drifted in and out of sleep. Since it was a Sunday, I had no obligations to attend to. I thought I at least deserved to rest myself, both physically and mentally, before I had to face another horrible week working side-by-side with The Mistress.

That thought alone sent me into a tailspin. I didn't manage to open my eyes again until four p.m. I was so tired, I wondered if I was coming down with something because I didn't think it was normal to sleep for fourteen plus hours a day. However, it seemed better than the alternative—watching reality TV, sorting through all of my e-mails, and dodging calls from people I didn't want to talk to.

I managed to get out of bed briefly at five p.m. This gave me just enough time to take out Madam and bring a bottle of wine back to bed with me. Yes, I drank straight from the bottle. So what? Since I had no one around to reprimand or judge me, it just seemed like a waste of a wine glass I didn't want to wash. I have to say, I now had a greater understanding of why people let themselves go. When I had seen freaky and disturbing people trolling the aisles of Wal-Mart, I always wondered, *where did they start to go wrong*?

Did they always have a horrible fashion sense? Did they lose their job as a powerful and highly paid executive, and now they were hovering just above poverty level? Did they find out the person they loved was cheating on them so they no longer felt attractive? Yes, that must be the reason someone would wear bright orange sweatpants, tennis shoes without laces, and a NASCAR shirt—with the sleeves cut off—midday at Wal-Mart. It could only stem from a broken heart.

My phone started buzzing crazily around seven p.m., yet I knew there wasn't one person's call I wanted to answer. Without exception.

I lazily picked up my phone to check who was calling, and wouldn't you have guessed it? It was Ron. Right now, Ron was very low on the list of people I wanted to talk to. In fact, he was likely to stay there indefinitely. I had forgotten to e-mail him to cancel our date on

Tuesday, but I knew I had more than enough time since it was a few days away. Right now, I barely had the energy to lift my head and drink out of my bottle of Shiraz while holding my remote control at the same time. Anything more complex, like breaking up with my boring boyfriend, would have to wait for a later time.

I wrapped up my evening by punishing myself in a sick and sadistic fashion as I watched a marathon of wedding shows on the *We* channel. My favorite by far was this strange and demented show called *Jilted*, which I was oddly attracted to. The premise of the show was that a woman who was dating someone who couldn't commit to her would pop the question on her boyfriend, giving him an ultimatum that he only had one week to marry her. The real kicker was the bride already had her wedding all planned out, with a venue and a date, and the groom had to decide whether or not he was going to show up the day of the wedding. Since I was in a very low place, I secretly hoped each and every groom would stand the bride up at the altar. But as disappointing as it was, most of them were pressured into saying, "I do" in front of their nearest and dearest. I guess I didn't blame them. Who would want to break up with someone on national television? Although if you ask me, it would have given the show much more dramatic appeal.

The punishment of the wedding TV marathon must have taken a lot more out of me than I realized. Suddenly, I woke with a start and looked at my bedside alarm clock. It read six-fifteen a.m. Where had the time gone? How long had I stayed up last night? Once again I had awakened in a pool of some wet substance in my bed. But this time it wasn't tears. It was wine. *Damn.* Drinking red wine in bed was a horrible idea. I would probably have to throw out my sheets and buy new ones. Not like it mattered anyway. I had the same bedroom set Adam and I had shared when we were married. It was probably good karma just to scrap the whole thing and start afresh.

With the sixteen to eighteen hours of sleep I had under my belt, I had a pretty difficult time getting back to sleep after that point. Still, I felt entirely unprepared to face the world after the weekend I'd had. I figured now was as good a time as any to use a few of my PTO days before they expired at the end of the year. I actually had ten PTO days left, and it was already October.

Since the likelihood of me going on a beach vacation anytime soon was slim to none, I decided there was no better way to waste my time off than by spending it alone in my house sulking and reading trashy magazines. I sent Gwen a quick e-mail telling her I must have caught a bug over the weekend, and I would be back to work on Thursday to work side-by-side with my new colleague, Cherry. I couldn't wait.

The next two days passed in a lazy and slightly drunken stupor—exactly the type of R and R I needed. Screw yoga, detox retreats, and the Hollywood cleanse diet. All I really needed to get myself back on track was a few good bottles of wine and some subpar television. I could start my own retreat getaway right here in my townhouse.

By the time Tuesday morning arrived, I had let my phone die because it had been vibrating like crazy. What was the point in charging it if I didn't want to talk to anyone? Gwen had sent me a few e-mails with follow-up voicemails explaining she had left some important information on my desk for me when I returned to the office. Amber had called me one more time to leave me a voicemail telling me she hoped things weren't weird between us, and I shouldn't worry about missing her wedding because she understood. Ron called seven times and left three voicemails saying he was concerned about me and wondering if we were still on for Tuesday evening. And last but not least, April had been stalker-calling me a minimum of ten times per day on Sunday and Monday. She told me she would be stopping by my house after work to-day if I didn't get back to her because she was afraid I had drowned in the bathtub or choked to death alone in my house since there was no one there to help me. Wasn't that sweet?

It was always great to be reminded you were absolutely alone and could easily die in a household accident since there was no one else there to save you. I made sure to eat very care-fully and chew my food thoroughly after that.

The Ron-situation was something I didn't want to deal with. So I just sent him a quick e-mail telling him I was sick. Sick in the head and sick in the body were all relative. I felt like it was a valid excuse. I just needed a few days to get my head together and get a grip on my fluctuating emotions before I was ready to either face him on another date or break it off for good.

Since April had left me a threat that she would be stopping by my house today, I surrendered to my fate. It took too much energy to call her up and explain what was going on with me. If she didn't end up stopping by today, then I'd just see her at work Thursday, so it was all good. The Amber message was one I put on my mental to-do list. It would take a lot of emotional work to handle. Yes, I definitely needed to call her back and explain that everything was fine between us. I didn't want to burn my bridges permanently. But I didn't have the strength or energy to do it just yet. Another day perhaps.

I felt just as tired today as I had the entire weekend. Fortunately, I still had a few nonperishable items around the house, like ramen, ravioli, and a box of cereal. By my estimation, I wouldn't have to leave the house until Thursday, when I had promised to return to work. But if there happened to be a nuclear fallout between now and then, I was screwed.

I also had a really adorable wine rack that was given to Adam and me as an engagement present. I had been clever enough to stock it up with a minimum of twenty bottles a few months ago in the anticipation of a lively social life. Thank you, past-Danielle, you have been so good to me. If it wasn't for my past-self having the foresight to stock up my wine rack to the max, I'd probably have to venture out to the liquor store or beg April to bring me some alcohol on her visit.

It appeared I had enough supplies to last another forty-eight hours, so I set myself up on the couch—in the same pajamas I had changed into Saturday evening—and began my daily television marathon began.

I always figured if I had the time to lounge around my house, I would do something truly interesting and innovative. Like read several books back to back, write some poetry, or learn Mandarin Chinese on Rosetta Stone. But I guess we are all creatures of habit. When I had four consecutive days to myself to do any-thing I wanted, I just watched crappy show af-ter crappy show. At least I managed to paint my toenails on the commercial breaks. I was on fire!

But really, the only time I moved from my butt-groove on the couch was to fill my glass with wine or use the bathroom. The hours flew by before I even knew it.

All of a sudden it was noon. After deciding to finally charge my phone, I saw that April had sent me a quick text, ominously telling me she would be at my home at five p.m., and I'd better be waiting for her. I just sent back a simple "K," since I didn't know what else to say to explain my troll-like ways.

I settled back on the couch to finish the glass of wine I had just topped off. Halfway into *TLC Baby Story*—I'd run out of wedding shows by that point—I decided that I was cold and wanted to grab a fuzzy hoodie from my closet. I knew just the one I wanted. It was Adam's warm and worn DU sweatshirt that was so incredibly comfortable, it was almost as good as wearing a snuggie—I swear it. Getting off my ass was a big move for me. I braced myself for the effort and slowly shuffled down the hall back to my bedroom.

When I got to my closet, I dug through all Adam's winter clothing that I had yet to give away to Goodwill—shrink me on that one, Sigmund Freud—and finally found the coveted hoodie. Just as I was about to hobble slowly back out of the closet and return to my post, I saw The Box I'd been hiding from for the past several weeks. This was the same box—with all Adam's belongings—I had chosen not to open when I was cleansing my home and channeling the peace and insight of Jesus.

Which was unfortunately *not* the attitude I had, moping about the house today.

No. I no longer peacefully and open-mindedly felt bygones should be bygones. Instead, I had the sudden urge to tear every side off of that box and get to the bottom of it. What if it had some kind of clue to the past that would shed some new light into Adam's psyche? As much as I didn't want to admit it, it was killing me that I didn't know what triggered Adam to cheat on me. I mean, you're going along, married, thinking that you're enjoying your life, and then BAM! Your husband's a dead cheater. What caused that kind of shift in character? Or had I even really known him at all? It was inconceivable to me that I could say vows to a person, link my life with his, and then uncover some very unpleasant surprises when he was no longer in the picture. I simply couldn't stand it.

I ripped one of the top flaps violently off the box, definitely not taking the polite approach where you slowly and carefully unwrap a Christmas present and then fold up all of the wrapping paper to be used for later.

Fuck that!

It was incredibly satisfying to tear the cardboard off Adam's memory box. I made sure it was sufficiently ripped in several places before I even looked at what it held. At the very top of the box was Adam's college yearbook. This I had expected. I highly doubted his yearbook held any sordid clues, but just to make sure, I double checked that no Cherry James was in attendance in his class at DU. Fortunately, there wasn't. I found his framed high school and college diplomas, a few other certificates of achievement, and even a picture of the first successful website he had designed and sold right out of college.

I remembered that website well. It was for a small natural and organic dog biscuit baking company in Boulder who paid Adam the hefty price of one thousand dollars to design the interface and logo for their new brand. As a new college graduate, being paid a lump sum like that was seemingly out of this world. Adam and I took a tenth of that money as a reward and stayed at a fancy hotel in downtown Denver for the night to celebrate. Today, one hundred seemed like a small figure, more like the amount of the monthly electric bill or a moderately priced pair of shoes. But just out of college, it was a magical achievement and Adam's first milestone on the way to a successful career. I'd printed out a picture of the website after it was launched and framed it for him as a gift—which he absolutely loved and set up in his office—and a reminder of where he started.

The next thing I pulled out of the box was a Ziploc baggie full of pictures of us—what was with guys and their hatred of photo albums? When we'd first met that fateful day at the Irish Hound Pub. Our first mini vacation together at a cabin in the mountains. Us drinking out of a keg with friends that summer at the Boulder reservoir. And a few strange and very hazy snapshots from our engagement party that started out innocently at the Cheesecake Factory at the Sixteenth Street Mall with all of our friends and family and then later turned into a drunken debacle that ended at The Front Porch on Fifteenth—where we both entered their weekly Tuesday Flip Cup Tournament and managed to win and lose at the same time. We concluded the evening by throwing up outside of the bar in tandem until a taxi came to take us home. A pretty epic way to start a marriage.

Those pictures made me smile a little at the memories. We had definitely shared some wild and fun times. I'd truly thought I was marrying my best friend who I could trust more than anyone else—until he stabbed me in the back when there was nothing I could do about it. As much as I was angry at him and couldn't understand why he'd cheated on me, most of all, I really missed him. And that was a very difficult thing to admit. I'd much rather have been angry at him or else just pretended he didn't exist altogether—which is what I'd done with all of the guys I'd dated recently. I'd neglected to tell Ron, and all of the others, I was even ever married. I didn't want to have to explain I was the "w-word," widow. That was like a four-letter word to me. I had no clue how to integrate it into my dating life. So I just didn't.

I thought getting to know all these new people would be the refreshing change of pace I was looking for. But there's something to be said for being married to the same comfortable person for several years. This was a person you trusted and looked forward to coming home to. I'd much rather have watched Netflix with Adam and eaten some takeout than worry about getting all dressed up to impress someone I didn't even know if I cared about.

Adam had hurt me beyond belief. But it didn't change the fact I legitimately missed him. Would we have been able to work it out if I had discovered his affair when he was still alive? That was a question I couldn't answer and would never have the luxury of finding out.

If I had been posed that question when Adam was alive, I would have probably said something empowering, like, "If my husband ever cheated on me, he'd be out the door. No exceptions." But of course, that's what all the women who have never been cheated on say because it's comforting. And it makes them seem independent and powerful. But what I would really have done was the mystery question of the hour—or even of the decade.

I continued to rifle through his box of important earthly possessions, finding things like ticket stubs to the Against Me! show we went to when they visited Fort Collins a few years ago, a picture of us snowboarding two winters ago, a picture of us at Coors Field when the Rockies finally made it to the World Series, and a little wax figurine of a seal we had made when we played hooky and visited the Denver Zoo for a day. All of these keepsakes seemed so important at the time. Yet they meant absolutely nothing to me now. Perhaps if I hadn't found out Adam was a big fat cheater, maybe I would have gone through his box "when I was ready" and then kept the most important belongings to gaze at tragically and longingly whenever I missed him.

But now, I felt guilty even caring about all of his old shit in his shitty old box—*boy, I have a way with words.*

It seemed wrong to still have feelings for someone who had screwed me over so horribly. The only thing I should feel for Adam was hate and resentment, plain and simple. Which would make it easy to wrap up our whole relationship into a neat little box and throw it out with the daily garbage. Right?

By the time I got to the bottom of his box, the leaking face phenomenon had started all over again and didn't show any signs of stopping. I didn't think I'd ever cried this much in my whole life, Adam's death included. It felt like something inside of me that I had been holding onto this whole year finally broke loose.

I decided to manage the constant crying by wearing a makeshift bib—constructed of used Kleenex—which prevented my tears from staining my perfectly good pajama tank top. If I marketed and sold this Kleenex bib concept for all the widows out there who needed something to cry into without ruining their clothes, I could make millions.

I spent the rest of the afternoon organizing Adam's box into neat little piles, rearranging them, and reorganizing them in the hopes I could make some kind of sense of our past together. I thought maybe if I continued to arrange and rearrange all of his keepsakes into specific patterns, they would somehow speak to me and point a clear arrow in the direction of where and how Adam met Cherry James.

This detective work was entirely time-consuming. Before I knew it, April had barged into my house, using the hidden key I kept under a very obvious fake rock on the porch. Any competent thief would immediately discover my secret key since it was inside a plastic rock, sitting on my porch for no reason at all—other than to house my secret key. But I hadn't had any break-ins so far, unless you counted April today.

She took one look at me surrounded by piles of photographs, ticket stubs, and yearbooks, with my handy Kleenex bib punctuating my entire ensemble, and said, "Oh my God, it's finally happened."

She stooped down onto the floor to give me a tight hug, cleverly avoiding my snotty and damp Kleenex bib.

"What are you talking about?"

"You've finally totally lost it. I was just waiting for this to happen because you've been prissy, self-righteous, and in denial about the whole thing. I'm just glad you cracked. It's not healthy to pretend nothing's wrong after something really big happens. Trust me on that one."

"What do you know?" I demanded, sniffling in between my tears. "You just married some weird older guy and got over it right away. How do you have any idea about denial?"

"Are you kidding me? I've been in denial since the moment I met Roger. It wasn't until I finally started dating again that I had to deal with all of the shit he put me through and the horrible ways he made me feel. If anybody knows about denial, it's me," she said proudly—which was rather strange in and of itself.

I ignored what she said and got back to work arranging my little piles of evidence against Adam. April kept right on talking as if my lack of response didn't even matter. This was actually a good thing because I didn't have much to contribute to the conversation.

Suddenly, I couldn't stand it anymore and interrupted her mid-sentence as she was going off on a rabbit trail about whether or not she should wear high heels on her online dates anymore since a few guys she had gone out with had lied about their height on their profile, and she stood a good four inches taller than them on the date. How embarrassing.

"I made a list," I blurted out as I shoved the wrinkled and tear-stained paper into April's face.

"What are you talking about?" She looked at me as if she were seeing me for the first time and had realized she'd basically been talking to herself for the last thirty minutes, the same way you would lovingly tell stories to your deranged grandmother who was hooked up to a feeding tube at the nursing home. It was kind of sweet if you thought about it. With a disgusted look on her face, April took my crumpled and snotty list from me and started to smooth it out. Once again, I didn't blame her. I was in pretty bad shape.

My list was something I made during the box-unpacking-ceremony that had taken the greater part of my afternoon. It held all of the conclusions I had come to for why Adam had possibly thought it would be a good idea to cheat on me while I thought we were perfectly happy in our marriage. The list had taken all of my mental stability and strength and I still hadn't come to any hard conclusions.

April began reading my slightly illegible and grief-stricken handwriting, "Reasons Adam Cheated on Me with a Slut." She laughed. "Nice."

I nodded my head vigorously so she would continue reading. My zombie intimidation must've worked as she hurried on.

"One, I was no longer attractive to him.

"Two, we spent too much time working.

"Three, my career wasn't smart enough.

"Four, I wasn't smart enough.

"Five, my hair wasn't blonde, shoulder length, and adorable, and I wasn't named after a fruit.

"Six, I always made nasty faces at him when I picked up his socks.

"Seven, I accidentally on purpose washed his black socks with his white clothes to teach him a lesson about putting his laundry away.

"Eight, I drank too much on the weekdays.

"Nine, Adam didn't drink enough on the weekdays.

"Ten, he proposed to me out of pity."

April finished and looked at me strangely. "Wow, Danielle, this is a very detailed list. But don't you think the majority of these reasons are a little farfetched? I really doubt his cheating had anything to do with laundry. And I would say it was probably a combination of number one and number two. No offense, but that just seems to be the reason why most guys cheat. It's really not rocket science, you know. And it definitely wasn't numbers six, seven, or ten because we all know how in love you guys were when you got engaged. "Sorry," she said with a wince as her last comment made my face leak even harder.

I hadn't wanted to show anyone my secret list because I didn't want them to confirm any of my greatest fears out loud—which were precisely the combination of number one and number two, respectively. I mean, who wants to admit to the fact they may have no longer been attractive to their spouse, forcing them to step out and cheat? Not this girl.

"I made another list on the back," I added weakly between sobs.

She turned the list over to see an even more stained and erratic handwriting on the back of the paper. "Signs Adam Was Cheating, and I Didn't Fucking Know It." She paused again. "You're really on fire with these titles."

I gave her a pathetic sneer/glare combination, and she went back to reading.

"One, he kept having strange work meetings at night.

"Two, he always kept his cell phone in the glove compartment of his car.

"Three, I didn't have a spare key to his car.

"Four, once he didn't come home all night and told me he had gotten really drunk and stayed at his friend Jason's house to avoid a DUI.

"Five, he started preferring linguini to spaghetti.

"Six, he sometimes ate standing up because he was in a hurry.

"Seven, he didn't really care when I turned all of his white clothes gray.

"Eight, he started singing in the shower.

"Nine, he stopped eating his favorite cereal.

"Ten, he changed all of his computer passwords."

By the time April finished my second list, I was nodding my head emphatically at how right on I was.

"Well, I have to admit some of these behaviors are a little strange, like number ten and numbers two and three," she said gently. "But half of this list is just the way a regular person acts. Adam totally had the prerogative to change his preference in pasta and eat standing up or sitting down. I think number seven just meant he was being nice to you."

I snatched my list away from her and crumpled it up into a little ball. "You don't know what you're talking about," I hissed belligerently.

The conversation got awkward after that since I went all Cruella DeVille on her ass. But she was still kind enough to hang out with me for the next three hours as I continued to reorganize my closet and drink to excess. Finally, she told me she had to go home to get ready to meet a new eHarmony date for drinks. I merely nodded in her direction as a goodbye. I also vaguely heard her telling me she was going to stop by at the same time tomorrow to make sure I was still alive. Good point. And she would break in again if she had to because she knew how.

Since my closet was thoroughly cleaned, and Adam's box of memories was thoroughly destroyed, I had nothing left to do but return to my post on my faithful couch, sip my wine, and watch hours and hours of reality television.

What's on the menu tonight? Six back-to-back episodes of *Sixteen and Pregnant*? Don't mind if I do!

There was nothing like a depressing teen documentary to put a little perspective into my situation. Better yet, many of the white trash baby daddies were also cheating on the baby mamas when they were about to give birth. Perfect.

As captivating as *Sixteen and Pregnant* was, it only lasted me a few hours before the natives got restless again. I didn't know how to pass the time in my depressing, miserable existence, so, in grubby pajamas and slippers, I took Madam for a walk —though it was cold and sleeting outside, and we only lasted half a block.

I cooked up two packets of ramen as a treat because I was worth the extra fifteen cents. And finally, I found myself in my bathroom, rummaging through all of my toiletries and Adam's old pain medications, wondering how many pills it would *really* take to kill myself?

Even though that sounded like a dangerous and suicidal thought, I knew I wasn't going to do it. I was just wondering. This was what led me to call the convenient twenty-four hour Suicide Hotline number, I found on a sticker on the bottom of a bottle of Adam's Ambien, just to ask their expert opinion on how many pills a person would actually need to knock themselves out for good. But, of course, the Suicide Hotline operator was all kinds of difficult. She adhered strictly to her scripted protocol and refused to give me that information.

After I finally hung up on the call so that more suicidal—*suicidaler?*—people could have their chance at asking for help, too, I went back to my station in front of the television—the place I now thought of as my Den of Despair.

Of course, the suicide thing was merely a distraction. I didn't want to give up my life just yet. My main motivation for living was so I wouldn't meet Adam in the Great Beyond. If I did, I would probably punch him right in the face and get kicked directly out of heaven. No, it was best that I spent my time in anger and un-forgiveness here on this earth until I was peaceful enough to spend eternity with a dead husband who cheated on me. It sounded like a fucking riot. I couldn't wait.

CHAPTER 18

I awoke the next morning the same as I had every other morning this week—lying on a pillow soaked with tears and a puddle of red wine on the bed with a little bit of crushed cereal sprinkled on top. I was definitely going to have to get new sheets. *If* I ever pulled myself out of this funk.

Today was Wednesday, aka my last day of depressing freedom before I had to return to work side-by-side with my best buddy, Cherry. I truly didn't want to think about that because I would consider suicide for real then.

I was almost out of ramen but still had plenty of wine, so I sent April a quick text asking her to bring me more instant soup and cereal when she broke into my house later in the day to check on me.

Her reply? "K. Glad UR Alive."

Ha ha. She killed me. My dark humor was getting the best of me in this sordid situation.

Today was a big day since I finally decided to shower. A pure phenomenon. After that, I upped my standards a bit and watched a few episodes of *Weeds* I had recorded, which I thought was a giant leap in the right direction away from reality television. Perhaps my emotions and mental states were improving after all. Although I highly doubted it.

Weeds took up the better part of my afternoon of drinking and sitting. Before I knew it, it was five p.m., and April burst into my house like a SWAT team. I reacted as any self-loathing vampire would by covering my eyes and shrieking at the first sign of daylight. I screeched at her to close the door before I melted. She grudgingly obliged but told me I needed to pull myself together before returning to work tomorrow.

Of course, I agreed. *Wasn't it obvious*?

April was like Santa Claus for the emotionally wounded and came with a sack load of fun goodies. Like three different flavors of ramen—hooray!—instant whole-wheat macaroni and cheese—my fave!—and several cans of tomato soup—what the hell was she thinking? Overall, a majority of good choices that would have lasted me several more days in my shelter of sadness. I thanked April profusely, but she quickly interrupted me, took me by the arm, and dragged me over to my computer desk in the far corner of the dining room.

"Log in," she commanded me.

I have to admit, I was a little intimidated by her at this point.

"Why?" Although I had no problem logging in to my computer at her request, I didn't like being bossed around for no reason.

"You'll see." She rifled through my purse on the desk until she found whatever she was looking for. I began to wonder if I was hallucinating. Or was my best friend actually taking advantage of my fragile state and robbing me blind? Part of me was pissed, but another part didn't really care. What did I need with my worldly goods at this point?

She shoved me roughly out of the way and started typing a URL into the browser.

"April, seriously, what are you doing?" I demanded.

She didn't answer.

She was moving like a whirlwind and had gone onto a travel website. I couldn't see what screens she was clicking on or what she was doing since she moved so quickly. Finally, she typed in the number from my credit card. I tried to stop her with physical force, but since all I'd eaten for the past five days was ramen with a few hearty splashes of wine it wasn't difficult for her to hold me back.

"Hey! April! You seriously need to tell me what is going on. Right now! I'm not kidding. I'm not kidding!" FYI, when someone says "I'm not kidding" twice, then they're probably kidding.

She continued to ignore me and, within a few seconds, stepped proudly away from my computer. On the monitor, I saw a "Thank You!" screen, showing a travel confirmation number.

"You're welcome," April said, handing me back my credit card.

"What have you done?" I snarled. I couldn't imagine who, when, or what she had booked a vacation for. With my luck, she had booked her and her latest e-boyfriend a cruise to France at my expense.

"I booked both of us a vacation for Thanksgiving weekend at the resort Adam and Cherry were going to stay at together." She grinned "You're acting like a total mental patient, and I think the only way for you to snap out of this is by confronting it head on. We're going to go, we're going to have a good time, and there's nothing you can do about it because it's nonrefundable," she concluded happily.

"But how did you even know where they were going? And how are we going to get the time off work?" I bombarded her with a string of anxious questions. "And what about Thanksgiving?"

"First, I'm your assistant so I receive all your paperwork, and I found your security deposit refund statement from the Grande Royal Antiguan Beach Resort where Adam booked the vacation. Second, you've only been loafing around your house for five days, so according to my calculations, you still have roughly five more vacation days left. And I have seven that I haven't used. We have the Friday after Thanksgiving off, so we're actually only using one vacation day on the Wednesday we fly out, since we'll get back on Sunday. Lastly, you don't even really like your family that much. You always get drunk, and afterwards you complain about how you should go on vacation instead of staying in town," she finished triumphantly. "Which is why you should thank me."

Wow! She had definitely covered all her bases. If I hadn't hated her for stealing my credit card and booking the "Mistress Vacation

Extravaganza Part Deux," I probably would have been just a little bit excited about it. Okay, a lot excited. But taking into account my current mental health, I had no clue how I was going to handle taking the beautiful vacation my dead husband had planned with someone else.

However, I really had to hand it to April—that bitch!

ℂℂℂ

As much as I didn't want to admit it, I spent the night dreaming of my upcoming tropical getaway, which was a little over a month from now. I had no time to lose! I figured if I could stick to my diet of ramen and wine, I'd be a good ten pounds lighter—albeit nutrient deficient—and completely ready for swimsuit season in the middle of the holidays.

Still, I didn't have a good feeling about traveling across the continent to visit the same tropical location Adam had wanted to take his beautiful girlfriend—never mind the fact he had a wife. I mean, what *was* he thinking?

He did occasionally go on work conferences to Atlanta for a company called Stompernet that claimed to teach insider secrets about the Internet, so I assumed he had been planning to take Cherry on vacation under the ruse of going to one of those conferences. If he were still alive— he'd have spent 9 days last August sipping piña coladas with that stupid slut under a huge umbrella on a white-sand Caribbean beach.

It was just like a Sandals commercial—if you take out the lies, betrayal, and infidelity.

Maybe they should market a new type of couples resort to that demographic. The chain of resorts could be called "Betrayal: Beach Getaways for mistresses and cheating scumbag husbands." It would sell big!

ം

I also wasn't sure how my family was going to feel about me ditching them on Thanksgiving, even though I had threatened to do so year after year. I would inevitably drink too much, and then my mom would say something "mom-like" to me, such as, "Don't drink too much this year." And I would get a "You don't know me!" attitude with my feathers all ruffled and become eerily silent at the dinner table, all the while continuing to drink heavily and glare at my mom in defiance. It was very mature.

There was one specific holiday where my feathers got so ruffled—love that figure of speech, by the way!—I told my mom I could drink when, how, and wherever I wanted to because I was well over the age of twenty-one. And if she had a problem with that, then I would proceed to sit in my car in the driveway and drink from a flask. I actually didn't *have* a flask at the time, but I just wanted to prove the point that I *could* if I wanted to.

In this specific circumstance, my mom dropped the subject and became eerily silent at the dinner table, glaring at me throughout the meal in defiance—which is obviously where *I* learned it from.

So, as anyone can clearly see, someone in my fragile emotional state didn't need to deal with that type of family drama. I really didn't feel I had the mental strength to "break up" with my family over the holidays. Instead, I decided to send them a lame and non-confrontational e-mail about how I had planned a vacation with April because I thought it would be good to get away from all my stress, given what I had had to deal with over the past year. I knew I wouldn't get any arguments because whenever you allude to tragedy, it's basically a get-out-of-jail-free card. That was the one thing I'd learned about having a dead spouse. You could get away with almost anything if you blamed it on being a twenty-nine-year-old widow.

After sending the mass e-mail to Lacey and my parents, telling them I would be out of town for the first time ever on Thanksgiving this year, I logged off of my computer and got ready for bed. Or rather, I got ready to sit in the crumb-infested, wine-stained mess I called my bed these days. Without a doubt, I needed to find new sheets as soon as I was ready to face the world again.

Speaking of facing the world, my return to work was a mere twelve hours away. I wasn't sure I was prepared to work chummily side-by-side with The Mistress just yet. I mean, wasn't it the worst form of torture that anyone should to have deal with their husband's girl-friend as their coworker? I truly thought there should be a law somewhere against it.

Or at least an amendment.

I drifted off to sleep with dreams of spilling a cup of coffee down Cherry's blouse—or im-paling the top of her foot with my razor sharp stilettos—dancing through my head. I also clutched a bottle of Cabernet to my chest as if it were my favorite teddy bear. If this whole picture hadn't made me appear to be a raging alcoholic, it would have been my preferred way of going to sleep every night. It was that comforting.

CHAPTER 19

Returning to work wasn't as bad as I thought it would be—partially because I was still buzzed from the copious amounts of wine I consumed over the past five days.

I woke up at my usual time of seven-fifteen a.m., but I just didn't have the motivation to put on my full face of makeup, false eyelashes included. Instead, I swiped halfheartedly at my eyelashes with one coat of mascara as opposed to my usual three, and I didn't even curl them.

Something was definitely wrong. If I hadn't known it before, I would have clued in to that fact when I saw the shocked and horrified faces of my coworkers as I entered the building. Sure, I hadn't swept my hair into a loose and stylish chignon. And maybe I hadn't dressed all that fashionably since I was sporting a faded old pair of jeans and a white button-down blouse, from a career day long passed, that I'd found in the back of my closet. And maybe my complexion was pale and sunken because of my lack of nutrients over the week, but I really didn't see what the problem was. Nonetheless, everyone I passed on the way to my office looked at me as if I were a ghost. Which was probably fairly close to how I actually looked.

Fuck it.

The only bright and shining face I saw was Cherry, who was lingering nervously outside of my office door, holding a muffin as a peace offering.

"Hey, girl!" she said with a nervous smile. "I grabbed you an extra muffin this morning at Pike's Perk! Hope you like banana nut."

I didn't feel I had the capacity within myself to even muster up fake friendliness today. I silently took the muffin and pushed past Cherry into my office, shutting the door behind me. If I happened to make enemies in the process, so be it.

Unfortunately, my ability to churn up fake friendliness was tested to the max over the next forty-eight hours, where I had to spend the majority of my days side-by-side with Cherry brainstorming, creating, and troubleshooting new interface ideas for the web design of our online magazine launch. We discussed such stimulating topics as whether or not raspberry pink was too bold a color for our background, or if we should instead have a background filled with thousands of tiny lipstick images. Although the decision was tough and took hours of grueling deliberation, we went with raspberry pink.

It was obvious the surly demeanor induced by my depression had frightened Cherry. She made it a point to direct every aspect of our conversations to our work on the project. This was fine by me. I, too, was frightened of the uncharted waters that lay between us. I didn't want to accidentally let it slip that I was going on her dream vacation, so I just kept my mouth shut unless we happened to be talking about what font was best for our blog, Georgia or Comic Sans.

I managed to make it through two arduous days that actually felt closer to an eternity, until it was finally Saturday. Now, I truly understood all of those Prozac and Zoloft commercials that played within my beloved daytime television shows, depicting a haggard-looking soccer mom staring longingly out the window, symbolizing she was trapped in her own prison of depression. I always thought, "Just go outside, bitch!" But now I understood she was living in a glass house of emotions. Or something profound like that.

I could relate. I was now the creepy soccer mom who stared at everyone and wished I was happy enough to participate in normal activities again.

Since I wasn't one for medication—I had vivid memories of my mom crushing pills and stirring them into my ice cream when I was eight years old and home sick from school—I decided I had to "tough it out" until I got over the deep sadness that was eating away at me. I didn't know what to do with myself over the weekend that stretched out before me. Before I settled down on my couch with a bottle of wine and a bowl of ramen, I decided to drive around to see if anything fun in Denver caught my eye.

ᘒᘓ

I could have predicted where this aimless drive was going to end up. It was very similar to the plot of a *Lifetime* movie—yet again. Yep, you guessed it. I blanked out behind the wheel, drove around in sadness, and ended up at Fairmount Cemetery where Adam was buried. If Fairmount hadn't been full of graves, it would actually have been a beautiful place to spend time since it was so peaceful. But I guess that was the irony of cemeteries in the first place. I'd spent more than a few days here directly after Adam's death, but my wifely visitations experienced a significant drop-off as soon as I learned about his affair. I wondered if Cherry had ever visited the cemetery, or if she even knew Adam was buried here.

I hadn't come prepared with flowers, keepsakes, or anything symbolic to place on his grave, so I just stood awkwardly in front of his headstone without saying a word. I could've been there for five minutes or five hours. It all felt the same to me. In my head, I ran through all the items on my lists of why Adam had cheated on me and the warning signs I should have caught beforehand, offering them up as a silent plea for him to tell me from beyond the grave why he thought it was a good idea to betray our marriage like that. That was the question I needed answered, even though I suspected it wasn't a profound or even particularly interesting reason. It probably had more to do with what April was trying to tell me. Some men just got sidetracked and didn't think about the consequences of their infidelity. It was a fact of life, and it also happened to be the plot of every *Lifetime* movie ever made— especially those starring Tori Spelling.

Halfway through my lengthy standing-and-staring-at-Adam's-grave session, I had an eerie sensation someone was watching me. Taking into account, I was currently in a cemetery, it really creeped me out.

I had automatically put my hand on the back of my neck to smooth down all the hair that had bristled up as a reaction when I heard the crunch of a soft footstep in the leaves on the grass behind me. I absolutely knew Adam's ghost had come to haunt me and tell me I was a horrible wife who deserved to be cheated on.

Whirling around, I expected to see the ghost of Adam carrying chains, similar to one of those ghosts from *A Christmas Carol*. This made it all the more surprising to see a real, live man. I was definitely losing it. I gave the man a quick smile and turned my full attention back to staring at Adam's grave.

A few more minutes went by, and I noticed that this person who had disrupted my grave staring still hadn't moved from his spot about six feet behind me. What the hell was this guy doing? *Am I going to get mugged at a cemetery of all places?* That was just cold. I turned around to give my attacker a menacing look while fumbling in my pocket for my keys. I'd heard you were supposed to stick them between your fingers to stab criminals in the eye if they tried to jack your car.

It was worth a shot.

The mugger came slightly closer and cleared his throat. If he was planning to attack me, he was definitely taking his time.

"Um, I don't mean to bother you," he said quietly. "But I was wondering if you would mind?"

Was he asking for my purse outright? What was wrong with this guy? "Mind what?" I demanded through clenched teeth.

"Um." He looked uncomfortable. "Well, I actually wanted to put this card and flowers on the grave, but you were standing in front of it, so..."

"Oh! Sorry about that."

I politely moved to the side without giving a second thought as to how random it was for a stranger to be placing flowers on Adam's grave. Did Adam also have a gay lover I didn't know about? The mugger didn't really look gay, but you never know these days.

"I guess you don't remember me that well," he continued. "But I was actually at your wedding a few years ago. I'm really sorry to hear about your loss. Adam and I went to school together from elementary to high school, and our families were really close. So that's why they asked me to bring this card and flowers up here. I live pretty close to the cemetery."

"And what's your name?" I asked. I didn't remember meeting him at our wedding. *But since it was a total drunken extravaganza, the odds were we had probably been introduced.*

"Derek. Derek Watts." I guess my purse was safe. I vaguely remembered his name from some of Adam's high school stories, although I couldn't pinpoint him exactly. "Well, that was really nice of you to bring all this stuff up here. Adam would've appreciated it."

Derek gave the standard reply. "He was an amazing guy. I really can't believe what happened."

"Yeah, kind of," I muttered quietly. Not a very wifely thing to say.

Derek looked at me strangely but kept his comments to himself. He probably assumed I was crazy and stricken with grief. And he would have assumed correctly.

"I recently found out that Adam was cheating on me," I continued, since I was on a roll, and when was I ever going to see this guy again? "And if he'd still been alive, he would have gone on a lavish tropical vacation with his mistress this past August."

My blunt comments brought social awkwardness to a whole new level. Derek seemed at a loss for words, but I really didn't care what he thought at this point. After several minutes of embarrassing silence, I threw him a bone. "So you and Adam were really good friends in high school?"

He answered immediately, obviously happy to get away from the excruciating portion of the conversation. "Yeah, we actually lived down the street from each other. We used to go to the pool together all the time. In high school we both ran on the track team together, and he even took my little sister to prom, which I wasn't too happy about." He laughed at the memory.

"That's interesting," I said unconvincingly. "So you live close to here?"

"Yeah, I have a little house pretty close by, off of Holly and Leetsdale, if you're familiar with the area."

"I live pretty close myself. In Cherry Creek, so I know where you're talking about. Nice area."

After a few more minutes of awkward silence, I said, "So where do you work?"

I had about as much charm as a doctor doing a routine checkup, asking standard questions I didn't really care to hear the answers to.

"I work as a recruiter for college athletes at DU. It's pretty funny because I went to the Art Institute of Denver to do something related to graphic design, but I just wasn't into it. I'd always loved sports, so I figured it was the best of both worlds to be a recruiter."

Whew! If he'd said he was a graphic designer like my douchebag husband, I would have turned on my heel and walked away, polite or not. As it was, I was more than ready to wrap up this painful conversation, so I said something vague about the fact I had a busy afternoon with errands to run, but that it was nice to meet him. As I started to walk slowly to my car—without my keys between my fingers for protection–Derek called after me.

I waited so he could catch up with me, and he said, "This is kind of strange, but I was wondering if you'd want to grab coffee sometime since we're practically neighbors. I just thought maybe it would be a good idea for us to hang out and talk, like maybe it would help."

I obliged by giving Derek one of my cards I carried in my purse with my contact information, thinking he was just being kind to a poor old widow and would probably never follow up on the offer. Although it would have been nice to go out on a coffee date with someone who was actually good looking with a seemingly-pleasant personality—and who said we had to talk about dead husbands at all?

I said goodbye to Derek and drove away from the cemetery, back to my depressing weekend of drinking and watching bad television. I had already missed several precious hours of the *Rock of Love* reruns that were on *VH1*. Fortunately, I had the foresight to record them. Thank you, past-Danielle.

When I got home and took up my station on the couch with booze in hand and a crappy plate of noodles on my lap—I decided to go wild and mix it up today by drinking white wine instead of red—it was nearly five o'clock. Where had my day gone? I could tell you where. I had wasted it at the cemetery, hanging out with my Adam's ghost and mingling with fellow cemetery goers. By the time eight o'clock rolled around, I was exhausted and almost ready to go to my filthy bed. Depression and sadness definitely made you much sleepier than normal. I'd never been the type to hit the hay just after the sun went down.

As I was performing my nightly ritual of washing my face and brushing my teeth, I heard my phone buzz. Since I had a long list of people I didn't want to talk to anymore, especially Ron who thought I was still recovering from a long illness, I just let it roll over to voicemail. I shuffled off to bed and completely forgot about my lingering voicemail, until I suddenly remembered to check it the next morning when I finally woke up at the early hour of one p.m.

Shockingly enough, the voicemail was from my new cemetery buddy, Derek. I guess he really meant what he said about having a cup of coffee with me. He asked if I was free to meet him at the Starbucks on First tomorrow, which was now today. Since I'd already wasted my morning and a small portion of my afternoon, I decided I didn't have anything better to do than catch up with Adam's old friend. It would be a great feat if I left my house more than once within the weekend.

I sent Derek a text telling him I was available, partially hoping he wouldn't see it right away and maybe I would be off the hook for our coffee meeting. No such luck. He probably had his phone on vibrate in his pocket. He texted me back within three minutes telling me he could meet me at three p.m., a little more than an hour away.

Although I was tempted to drink heavily before this strange meeting, I decided to go the sober route. The last thing I needed was an afternoon DUI on my record. That would confirm without question I had hit rock bottom, and I didn't think I was there just yet.

I took my time showering for the first time in several days, slicking back my hair into a disgusting ponytail since I had no one to impress anyway. Makeup was also off the table since I wanted to let my new ghoulish complexion shine through. I decided to keep the faded sweatshirt I had on and just change from my pajama pants into a pair of jeans.

I was living in style.

I got to the Starbucks only fifteen minutes late. I figured this was close enough to our initial meeting time so I didn't have to apologize or acknowledge my lateness. This was a far cry from the crazy punctual, anal-retentive-Danielle, but I had kissed that girl goodbye weeks ago. Where had she ever gotten me in life, anyway?

Derek seemed surprisingly happy to see me even though I'd kept him waiting. He stood up from his table in the back to give me a warm hug. I took a closer look. He was actually hotter than I remembered. Which only proved how bad I would have been at picking him out of a lineup if he had actually mugged me. He had dark brown hair, well groomed in a short cut, even darker brown eyes, and olive skin to match. I was wondering how he managed to maintain such an excellent tan in the cold month of October when I realized he had already started the conversation without me.

"...so, I spent the rest of my morning catching up on a little bit of work, and I also decided to rake my back lawn since there's this huge tree from my neighbors' yard that always spills its leaves all over mine. I've talked to them nicely about it, again and again, but they never actually trim the tree even after they promise to do it. So every fall I have to spend hours on the weekend raking up the leaves, but at least it's a good workout," he said, smiling happily.

"Mmm-hmm."

Derek was happy to completely dominate the conversation. Maybe he sensed my underlying depression and lack of motivation to talk to a human. He entertained me with stories of the trouble he and Adam had gotten into in high school—sneaking liquor into school in a water bottle, those little rebels!—how he had lived for a few years in San Diego when he went to college but actually much preferred the mountains—me too!—and how he was excited for Thanksgiving this year since he was hosting his family at his house for the first time.

That was when I interrupted his rambling monologue. "I'm actually going out of town for Thanksgiving for the first time. My best friend booked both of us a vacation to where Adam was going to take his mistress last August. My friend thinks it'd be good for me to check out the resort, even though I disagree."

Once again, I had a knack for making an everyday conversation crazy awkward. Derek ran his hands through his short hair and laughed nervously. "Wow, that sounds like it'll be interesting, to say the least. Where did you say the resort was again?"

"I didn't. Antigua." And that was all I had to say on the subject.

Derek took that huge and uncomfortable pause in the conversation as an opportunity to go grab me a soy latte—very gentlemanly and greatly appreciated. By the time he came back, he seemed to have pulled it together and had even thought of a few new conversation topics he could discuss with exuberance, not requiring any response from me.

I listened to him talk about how track had become a much more popular college sport than many people realized, even though he primarily had to recruit for the DU football team. I only interjected one time to ask him about the regulations for college athletes who did illegal drugs, like steroids, which made Derek launch into a long soapbox speech about how so many people associated college athletes with illegal substances, when really most of those drugs were reserved for professional athletes who had the money to buy them.

Before I knew it, two whole hours had passed. I was surprised I hadn't missed my wine or ramen noodles once. I told Derek I'd had a wonderful time, and I wished him a great week ahead—in a very generic way that implied I would never be seeing him again. I mean, one pity-friend date was more than kind of him since he was old friend of Adam's, but two meant I was officially a charity case.

Derek interrupted my goodbye speech by saying, "I don't know if you're busy, but would you be interested in coming with me to a swimming match at DU on Saturday? I don't know if it's your thing, but I have a few new recruits I wanted to keep an eye on to make sure everything was going well."

If I wasn't mistaken, Derek looked positively nervous awaiting my reply. Why did he even care what I was doing on Saturday anyway?

"I don't mean to be rude, Derek, but you don't have to hang out with me just because I'm dealing with this loss. I'm perfectly content hanging out at home, and I'm actually doing fine." What a horrible liar I was.

Derek flushed deeply and said, "No, that's not what I meant at all. I'm really sad to hear about what happened with Adam, but I just like spending time with you. We live really close to each other and seem to like some of the same things, so I thought it'd be great to see you again. But if you don't want to—"

I cut him off. "No. I think that could be fun, so just text me the details later on in the week."

He walked me to my car outside and gave me another warm hug. I suddenly noticed he smelled absolutely incredible. I drove home in a confused haze, not wanting to consider our upcoming meeting was anything more than one friend helping out another. I had already alienated all the girlfriends in my life besides April, so I'd take any friends I could get.

CHAPTER 20

The next week flew by at lightning speed. Probably because I had mentally checked out and didn't give a shit about what was going on anymore. I could only assume this made me an excellent boss to April since I had nothing more to say about how often she took breaks, how quickly she answered the phone, or whether or not she got my messages right.

I was also doing surprisingly well working side-by-side on the project with Cherry. I was using the clever tactic of pretending she was an absolute stranger who'd never spread her legs for someone I was once married to. I didn't think that approach would last, but if it got my mind off of all of my inner turmoil for a few weeks, then I was one happy camper.

I guess you could also say my week seemed to go by quickly because I had agreed to a date on Saturday that I wasn't exactly looking forward to. Let me explain. On the one hand, I had no issue with going on what appeared to be a second date with a good-looking guy my own age who had a normal job and was easy to talk to. On the other hand, I didn't want to get too excited about anything because I had a strong suspicion Derek was only fulfilling his friendly duties to Adam by taking out his widow a few times so he would feel less guilty. Anyone in his shoes would do the same thing.

Oh, and I didn't know if I was exactly free to date since I still had Ron in limbo. I had never directly told him I was done seeing him. I had just put him off for another week by e-mailing him that I was still under the weather. I had never been a fan of lying by omission, but it just seemed to be too complicated to tell Ron I was close to hitting rock bottom and was busy drinking myself to sleep every night. Much too complicated.

By the time Friday rolled around, I decided the humane thing to do was to put Ron out of his misery since he kept asking, via e-mail, when we could reschedule our date. No. I didn't go over to his house with a shotgun and put him down as you would an old mare, but I did finally send him an e-mail, telling him I didn't think I was ready to date anyone since I was a widow of only one year. Again, it wasn't necessarily classy pulling the widow card to get out of this situation. But it seemed appropriate.

He, true to character, e-mailed me back within a mere ten minutes telling me he was very sorry and had no idea what I was going through. Of course, he didn't. I'd never told him. Yet, he was overly apologetic, nonetheless. He also told me he would be more than happy to see me again if I was ready in a few months and to keep him posted. I guess I could consider it comforting that I had a man on call if I ever really, really needed a tight-lipped and uncomfortable kiss.

I went to bed early, and a little more sober than usual, on Friday night. I wanted to be coherent and ready to take in every aspect of my non-date the following day. You could possibly call it a pity outing, but I was kind of looking forward to it anyway.

 C/3C/3

I woke up bright and early on Saturday morning at eleven a.m., which was actually good for me these days. It gave me four whole hours before I had to meet Derek at his house to get to the match by three-thirty.

I didn't think a swim meet was the appropriate time to bust out the costume jewelry and high heels. So I instead decided to go for a comfortable and stylishly worn-in pair of boyfriend jeans with a tight knit top that made my boobs look a lot bigger than they actually were. If any observers were to take any cues from the way I carefully dressed myself, they would see I was more than a little excited about this meeting. Even though I didn't want to admit it.

The anonymous observers would speculate as they peered into my bedroom window. *"Did you see the way that she chose that top to accentuate her breasts? And did you see how long she took to apply her makeup so that it looked as if she wasn't wearing any? And can you believe she spent forty-five minutes finger curling her hair so it looked fresh and tousled? It's obvious that the girl's got it bad!"*

I was ready for Derek in record time. I didn't want to get comfortable with the hour I had to spare for fear I would start drinking or eating ramen and wouldn't be able to stop myself in time. So I sat primly on my filthy couch and watched the National Geographic Channel while I sipped a glass of water. Just so I wouldn't get too relaxed or distracted before I had to leave.

Derek's house was surprisingly close to mine, so I actually arrived a full ten minutes early. This sent me into a state of panic. I didn't want to appear too eager, so I drove around his block six times before I parked in his driveway.

He answered his door and greeted me with, "Did you get lost? I thought I saw you driving by the house a few times. Wasn't it easy to find?"

I lowered my head and blushed deeply. "Oh, yeah, I think I was just a little distracted, so I ended up passing it by accident."

He took the gentlemanly approach and drove both of us to the swim meet in his car, since I had no idea where it was located, finally allowing me the opportunity to participate in some human conversation. Not like I was bubbly or fun to talk to or anything. But I did throw in a few random contributions about how my week had gone, and I also made sure to morbidly tell the story of how I was now working with my husband's mistress.

Derek seemed absolutely shocked by that fact. "So you've actually met her? How did that happen?"

I replied, "Well, I would say that it's a long story, but I actually caused the whole thing. I spied on her, trying to figure out who she was, and then I invited her to one of our work functions under the guise that we were interested in her as a graphic designer. Long story long—the whole thing blew up in my face. My boss actually decided to hire her to work with me on our website launch, so now I have to spend a pretty good amount of time with her."

He hesitated. "How's that working out for you so far?"

I gave him a look that said it all—his cue to chat happily about random subjects that had nothing to do with Adam or his infidelities. We talked about when we thought the first snowfall would be—I said December, but he insisted that it would happen by Thanksgiving—what we both thought of *Inception*—so was it really all a dream in the end?—and how he was excited about going to a Rockies game before the season was over.

You know, the usual.

We were at DU in what felt like a matter of moments. Derek rushed me in to the indoor swimming pool, where we were able to sit on the very front row with a few other coaches. It would have been exciting if there had been more than twenty people there. But, again, beggars can't be choosers, right? Derek explained that swim meets weren't very popular with the college crowd, so this was actually a fairly good turnout.

I hadn't thought I would be interested in watching a swim meet since I wasn't a big sports fan. But something about the fluid motions of the swimmers and their peaceful expressions entranced me. Or maybe I was just acting like the depressed soccer mom in the Zoloft commercial again. There was one particular female swimmer I had my eye on the entire time. She seemed like she was always stuck in second place. She had an impressively strong upper body and sliced through the water so quickly I barely saw her arms break the surface. She swam in three different races, "heats," and placed second, third, and second respectively. Even though it was just a race, it all seemed so depressing. This girl had probably trained for years and years, yet when it all came down to it, she was still only second best. Maybe that was a pessimistic point of view, but I didn't think I could be expected to come up with anything more positive in my current mental state. It just seemed like a lot of wasted effort for someone who was trying so hard.

I lost my focus on my favorite second-rate female swimmer as Derek pointed out the girl he had recruited. Fortunately for her and unfortunately for the second place swimmer, his recruit placed first in all of her three races. I didn't know her, but I could only assume she was "that" type of girl, an overachieving perfectionist that probably broke up people's marriages.

I faked enthusiasm as I congratulated Derek on his amazing find of a new champion swimmer and sat tight while the rest of the heats finished. When the match was over, Derek's recruit placed first overall, which put him in an exceptional mood. The girl I had my eye on didn't even make it to the top three winner's block.

Such is life.

Derek spent about thirty minutes after the match congratulating his recruit and talking with a few other coaches about how she was doing and what her prospects were. Or something along those lines. I wasn't really paying attention.

He finally trotted back to me and said apologetically, "I'm so sorry it took me so long. I guess I should've explained to you about all of the recruiter politics, and how I'd have to talk to a few people afterward. Can I make it up to you by taking you out to dinner?"

I happily agreed since I was suffering from a serious case of low blood sugar. But I couldn't help thinking to myself that this was beginning to sound like a real date. I mean, I would go to a swim match with my brother on a Saturday afternoon, but I highly doubted he would then take me to a low lit restaurant where we would sit in a cozy booth together and sip wine? At least I hoped not. I didn't even have a brother, but the idea was really gross.

We actually ended up at a place called the Sushi Den a few blocks away on South Pearl. Even though Derek couldn't have had any idea sushi was my favorite food, it seemed like it was planned just for me. Since I was under the impression this wasn't a real date, I didn't have any of those first date jitters where you feel obligated to act like a girl and don't want to order too much food to make you look fat, causing you to go home hungry and chow down on SpaghettiOs at two a.m. because you're starving.

Nope, I went totally crazy. I ordered a seaweed salad as an appetizer, a spicy tuna roll, a unagi roll, a California roll, and a little something called a Rocky Mountain roll that I'd never tried before. And that was just for me. Derek looked at me with surprise but ordered just as many rolls for himself.

After our massive amounts of sushi finally arrived, we settled into a comfortable conversation. Since this was a non-date, I appreciated the fact we didn't have to talk about our jobs, where we grew up, and our idea of a dream vacation. Bo-ring.

My spirits were lifted because of the offensive amounts of sake I consumed, so I went on and on about the plots of all of my favorite television shows since they were the closest things I had to friends lately. Derek seemed mildly amused and didn't stop me, even when I broke into a long soliloquy about how I thought the *Real Housewives of New York* cast was better than all of the other *Housewives* seasons and why.

Finally, I took a break from my reality drama dissection to make a dent in my tall pile of sushi.

At last, Derek had a chance to speak. "You're funny, you know that," he said with a smile as he crammed a piece of spicy tuna into his mouth.

I had to finish chewing my own substantial bite before I could answer. "Why's that?"

"Well, at first you gave off this impression you were distraught and having a hard time, but today you're like a totally different person, he answered, grinning yet again "I'm just saying, I'm having fun spending time with you.".

"So you weren't having fun on our coffee date? Or at the cemetery?" I shot back.

"So our coffee date was a date?" he rebounded expertly.

I had no idea what to say to that and blushed. Then I went with my go-to response of laughing like a total airhead and slamming a shot of sake. It worked every time.

The rest of the meal was enjoyable, and the awkward silences I normally dreaded and felt so desperate to fill, didn't seem to be an issue. We both took our time chowing down on our separate piles of sushi, and we talked a little in between.

On the ride home, I automatically brought my hand up to change the radio station, which was playing the only Chumbawumba hit that also happened to grate on my last nerve. But I brought my hand back down to my lap as I thought better of it. I didn't want another repeat of the passive-aggressive assault from Ron when I tried to change the NPR station. No, thank you.

Derek immediately noticed my strange hand flapping and asked, "Did you want to change the station?" He started rapidly scanning through all the radio stations and instructed me to tell him when to stop.

Since I considered myself to be a professional radio Mix Master, even more so when I was drunk on sake, I took the task very seriously. Finally, I heard the familiar riffs of "Eighteen and Life" by Skid Row. "Stop!" I commanded and held up my hand like a traffic cop.

"Skid Row? Excellent choice." He nodded approvingly at my amazing hair metal selection and cranked up the radio. We spent the last few minutes of the drive home basking in screechy 'eighties rock that never truly got the credit it deserved.

As we pulled into Derek's driveway, I hopped out of the car and started to stumble over to my own car a few feet away.

"Hey, wait!" he said as he hurried to catch up with me. "Aren't you going to say good-bye?"

"Oh, sorry," I replied. "Um, goodbye! Thanks for dinner!" I rummaged around in my purse for my car keys.

Before I knew what was happening, Derek put his hand behind my head and pulled me toward him for a kiss. I immediately tensed because I still hadn't gotten over my initial impression of him as a mugger. But as soon as his lips met mine, I completely forgot about him stealing my purse. I know there are many cliché ways to describe a good first kiss, so all I will say is that when it's good, it's *good*.

The kiss only lasted a few seconds. When he stepped back, I was completely speechless. He gave me a sheepish smile, and since I had nothing to say in response, I opened my car door, climbed in, and drove away. I'd have to chalk that one up to yet another time I made a seemingly perfect situation completely awkward.

CHAPTER 21

Even though I didn't want to make too much of the exceptional kiss I received at the end of my date with Derek, I did the girl thing, anyway, where I automatically expected him to call me the very next day and tell me how wonderful I was. Why wouldn't he?

No matter how much I tried to tell myself what happened between us didn't matter and was probably a result of too much sake, in the back of my mind I was convinced he would call me before the weekend was over and set up our next date.

Maybe I was already brainwashed from my brief experience with Ron, but that definitely didn't happen. I waited with anticipation for Derek's call for a good three days until I considered blocking his number altogether, although April begged me not to. I had told her every detail of our date number two, including the big kiss finale, and she assured me it was totally normal not to hear from a guy for a few days afterward. Ron was obviously a human robot and the exception to the rule. She reminded me I couldn't expect an eligible guy with attractive male characteristics to call me even within a week of a date. It just wasn't going to happen.

For that reason alone, I didn't delete Derek's number. But I vowed to myself I would screen his first and maybe second call, just to show him I was busy with my own life and not waiting around for anyone. That was a classic dating move that perpetuated all of the dating games I so detested, but I didn't have any other ammunition. While it was a possibility for me to have my own set of balls and call Derek myself, I just didn't feel right about it since he was the one who kissed me in the first place. Pick up the phone, dammit!

By the time the second week came and went without hearing from Derek, I was desperate for him to call and had thrown out my screening plan altogether. I had no idea why the only normal human guy that I'd met in a very long time, ironically not from a dating website, didn't seem interested in seeing me again. Or maybe I did have an idea. In the back of my mind lurked the reality that the guy in question was one of my dead husband's life-long friends. Maybe it had finally occurred to him that it was not so kosher to make out with your dead friend's widow. This was a word of advice I'd never specifically found inside of a fortune cookie, but it seemed wise, nonetheless.

Instead of moping around about Derek, I chose to direct my energy elsewhere and moped around about my impending Thanksgiving vacation/punishment instead. It was difficult to grumble and complain about going to such a beautiful paradise, especially since my best friend would be with me, but I felt guilty looking forward to this trip in particular. It didn't seem right to celebrate a trip my husband had been planning to take with Cherry. Even though we were going for purely psychological reasons to help me confront the ghosts of my past, or some shit like that.

April took me on a fairly fun shopping trip with depressing overtones, where we cleaned out every off-season sale rack. I walked out of the store with bags of bikinis, wooden wedge sandals, gauzy swimsuit cover-ups, and over-sized beaded hoop earrings that seemed completely appropriate for a tropical setting. I was having a little bit of fun shopping for a beach vacation in such cold Colorado weather. But I wouldn't admit that to anyone, including myself.

April made me try on bikini after bikini. I had to hand it to her, she dealt with someone in my emotionally crippled state exceptionally well by ignoring the way I was acting and talking to me like a normal person. No matter how much it irritated me.

"I really love the gold bikini," she commented happily. "It brings out the warm coloring in your skin tone. You should get it!"

"I guess," I said as pathetically as I could.

She smiled. "If you think about it, you're probably going to need a minimum of five swimsuits, one for every day we're there. Since these are half-price, you should just get them all."

I sighed much louder than I needed to and rummaged through my bag for my credit card so I could buy exotic beachwear in bulk for a fraction of the price. If I was in a better mood, I would have patted myself on the back for how much money I saved and then proceeded to spend the savings on something ridiculous. Like silver boy shorts that said "Too Hott 2

Handle" across the ass. But I wasn't in the mood this time.

After I "shopped 'till I dropped" for everything I could possibly need for vacation, I spent the next two weeks pretending I had never heard the name Derek before, deleting every single eHarmony e-mail in my inbox—those from Ron included—and getting along surprisingly well with Cherry . The odd thing about it was we were receiving compliment after compliment from Gwen, telling us how pleased she was with how we had collaborated on our rough design for the website launch. Of course, the design and content of the website was something we were going to have to work on together for a complete year, but it seemed to be off to a great start.

When I pretended Cherry was a total stranger to me, I actually appreciated quite a few aspects of her personality. Firstly, she was self-deprecating, much like me, making it interesting to work with her. Secondly, she never ceased to buy a little something extra for me when she grabbed coffee, lunch, or even an afternoon snack for herself—a generosity I couldn't help but to be grateful for. Who would turn down a free muffin every day, I ask you? Lastly, she was actually laid-back and very easy to communicate with. We didn't have any underlying tension or catty arguments about one of us wanting a different color, font, or graphic for the website design. That was actually a pretty rare find in a female coworker, especially in the magazine world.

Of course, all of the seemingly good qualities about her bothered me deeply because she was...well, The Mistress—plain and simple. The fact I even *wanted* to like her messed with me psychologically so I absolutely couldn't wait to get away to the upcoming reenactment of Adam and Cherry's beach rendezvous. But instead of a beautiful couple on the beach holding hands and drinking piña coladas as the sunset, it would be me and April, with her trying to make sure I didn't drown myself in the ocean out of despair while her back was turned.

With our trip just a few days away, I was in an absolute frenzy trying to tie up all the loose ends for both of my workload as well as April's. I made a long list for Cherry of every possible detail she would need to know in my absence, although I was only going to be gone for one day. On top of that, the holidays were an intensely busy time at *High Life*. We had to put together holiday gift lists for our readers, focusing on beauty, fashion, and eco-friendly "Gifts for Him." I was in charge of the beauty aspect of it and had countless e-mails and voicemails to deal with from product reps trying to push their latest concoction on me to make sure it was seen by our readers before the Christmas season.

That being said, I was stuck in front of my computer and on my phone every moment of my workday for the last forty-eight hours before we were to leave the country. I could barely see straight, let alone keep straight each beauty product rep who was vying for my attention for our Christmas issue. The standard protocol with all of the calls coming in for me was that April would knock frantically on the window separating my office from her desk. I would then give her a thumbs-up or thumbs-down as to whether I was available to take a call. It was a pretty prehistoric method of communication, but I couldn't think of any better way to let her know when I was swamped or available for a phone call.

On Tuesday afternoon, I was in the middle of replying to my last batch of e-mails from skin care reps who were desperately inquiring as to whether their products would be in our Christmas issue this year. Since only a slim minority of the beauty products made it to our "Wish List," I tried to let each rep down gently, yet clearly, so they wouldn't be tempted to call and leave me angry voicemails about their rejection.

In the midst of my fourth or fifth e-mail, April gave our signal by knocking on the window to see if I was available for a phone call. I gave her the cutting motion across my throat, which meant a definite *no* for answering a call right now. Oddly enough, she kept knocking and knocking, and I kept cutting and cutting. I wasn't in the mood, nor did I have the time, to take a call at the moment. Finally, April got up from her desk, popped her head in my door, and said, "I'm putting a call through."

I shook my head vigorously, but it was already too late. My phone buzzed and I answered, "Danielle Starkey."

A man's voice said, "Danielle."

"Yes, how can I help you?" It was probably just an aggressive product rep trying to twist my arm into putting their product on our Christmas wish list at the last minute.

"It's Derek."

I had absolutely nothing to say to that. Since I had recently omitted the name Derek from my vocabulary, I was speechless. First of all, it was strange that he was calling me at work. Second of all, what was he thinking calling me almost a month after our second date?

"What can I do for you?" I replied a little too coolly. Oops.

Derek hesitated. "Um, I just wanted to get a hold of you because I know you're going on vacation over Thanksgiving."

After an excruciating pause I was tempted to fill with inane anecdotes, he continued. "I wanted to tell you I hope everything goes well because I know it's kind of a big deal."

"Why are you calling me at work?"

"I actually left you a few voicemails last week, but I didn't hear back from you. I had your work number on the card you gave me, and I just wanted to talk to you before you left. I'm sorry I didn't call sooner. "

Oops again. Although I had waited with bated breath for Derek to call after our date, and even slept next to my phone—my dirty little secret—I had been crazy busy with work over the past several weeks and hadn't even bothered to check my personal voicemail which was clogged with business messages rolling over from work. I figured whoever really needed to talk to me would call my work number, and I guess, in a way, I was right.

"Why?" I said.

"Why what?"

"Why didn't you call me sooner? I haven't heard from you in over a month, so it seems a little off to try to wish me well on my vacation after all this time."

"Yeah." He paused dramatically. "I don't really know what to say to that other than I was worried I overstepped my boundaries with you. You jumped in your car and drove away so quickly after we kissed, I thought I'd offended you. It just felt like I went too far, especially since Adam was a good friend of mine."

Hmm, his story seemed to line up. I was always wary of guys and the fake sob stories they used after blowing you off for months, just to get back in touch with you when it was convenient for them. But he did have a point. I had acted really strange. I probably would have been put off by anyone who slammed their car door in my face and drove away with wheels screeching after a really great first kiss too.

"I'm sorry." I said, surprising myself. "I'm kind of having a hard time adjusting to the whole dating scene, and I know I acted a little weird. But I did have a really good time. Really."

"Really, really?" Derek said jokingly. "Me too. I don't want to keep you, but now that we know we're on the same page, why don't I give you a call after Thanksgiving? I really meant what I said though. I hope you have a great time and that the trip helps."

I did too. I hung up the phone with a smile on my face and gave April a quick thumbs-up through the window since she knew exactly who I was talking to, the sneaky little bitch. I'd have to save all of the juicy details for our marathon packing session scheduled for tonight before we left on vacation tomorrow.

As much as I wanted to tell myself I wasn't looking forward to this, there seemed to be a small light at the end of the tunnel. I never envisioned myself spending the holidays investigating my husband's infidelities, but I figured that if I was forced to spend a few days in a beautiful tropical getaway, then I at least ought to have some fun while doing it.

Game on.

STAGE 5: ACCEPTANCE

CHAPTER 22

Stepping onto a plane headed for Antigua sounded like the beginning of a beautiful vacation/romantic comedy, although the actual trip from point A to point B was far from fabulous. First of all, April had never been an excellent trip planner. Something I completely forgot when she hijacked my credit card and booked our "love getaway" the month before. She had a horrible tendency of never paying attention to the itinerary and always making it to the plane at the last second. Or missing the flight altogether, which almost caused a family rift when she was mere hours away from being late for her own brother's wedding several years ago. But that's another story altogether.

I, the organized/anal one, had also neglected to check the itinerary because I didn't want to go in the first place. So that meant we happily sipped mimosas on the redeye out of Denver to Miami, where we then realized our next flight wasn't scheduled to leave for Antigua for nine more hours. Meaning we would finally arrive at our tropical getaway just as the sun was setting.

If you did the rough calculations, that was an entire day wasted. Time we could have spent getting sloshed on the beach. Instead, we spent it sitting upright in hard plastic chairs in the back of a Miami airport terminal, where they must have had a great sense of humor because the air conditioning was blasting at fifty-five degrees, although it was eight-five outside. And we hadn't brought any jackets or sweaters in our carry-ons. And Kenny G was playing on the Muzak at such a loud volume it was impossible to take a nap or even talk to the person sitting next to you.

To remedy the prison-like conditions that felt just as torturous as being water boarded in a Chinese jail—at least I would imagine—we hightailed it to the nearest bar, parked ourselves on barstools and drank margarita after margarita until it seemed almost fun to be stranded at the airport instead of drinking for free at our all-inclusive resort.

That's the beauty of alcohol for you.

Not to worry, we did finally arrive at the Grande Royal Antiguan Beach Resort a little after dark. The air was hot, sweet, and definitely thick with the smell of mistresses.

The resort itself was beautiful and exclusive. Yet, I couldn't help but be aware of the fact it seemed like the perfect place to take a sordid secret vacation if you were a cheating husband. I pushed all foreboding thoughts out of my mind as we were greeted by a gorgeous island girl, wearing a festive head wrap and shoving glasses of rum punch in our faces—something no one with a pulse could resist.

I gulped down my very strong drink in just a few minutes, itching to see what the resort was all about. I wanted to throw our bags in our rooms and get into swimsuits as quickly as possible. Now that I had been forced out of the country on a dream vacation, I was literally going to make the most of every second. I highly doubted I would be going anywhere near this beautiful with a man anytime soon.

April and I were handed our room key on a silver tray with few more glasses of rum punch when I noticed something peculiar. Yes, I said "room key" not "keys". There must have been a mistake. That's exactly what I said to April with a slight slur in my speech already—

always a good sign on vacation!—as she gazed back at me sheepishly and didn't respond.

"We got two rooms, right?" I said again, growing angrier by the moment.

"Um, I didn't want to tell you this in Miami. I actually thought I booked one room with two queen beds, but it ended up being a suite with one king bed. But the good news is that we get a romantic breakfast on our last morning here!"

Great. Now we were going to be cast as the lesbian couple at the resort. At least it would keep creepy single guys from hitting on us so we could really relax and enjoy our vacation.

"I kind of hate you, you know," I said only half-jokingly as I swigged of the rest of my punch and made my way toward our shared lovers' suite on the sixth floor of the hotel.

If I hadn't been sharing a romantic room with my best friend on a vacation that Adam had planned with his mistress—try to wrap your mind around that one, *Days of Our Lives*—I would've been really impressed with our room setup. We overlooked a beautiful, bright blue ocean that looked as if it had been enhanced with food coloring. It was that vivid. It would have inspired a double-rainbow-type-freak-out in anyone.

We also had a private balcony and a huge bathtub/Jacuzzi filled with bath salts, Jasmine scented bubble bath, and sensual massage oil. I guess I could have a spa day for one with all of the goodies because there was no way in hell I was going to let April massage my back with scented oil. No matter how sorry she was for booking us only one room.

I opened my suitcase and hung up all of my beach and cocktail dresses within ten minutes. April still had yet to change into her swimsuit. That was classic April-behavior anywhere we went together, but I decided it was high time to lay down the law.

"If you don't get ready in five minutes, I'm going to leave without you," I said unconvincingly to her back as she slowly smoothed her eyebrows down with clear brow gel.

"Mmm," she murmured.

I waited a full fifteen minutes after my ultimatum, drinking half of a bottle of free champagne I found in our hotel room refrigerator, before I finally gathered up my bag, camera, and a book and went to explore the resort by myself. I made it as far as the tiki bar near the pool in front of our hotel when she caught up with me, breathless from running.

"I didn't really think you were going to leave me," she wheezed.

"You were taking too long," I replied over my shoulder as my new best friend, Rodney the bartender, handed me a beautiful concoction made with banana rum, banana liqueur, and a scoop of chocolate ice cream. Fittingly, it was called the Chocolate Monkey, and it was about to kick off my fantastic evening flying solo before April tracked me down. She ordered the same drink and happily took a seat next to me at the bar. Even though it was already eight-thirty and dark, the weather was warm and humid. I broke out in a little bit of a sweat. Still, no matter how hot it got here on the island, I could always remind myself that it was a good sixty degrees warmer than Colorado. I was one lucky girl to be here.

My attitude had slowly changed about the whole vacation. Stepping into paradise has a way of taking your mind off all of the petty bullshit you complain about on a daily basis. In fact, after just an hour of drinking at a poolside tiki bar, I felt this experience should be doctor's orders for anyone who was depressed, having difficulty liking their dead husband's mistress, or all of the above.

April and I blew through three more tropical cocktails apiece at an impressive speed, until the bar and surrounding pool area started to have that nice, fuzzy tint that signified I was definitely drunk. I didn't want any repeats of my last crazy drunken outing with April where I ended up with a black widow tattoo—which I was extremely nervous to bare at the beach, by the way—but I had quite a bit of inner tension to release. I felt I was entitled to a good time.

Just as April and I were talking about all of the fun activities we wanted to do the next day, my favorite bartender Rodney asked us why we weren't at the beach bonfire that night.

"What beach bonfire?" was my honest reply.

Rodney looked at me as if I was totally crazy in addition to being obviously drunk. "The resort has nightly activities for all of the guests. They're holding a special beach bonfire tonight since a few hundred guests are arriving for the holidays. It's right over there actually."

He pointed past the end of the tiki bar where I could see the subtle glow of a fire. I also heard pounding, island beats, which I had assumed the resort was pumping through speakers in fake rocks to create a tropical ambience. I guess not.

Before April even had the opportunity to give her approval, I grabbed her by the hand and waved goodbye to Rodney. That's the true beauty of an all-inclusive resort. You don't even have to think about your tab. If you order a drink you don't like, you can just pour it out on the ground. When no one's looking, of course.

As April and I stumbled through the sand around the side of the tiki bar, we saw a massive celebration, surrounding a wall of fire at least ten feet high. I thought maybe I was hallucinating from all the traditional island beverages I had already consumed, but April looked just as taken aback as I was.

"Whoa," she said in a daze, her mouth hanging open.

As I tried to think of something clever to say in response, we were suddenly surrounded by a group of four guys. They handed us each yet another rum punch and pulled us closer to the fire to dance to the Black Eyed Peas. Although the music was typical American club music as opposed to traditional island reggae, it felt liberating and free to be dancing in a huge crowd of strangers, with a few hot guys included as an added bonus.

The guys were total gentlemen, bringing us drink after drink. Which could have also meant they were sleazy and had ulterior motives—like trying to get us drunk so they could take advantage of us. But I wasn't going to argue. By shouting over the music, we gathered the guys were here on a fall break from the University of Mississippi. The specific guy I spent the most time dancing with was named Scott. Or Todd. Or Don. I couldn't say for sure.

As the bonfire wound to a close several hours later, April and I and our new male entourage collapsed on the cool sand near the water. Now that the music had been turned down and replaced with soft reggae grooves, I finally had the chance to figure out the guy I was dancing with was named Brad—oops! He happened to be celebrating his fall break in his *sophmore* year of college. That fact alone made me recoil as if someone had threatened to brand "child molester" across my forehead.

A few feet away, April seemed to be having the time of her life. Her barely-legal male companion had his arm draped affectionately around her shoulders and appeared to be pulling her closer and closer to him. Maybe she hadn't discovered yet that she was cuddling on a beach with a man-child a decade younger than her.

She turned to me and screeched at the top of her lungs, "This is Andrew! He's a sophomore in *college*!" She giggled hysterically and continued shouting as if I were deaf and in need of sign language.

She yelled, at a surprisingly high decibel, to the rest of the guys in the group that we were here on our Thanksgiving vacation and that we were almost thirty. I didn't see what was so funny about that dirty little secret. But all the guys laughed as if it were the funniest thing they'd ever heard in their lives. I suspected they had been too ingrained with the *Desperate Housewives* and the growing popularity of MILFs these days. Perhaps we were a treasured prize for them in conquering boredom on their college break.

That thought worried me even more. I tried to scoot away from Brad/Scott/Todd without him noticing. Obviously, in my drunken state, I wasn't as stealthy as I hoped as Brad said, "Hey there, cutie, where do you think you're going?"

I didn't have a specific answer other than I really needed to pee due to a bladder full of rum punch. I giggled and settled back into place as he wrapped his arm tighter around me. The drinks kept coming. April had already drifted off to a more secluded spot on the beach to make out with Andrew and probably get sand in places she was going to regret. Brad seemed to have the same idea. As I turned to answer a question he'd asked me, I found myself with his tongue down my throat. I went with it for a few minutes—since I was on vacation, which was supposed to give you a license to do anything stupid—but the random make out wasn't as much fun as I'd hoped it would be.

One bad sign was I found myself thinking of Derek during the very wet and very sloppy, drunken kiss. I actually wasn't thinking of our epic first kiss, as impressive as it was. I was thinking more about how much fun he was to talk to and how I couldn't wait to see him when I got back. I didn't care what we did. I just wanted to be around him and feel relaxed, as if I didn't have the weight of the world on my shoulders. Any epic kisses were simply icing on the cake and a welcome bonus.

I finally pulled away from Brad, due to the string of drool dripping down my face and threatening to dampen my beach cover-up.

Since I'd not yet mastered the art of the tactful getaway, I just said, "Thanks!" in an overly cheerful voice that made me sound like I was thanking Brad for taking my groceries out to my car for me. That in itself was ironic since Brad was just a few years past being employed as a grocery store bagger anyway. *Awkward.*

I limped over to April. It was much more difficult than it seemed to walk in the sand, especially after more than a handful of cocktails. I kicked at her legs a few times to get her attention, she wasn't having it. She literally waved me away with her hand without breaking her lip lock with her college make-out partner. I whispered to her that I would see her back at the room and was given a thumbs-up without April even coming up for air.

I had no issue with going back to our room alone. Especially if my only other choice was hanging out with a college guy a generation younger than me who was still learning how to kiss. I didn't necessarily blame him for his poor make-out skills, but I did blame myself for consenting to be molested publicly by someone who had just finished puberty.

I was proud to say I found our room in only three tries—I'd had to circle our hallway because I thought the numbers were going in the opposite direction. I didn't think April would be home for several more hours, so I made myself comfortable in bed and attempted to read a book. Unfortunately, all the words on the page were so blurry it was difficult to string them together into a sentence. I closed my eyes, for just a little while, to rest as I waited for April to get back so I could reprimand her for being a creepy cougar.

☙☙☙

Before I knew it, hot sun was streaming onto my face. I'd forgotten to close the blinds in our room the night before. The room itself was baking like a sauna since, in our drunken state, neither of us had managed to turn on the air conditioner. I was soaked in what I hoped was sweat—as opposed to vomit or Brad's drool. I looked over and was relieved to see April sprawled out next to me in the bed, still fully clothed and holding what appeared to be a quarter-full glass of rum punch in her hand.

Now that was talent!

The bedside clock read seven a.m., but I was suddenly wide awake and alert. It seemed all my depression-induced sleeping had finally paid off. I was ready to face the day a full five hours earlier than normal. That, or maybe I finally had nothing I was trying to escape from or avoid in my life to merit nightly sleeping marathons.

I remembered reading on the bulletin slipped under our door the day before that water aerobics were at eight a.m. I thought at the time that seemed like an absurdly early hour for exercise. I also thought exercise and vacation were two things that didn't mix and were only reserved for lame Hollywood celebrities like Kelly Ripa—who wanted to be photographed on vacation running with a rippling six-pack on the beach. Since I didn't have any danger of being photographed with a six-pack—only a black widow spider stomach tattoo for me, thank you—I felt oddly energized at the thought of jumping into a pool and getting a little bit physical, to quote Olivia Newton John.

I slipped into my swimsuit, thanking God above I had thought to bring at least one one-piece that would cover up my horrendous tattoo. I left a note for April that I would be back by nine a.m.—if she even happened to be awake by then. The bulletin said the water aerobics class was in the main pool, located in the courtyard directly in front of our massive high-rise hotel.

As I had suspected, the pool was full of senior citizens—although they were probably middle-aged. I had a difficult time guessing anyone's age after they passed fifty. That was a horrible quality, I knew. But it didn't change the fact that all old people looked the same to me. A few of the other middle-aged ladies in the pool made room for me right next to a very pregnant woman, who I was concerned had shown up to water aerobics by accident, thinking it was a water-birthing class.

The water aerobics instructor was much more aggressive than I was used to. I hadn't stepped foot into a gym in several years and preferred to run and hike on my own without anyone blowing a whistle for me to hurry up. I was also concerned all the old people could possibly have heart attacks and drown right before my eyes. But they seemed to be doing better than I was since I got winded before we even ended our warm-up of running in place in the water.

Still, it felt surprisingly good just to be doing something physical to get my mind off the long list of things bothering me. I was amazed I made it through the entire hour, given I hadn't exercised in a whole month and had also been living off ramen and wine. I guess I still had it going on.

After the class was over, I thanked all the senior ladies around me for helping me understand the unusually complicated instructions. A few of them were even kind enough to tell me they'd see me around for a drink later.

Glowing with confidence and feeling good after sweating out all my drunken toxins, I made my way back to April so I could check her pulse and see if she was still alive. But she was better than barely alive. She was vomiting violently into the toilet. I didn't want to laugh at her. I had been there many, many times before. Instead, I offered to grab her a sparkling water from the lobby bar so she could sleep and try to nurse herself back to health before lunch.

Apparently, her definition of "nursing herself back to health" was vastly different from mine. She didn't emerge from our darkened lovers' suite until nine p.m. That meant I had the entire day to myself. I made it a point to head to the beach, where I slathered myself from head to toe in SPF 45 non-comedogenic sunscreen—I had to represent myself as a beauty editor, you know. This was also the big day for my massive black widow spider tattoo. It was going to make its debut for the first time. I prepared myself for the collective gasps of the beach crowd as they saw the horror of what I had done to my body. But no one said a word or even batted an eye. I guessed Antiguans were used to this kind of crazy American behavior. A very ugly tattoo was no longer a showstopper.

I spent a good four hours soaking up the sun at the beach—while simultaneously waving away the resident beach drug dealer, who not only had a very large goiter but also told me he wasn't going to stop asking me if I wanted to buy "gonja" or beaded necklaces until I left the island at the end of my vacation. You had to hand it to him. He was a go-getter.

The beach in front of the resort was actually public, so there was nothing the resort could do about the goiter-sporting drug dealer. Maybe I had sunstroke already, but I found his creepy demeanor kind of charming—a cherry on top of my already perfect vacation.

I had assumed I would stew angrily on the beach with my arms crossed as I watched happy couples frolic in the waves together, reminding me of Adam and Cherry potentially enjoying their own love vacation. But they hardly crossed my mind. I actually had the strangest sensation as I sipped yet another free Chocolate Monkey on my beach chair. I felt absolutely nothing, and that was a good thing. I'd spend the past year slugging through a myriad of emotions. My recent bout with depression had thrown me for a loop, and I hadn't felt like myself since Adam was alive. Even then, I didn't know if that was the real me. Because apparently our marriage had been built on lies, and no one had thought to tell me about it.

Looking out at the crystal clear water of the Caribbean Sea around me, I was amazed to realize I had nothing on my mind. No mistresses, no worries about why my husband had betrayed me and then died on me, and no strange online date I had to call back or reject for the last time. Maybe this was what it felt like to truly be myself, black widow spider tattoo and all. To tell the truth, my gargantuan and offensive tattoo was actually starting to grow on me. It was one of the only things I had done all by myself, without anyone's permission. Of course, I knew I was going to have to spend my next five paychecks on a series of very painful and potentially damaging laser tattoo removals. But for the moment, I thought the overwhelming-spider-on-the-belly look suited me perfectly.

Just as I was about to get up from my comfortable beach chair to head to the nearby cabana for another intoxicating banana drink, I saw my make-out nemesis, Brad, making his way toward me across the sand. I wanted to make like a tree and leave—yuk, yuk, I couldn't resist—but instead, I pulled my wide straw hat down over my sunglasses and hoped he wouldn't recognize me. But why would he? I didn't have his trademark drool dripping down my face any longer, did I?

Surprisingly, he walked right past me, only stopping briefly to say, "Sweet tattoo, man."

Just a few feet behind my beach chair, he opened his arms wide to greet a very tiny and very adorable blonde girl who was obviously excited to see him—evidenced by the fact she jumped up and down in the sand and clapped her hands like a toddler. He kissed her in a semi-passionate way I was sure left drool all over her face—as was his style. They both settled down onto their side-by-side beach chairs together and sipped daiquiris.

Whew. That was a close one. I was almost in danger of wearing a bib for the rest of the time I spent with Brad on my vacation. Or else wearing a disguise so he wouldn't figure out the "man" with the "sweet tattoo" was the same drunken cougar he'd made out with at the beach bonfire. I guessed that his girlfriend, who appeared to be between the ages of fifteen and eighteen, wouldn't have been too happy about my existence. So I was fairly confident I was free from my college boyfriend for the rest of my stay.

I wrapped up my morning with five—*yes, five!*—more Chocolate Monkeys. When I was positive I was pleasantly buzzed, and possibly diabetic from all of the chocolate ice cream I'd consumed, I enjoyed a nice lunch on the open-air deck facing the beach.

The strange thing was that April's hangover was truly a blessing in disguise. This was the first day I'd spent enjoying time by myself in what felt like more than a decade. I was always waiting for Adam to come home, waiting for Adam to get off the computer, or waiting for Adam to finish watching CSI so I could get his attention. My life literally revolved around him. When he died, my life still revolved around his memory. I had spent the last year waiting to find out about his mistress, waiting for a new date to call me back, and waiting to feel better about the shitty, shitty thing Adam had done to me.

I didn't want to jinx anything, but this day was one of the best I'd had in a very long time. I spent the rest of the afternoon watching my new senior-citizen friends play beach volley-ball, oddly inspired by how agile they were for being so elderly. When one of the frosted haired ladies made her fifth spike in a row, I made a weak joke about having to "learn from my elders." She reminded me she was only fif-ty-five. This absolutely horrified me. She looked about seventy-five, with her sagging breasts and flat ass. I made a vow to myself then and there to start buying that expensive facial cream the department store girls at Ma-cy's always tried to sell me—because you never could be *too* careful.

My senior-citizen crew invited me to have dinner with them at the Asian restaurant on the resort, and I gladly obliged. There I learned much more than I ever needed to know about what things were *really* like in the 'sixties and early 'seventies, and why it was never a good idea to do opiates. Ever.

After I left my lively and entertaining re-tirement-home-style dinner, I decided it was finally time to see if April was still alive.

When I opened up our hotel room door, I was briefly reminded of the Oregon Trail game of my youth. I was absolutely sure there was someone in there dying from cholera, or dysentery, or yellow fever. But no, it was just April, still lying flat on her back on the bed, wearing her clothing from last night. And that funky smell that made me think of people dying was actually the smell of vomit since April had filled up the hotel trash can next to our bed with puke. Lovely.

I shook her awake. It only took me three tries to get her to open her eyes. I pulled her up like a limp rag doll and forced her into the shower. She stood under the hot water for a good forty-five minutes until she decided she was human again.

We both happily freshened up and hit the little club located on the resort for karaoke night. I did have to hand it to April. She always bounced back—*always*—even if she looked and smelled like she had been retching all day long.

At the karaoke bar, I switched from Chocolate Monkeys to vodka with a splash of cranberry, and I was on fire. April switched from sparkling water to shots of tequila, and she was looking positively radiant. In retrospect, that seemed like the true sign of an alcoholic. But I wasn't going to hold it against her on vacation.

We bombarded the karaoke set with our insane requests, like a harmonized duet to "Mr. Roboto," followed by April singing, "I Saw the Sign" as I vigorously danced the running man next to her. We completed our epic karaoke concert for the five bar patrons by singing a husky throated rendition of "Total Eclipse of the Heart" in unison. That definitely brought down the house.

For our efforts, which brought sweat to our brows from the nonstop singing, we were rewarded with a few more shots of tequila from the friendly bartender. We then struck up a conversation with a few middle-aged couples who told us they enjoyed our concert—in the same way your mom tells you she absolutely loved your ballet recital—and we finally decided to call it a night. Our shared bed was calling our names. I was positively exhausted from all of the "forced relaxation" that had filled my day.

CHAPTER 23

It wasn't until I awoke the next day that I realized yesterday had been Thanksgiving. I hadn't even thought of my family once.

I turned on my laptop—I had brought it with me in case of emergency—and shot them an e-mail, pretending the time difference had something to do with why I was late on the holiday greeting. As I was plowing through the rest of my inbox and checking up on Facebook, Lacey shot me back an e-mail immediately, telling me how much she missed me since she was stuck alone for hours with my dad's tiny children. Apparently, the entire family had run out to "grab more wine" but ended up stopping by one of the only nearby bars open on Thanksgiving to grab a few drinks and catch up—Lacey's husband included.

Lacey was conned into playing babysitter for three straight hours on Thanksgiving Day, "starving to death"—her words—since she hadn't had any turkey yet. Although I felt sympathetic to her plight, her story solidified how necessary it was for me to ditch my family on Thanksgiving and finally do something for myself. Besides, April had kidnapped me. I was just being a wise consumer and enjoying the vacation that was charged to my credit card.

When April woke up two hours later, I'd already had coffee on the deck, taken a luxurious bath with tropical bath salts, and read half of the book I brought with me. She was finally in the mood to be active, so we hightailed it to the "activities area" of the resort, where they claimed to have free water sports available.

The water sports turned out to be a handful of canoes and a giant plastic tractor that was called a "water trike." I was initially intrigued by the water trike. But April refused to ride with me because she thought it looked like too much work. I ended up being paired with a middle-aged man whose severely overweight wife just "wasn't feeling" the water sports today. Once we got onto the giant tractor together side-by-side and put our feet into our pedals, my middle-aged sports partner complimented me profusely on my hair, my body, and even my teeth, emphasizing that I "must work out."

Even though it kind of creeped me out that I was being hit on by a middle-aged man, I figured I could use his compliments to boost my esteem and water trike my ass off. As we set off on our journey, to pedal away from shore within the roped off barriers that seemed to be a mile away from the beach, it became obvious my soon-to-be-elderly water sports companion was only flattering me because he didn't plan on pedaling one bit. It appeared he only hoped to show off to his wife, who couldn't tell if he was pedaling or not from that far away, by turning around in his seat and waving at her while I pedaled in the hot, hot Antiguan sun. Total bullshit.

I thought I had enough stamina to make it all the way to the end of the roped off barriers. But since I was pedaling for two, I barely made it halfway before I decided to turn around. Turning around was another feat in itself. The water trike wasn't meant to be operated by one person—that's why it had two sets of pedals. Duh. I basically begged Mr. Middle Aged to pedal at least a little bit. Or even with one leg, if he felt inclined. But he wasn't having it. I managed to turn us slightly around after what felt like fifteen full minutes of trying. I was definitely feeling a burn in my thighs. Yes, I was, Suzanne Somers. I was also fully convinced I was sweating out alcohol because of all the rum I'd enjoyed in the past two days.

The man's wife seemed very happy with his progress and waved at us with both arms from the safety of the beach. I was jealous of her. I spent the rest of my energy trying to get closer to shore so I wouldn't have to throw my tubby water trike partner overboard to ease the weight limit in order to make it back to the beach. Just to rub a little bit of salt in my wounds, April sailed past me in her one person canoe, laughing and looking like she was having the time of her life. Bitch.

When I got close enough to the beach, the resort workers running the water sports station pulled me to safety. I collapsed with exhaustion on the hot sand. I begged April to bring me a glass of water, but apparently, she thought I was joking because she forced me to walk a quarter of a mile back to the tiki bar with her. A few Chocolate Monkeys made everything right and almost made me forget about my intensely sore muscles and my body covered with sweat.

April and I spent the rest of the afternoon napping in the sun next to the Great Pool—as they called it around here—where we were given complimentary cocktail service by some very good-looking male servers who appeared to be wearing loincloths.

Being caught up in this epic paradise made the last two days of vacation go by in a flash. I initially started out incredibly mad at April for pushing me out of my funky depression and onto a beautiful tropical island. But how can you hate anyone who made you go on vacation in Antigua? It could have been the heavy drinking, but I felt fresher and lighter than ever before—they probably don't tell you that in AA.

On our very last night on the island, April and I made it a priority to go to the beach after dark and look at the stars, double checking that there were no college boys lurking around to pounce on us. There, we had one of the most honest conversations we'd had in a long time, surprisingly without the help of Bailey's.

The two of us sat in silence for several minutes, taking in the beauty of the clear stars above us, unpolluted by smog or covered by tall buildings, as we were accustomed to in city life.

I finally decided to break the ice and "get real," as Dr. Phil would say. "You know, I didn't want to admit it, but I think this vacation really helped. So thank you."

She tossed back her long, thick, and enviably dark hair and smiled at me appreciatively. "You're very welcome. I know you thought I was out of line to book this, but I could tell you just needed someone to kick you in the ass and get your butt in gear. You know that's what I'm always here for." She laughed.

"True, true," I agreed. I paused again for a moment. "You know what?"

"What?"

"I never wanted to admit this either, but Adam was never really honest with me. I mean, he wasn't horrible to me or anything, but when I think about it, he would always lie about the stupidest things. For as long as I'd known him."

"Like what?"

"Well, obviously, there was the big affair at the end, but he would lie about what he did sometimes for no reason, or what he was looking at on the computer, or sometimes even what friends he went out with. If I ever asked him about it, he would just say he forgot to tell me. But lying by omission is really the same thing, if you think about it."

April nodded. "I know exactly what you're talking about. I know Roger's not a good example, but it does seem like there was always this weirdness between us, like we weren't being honest. Even on our wedding night, I was still really worried about how he felt about his ex since they were recently divorced, but we never talked about it."

"Yeah, exactly! It wasn't like any specific lie I caught him in, but it just felt like there were a lot of things we didn't want to talk about. But I just thought that was normal, and it turns out I was totally wrong. I just wonder how long it would have gone on if he was still alive."

We sat in silence a while and listened to the ocean. I didn't have any hard or fast answers to the unfortunate demise of my marriage. But at least I finally had some clarity about what was really going on all along.

૯৩૯৩

Sunday morning we were on the airplane at the crack of dawn, waiting for another unfortunate eight-hour layover in Miami. If there's one thing I learned from this entire trip, besides quite a bit of soul-searching, it was that I would damn well check my itinerary the next time I traveled with April. Seriously.

Our layover back through Miami went much faster than on our way to Antigua. That always seems to be the way it is on your return from vacation. You never wanted to go home. The only thing I happened to be looking forward to was calling Derek as quickly as possible. I finally felt like a normal person who could contribute to a thought-provoking conversation. If he felt like I was interesting and fun when I was the most depressed I'd ever been in my life, then he was definitely in for a treat now.

I called him the moment I threw my bags down in the hallway when I arrived home, even before I made my trek to Lacey's house to pick up Madam and catch up with her about my trip. Unfortunately, Derek wasn't sitting by his phone in anticipation of my call. His phone went straight to voicemail. I tried to think of something amazing and clever to say, but I wasn't expecting to leave a voice message. So it went a little something like this: "Hey...Derek...It's Danielle. I just got back from my vacation, and I hope you had a good or nice or interesting Thanksgiving, or whatever. I'll be around and would love to talk to you, like we talked about before—when you called me at work, you know. Bye."

Ugh. At least I could count on the fact I hadn't lost my touch when it came to ensuring any social interaction was awkward, even if it happened to be on a voicemail. I decided to hold off on unpacking until I picked up my precious Madam from Lacey's. I knew Lacey would be pissed if I came over any time after nine p.m. She had a little kid that she had to get up for school early in the morning. As I made my way north of Denver, I realized there was someone else I needed to call upon my return to the real world after vacation.

This time, I was begging and pleading and praying the phone would go directly to voicemail. As irony would have it, Amber answered on the second ring.

"Hey, girl!" She said excitedly.

"Hey, Amber. How are things with you?"

"Great! We had a really fun Thanksgiving, and we got to tie up some loose ends with the wedding planning," she replied happily. "How was yours?"

"Good, good. I went out of town with April on vacation, so it was really relaxing. Actually, that was what I wanted to call you about in the first place. Um, I felt like I was a little weird last time we talked on the phone about your wedding. But I want you to know how very happy I am for you," I said nervously.

"Oh! I totally understand. I know all this must be hard for you, but I just wanted you to know I still think about you a lot."

"Well, there's more." I paused. "I actually think I'd really like to be your maid of honor, or even a bridesmaid, if you'll still have me. It meant a lot to me that you asked, and I'm sorry I didn't tell you 'yes' right away."

I almost had to drop the phone due to all of the screeching coming from the other end of the line. "I guess that was a yes?"

"Absolutely!!! I'm so pumped! This is, like, totally perfect, and I hadn't even found anyone else to be my maid of honor yet because I'd really hoped it could be you! We have so much planning to do! Maybe we can get together for lunch later in the week, or I could just come over to your place, or something?"

I smiled. "Sure, I think that's a wonderful idea. I'm really excited too."

I wrapped up the call as I pulled into Lacey's driveway, hoping Madam hadn't been strangled or choked by Jackson playing too roughly with her. He seemed to have a wrestling fixation lately.

I felt good about finally making the decision to be Amber's maid of honor, even though I hadn't yet planned exactly what I would say to Adam's parents on her big day. I was probably making too much out of it anyway. Who said we had to discuss Adam's infidelities on his sister's wedding day? Ignorance is bliss, right?

Lacey met me at the door and immediately wrapped me in a huge embrace, as if I had just gotten home from war. I was definitely going to have to go on vacation more often.

Apparently, she disagreed. "You have no idea how horrible the holidays were without you! You *have* to promise me you are never ever going to go away again. I think I was the only sane and slightly sober person all day on Thanksgiving, not to mention the fact that after being abandoned, we didn't even get around to eating until eight p.m., and we had to get up early to go to Mom's the next day. Oh, and Rob Lowe died on *Brothers and Sisters*."

"Why the fuck would you tell me that? To punish me? What kind of a person are you to ruin the whole season for me?" I was completely disgusted, no matter how bad of an experience Lacey may have had over Thanksgiving without me. But she was always doing stuff like that. She had the older sister complex, where she always seemed to know better and wanted to be the bearer of news. Whether or not that entailed spoiling the plot of one of my favorite shows.

Since I was beyond exhausted from our long layover in Miami, I spent just a few minutes catching up with her before I gathered up Madam to go home. I was looking forward to nothing more than taking a hot bath and getting to sleep early. I didn't even want to think about the piles and piles of e-mails in my inbox waiting for me. That was one of the sweet ironies of going on vacation. You got five beautiful days without being bothered by technology, but as soon as you got home, you paid for it dearly.

As I cruised South on I-25 while listening to a little bit of Katy Perry on the radio—to boost my mood, I'm ashamed to admit—my mood instantaneously skyrocketed. My phone rang, and I saw Derek's name displayed on the caller ID. Hooray! I tried to play it cool, which was pretty difficult to do since I had to simultaneously turn down the radio, keep my car on the road, and deal with a little Chihuahua trying to make herself comfortable on my lap.

I answered the phone breathlessly. "Hello?"

"Hey, Danielle! Sorry I missed you earlier. I was at the gym. How'd everything go on your vacation? Any big breakthroughs?"

God, he was sweet.

"Oh, no problem! Yeah, I actually had a much better time than I thought I would. I feel really relaxed, although I'm not looking forward to work tomorrow." I paused. "Getting away for a little while gave me a whole new perspective. I just wanted to apologize if I acted weird before. I've really been dealing with a lot of stuff, and I probably didn't handle it well, to say the least. But I appreciate you spending time with me."

"No, no, there's no reason for you to apologize at all," he replied. "I really like you, Danielle. I just wanted to respect you and give you space if you needed it because I can't imagine how difficult Adam's death and cheating must be for you. Now that you're finally back, though, you can make it up to me by having dinner with me on Friday, if you're interested?"

I had to keep myself from screaming "Yes, yes, *Oh, yes*!!" into the phone like a total blithering idiot. Instead, I demurely agreed to our Friday night date and wrapped up the call by telling Derek I needed to go home and un- pack, and that I looked forward to seeing him later on in the week. "Looked forward to" was an understatement. I was hugely, immensely, and over-the-top happy about getting a second chance. With all the strange and potentially psychotic dates I'd been on in the past several months, this was legitimately the first time I'd felt butterflies in my stomach since meeting Adam.

My only assignment for the week was to figure out how to handle everyday social situa- tions, like a good night kiss, without my cus- tomary extreme awkwardness that could po- tentially alienate my date. Good luck to me.

CHAPTER 24

To my surprise, Cherry was out sick for the week. Our assigned days of working together were temporarily null and void, bringing me great relief.

Yes, getting out of my comfort zone and facing a few unpleasant truths had definitely unburdened me. But that didn't mean I was instantly mature enough to become buddy-buddy with The Mistress. No matter how much perspective and inner peace I achieved, Cherry was still Adam's mistress, plain and simple.

Due to lack of conflict and stress, my work week breezed by, for once, and it was Friday before I knew it. I forced April to come home with me after work to watch a long and very detailed fashion show of all of my top potential-outfit choices. I didn't know where we were going since Derek wanted it to be a surprise, which was another issue altogether. Was I supposed to wear a beaded evening gown? A casual cocktail dress? Hiking boots? It seemed men in general just didn't understand how many details a girl needed to get dressed to even step out of the door for a date in the first place.

April ultimately gave me the go-ahead on a white billowy, long-sleeved top paired with black cigarette jeans that were gently worn and frayed to give me a little bit of a rock star edge. I went with a simple silver necklace, fake-diamond stud earrings, and bright purple ballet flats to add a touch of Audrey Hepburn inspiration. I was dressed to kill.

I suspected April still didn't have full confidence in my now-healthy mental state since she chose to hang around my townhouse until seven-thirty p.m. on the nose when I had to leave to meet Derek at his house. We wasted time talking about her top two eHarmony date contenders who were both in the running for potentially becoming a steady "dating relationship."

She had gone on several dates each with Jack and Trevor, although nothing was exclusive just yet. She didn't know how to make up her mind between the two. Should she go for Jack, the shy, quiet, thin artist type with an amazing sense of humor once you got to know him? Or would it be Trevor, a guy's-guy corporate lawyer who was a gentleman to the max, always opening every door and even pulling out chairs?

Personally, I was on Team Trevor. I thought chivalry was almost dead, and he seemed like a potential gold mine. April couldn't make up her mind if her life depended on it since she preferred, in her words, "a guy that was a mixture of the two." I politely pointed out to her that it was impossible to construct your dream guy as if you were making a Build-a-Bear, and she should just choose the guy that seemed to be the most honest and least psycho, at least based upon my personal experience. While that may not have been the most profound dating advice ever given, I was confident it was true.

I finally pushed her out the door so I could leave. I was beyond excited. The simple fact Derek had chosen to make the entire night a surprise had me totally intrigued. Even if we pulled up in front of his favorite McDonald's, I think I'd still be happy. April wished me luck, waving to me out of her car window as she sped away. I made the short drive over to Derek's house with my hands shaking violently the entire time as I clutched the steering wheel. That had to be a good sign, right?

When I arrived at Derek's and knocked on the front door, there wasn't an answer right away. I wondered if maybe I had gotten the time wrong. Or if I missed the fact I was supposed to meet him at a restaurant. I peered into his front window, which immediately fogged up from my steamy breath reacting with the cold weather, but it didn't look like any lights were on. What the hell? I was going to be really, really bitter if this date didn't turn out as planned. I'd been looking forward to it all week. Not to mention the month before *that* when I was waiting—unsuccessfully—for Derek's call.

I was just about to call him on my cell phone to see if he was even home when the door burst open. He looked much handsomer than I remembered him, if that was even possible. His dark hair looked freshly cut, his skin looked healthy and Greek-god-like, and his dark brown eyes sparkled with excitement.

"Hey!" He gave me a warm kiss on the cheek. I wanted to close my eyes and take in every moment, but I thought I should avoid making him uncomfortable in the first few minutes by trying to smell him without him noticing. That was creepy and probably a dating faux pas.

"Hey!" I replied, a little too enthusiastically. "So what are the big plans for tonight?"

He didn't reply but simply opened the door a bit wider to reveal a picnic set up in his living room. I'd actually never been inside his house before, but it looked as if he had covered his coffee table in white linen and set up plates, silverware, wineglasses, and beautiful long stemmed candles. On top of that, all of the other surfaces in his living room, like the side tables, entertainment center, and mantle above the fireplace, were glowing with candles.

As cheesy as this scene was, the fact someone had taken the time to set up a candlelit dinner for me took my breath away. All the elements of wine, candles, and romantic music usually made me want to laugh and make fun of the cliché. But tonight, it was absolutely perfect.

My jaw must have dropped visibly. Derek took one look at my face and started to smile. "I wanted to surprise you, and I thought it would be fun to stay in so I could cook for you. I'm not trying to brag, but I did pretty well in a cooking class I took in college.

Meaning that I passed with a C because I didn't burn my final project."

"Wow." I replied. "I don't really know what to say. Thank you so much for doing this. It looks absolutely beautiful, and I can't believe you'd do this all for me!"

"Of course I would." He hung up my coat, poured me a glass of Riesling—did I even tell him that was my favorite wine?—and instructed me to get comfortable on the couch while he put the finishing touches on our meal.

When he said he "took a cooking class in college," he obviously meant he studied under the tutelage of Julia Child for several years as her sous chef. He was that good. He also won quite a few points for not bragging about it. I was served grilled halibut with cilantro garlic butter and sautéed asparagus drizzled with olive oil and vinegar. Not only was the meal mouthwatering and truly decadent, but it was also a much-needed treat since I'd never mastered the art of cooking nice meals for two, let alone one. That would explain my ramen fixation.

Derek and I fell back into our familiar rhythm of relaxed conversation. I couldn't believe how at home I felt with him. On all the other dates I'd been on, I always felt anxious, constantly thinking of what I was going to say or do next to make the best first and second and even third impression. It was exhausting. Even with Adam, it took me about nine months before I calmed down around him—not coincidentally, right around the time he proposed—and could relax and really be myself.

But with Derek, it seemed like all I could do was be myself. He'd managed to see something likable in me when I was at my worst and that made it much easier to be my best self. We chatted and caught up about the last month that we hadn't seen each other. I told him all about my amazing tropical vacation, emphasizing that he absolutely must go to Antigua some time because it was incredible.

When I said that, he squeezed my hand meaningfully and said, "I'd like that."

Whoa. I blushed furiously from head to toe and thanked God the room was lit with candles so Derek couldn't see me turning the color of a tomato. I offered to help clear up all the dishes, but he insisted he'd do it since our fine dining experience was not yet over. For dessert, he brought out crème brûlée he had made himself. *Made himself*! It was at that point I felt like I was being punk'd or that perhaps Derek had an indentured servant I didn't know about, toiling away in the kitchen on these culinary delights.

After dessert, we sat together on the couch, drinking wine and watching the fire crackle. This was definitely another cliché moment you would see in a *Lifetime* movie, but it just felt right. Besides, it's not like he had a bearskin rug or anything. That was where I drew the line.

When we finally reached a lull in our conversation, he turned to me slowly in a way that made it obvious he was going to kiss me again. I didn't move a muscle because I didn't want to say anything weird or interrupt our second kiss. And would you believe it? It was better than the first time. Better than I remembered.

I sat mesmerized in my own little world, closing my eyes, smelling Derek, and savoring the kiss. He pulled away and said, "I've already told you this, but I really like you. I know we're in a unique situation since I was a friend of Adam's, but I just wanted to put it out there and tell you I want to keep seeing you, if you want to."

Um, what could I say to that? Was "hell yes" appropriate? "Derek, I can't tell you how much I appreciate your honesty and everything you've done for me tonight. I guess it's kind of strange that you knew Adam so well for so long, but I've also realized I didn't know Adam as well as I thought." I paused. "I guess what I'm trying to say is that I would love to keep seeing you, and I really like you too."

After that fantastic ending to a romantically cheesy evening, I didn't want to push my luck and leave any openings for my embarrassing social awkwardness. Instead, I decided to head home since it was already eleven p.m. Derek walked me to my car like a true gentleman, giving me a few more passionate kisses to relish on my ride home.

CHAPTER 25

The saying, "Time flies when you're having fun," could also be said, "Time flies when you're under an overwhelming amount of stress due to an unrealistic workload." Or "Time flies when you're a maid of honor helping plan an elaborate, expensive, and over-the-top wedding." Or even, "Time flies when you're getting to know someone you really care about and being constantly whisked away on mini-vacations to the mountains for the weekend, fancy dinners at exclusive downtown hotspots, and romantic afternoons of playing in the park with your Chihuahua."

Yes, you heard me right. I had been one busy girl over the past four months. Now it was the beginning of March, and Amber's wedding loomed a mere week away. As much as I hated the high-maintenance attention given to weddings these days, I couldn't overlook the fact I absolutely loved spending time with Amber again. As horrible as it sounds, it was almost better and fresher the second time around without Adam there, demanding my attention. Although, I would never in my life admit that to Amber since she really did miss her brother.

I was Amber's right-hand woman when it came to all the important maid of honor type duties. Like throwing a bridal shower—where I had been manipulated into planning a long list of very lame games, in my opinion—to dress shopping—where friendly, bubbly, and easy-going Amber had a catastrophic tantrum/meltdown about the five pounds she'd gained over the holidays—to planning a bachelorette party that was held two weeks earlier in Boulder on a cold and snowy Saturday night.

We ended up throwing the bachelorette party early because Amber's fiancé wanted to go to Vegas for a bachelor party weekend with a few of his guy friends. The last weekend in February was when they found the best ticket prices. So I ended up corralling eight twenty-one-year-old "ladies," trying to get them into a party bus and hit all of the clubs in Boulder. I had to walk a fine line between drinking enough to have a good time and staying sober enough to make sure Amber didn't vomit in the party bus and make me lose my deposit. It was perhaps one of the most stressful nights out I'd had in a while, but at least Amber was happy—with the parts she remembered.

I even found this hilarious idea online that involved making Amber wear a tank top I had written "Suck for a Buck" on with fabric paint. As if that wasn't classy enough, I then attached Lifesavers on safety pins to the tank top. Men in all the bars had to pay her a dollar for the great prize of sucking a lifesaver off of her chest. The money was then ceremoniously placed into the garter she was wearing over her jeans. It was an ingenious idea that got bunch of creepy men talking to us, not to mention several rounds of drinks bought. At the end of the night, Amber ended up earning twenty "Suck Bucks," including ten dollars Canadian, which was baffling in itself. Not bad. Not bad at all.

Amber thanked me profusely that night, drunkenly calling me "the best sister ever," before she daintily asked the bus driver to pull over into a gas station so she could puke her guts out in a trashcan. Fortunately, she didn't remember any of the puking incident. She probably would've been greatly embarrassed. For her sake, we all pretended she was the perfect lady on her last night out as a single gal.

That was one of the only nights I hadn't spent with Derek in a long time. We'd fallen into the practice of spending every evening together. But the weird and amazing thing was that it wasn't all boring couple stuff, where you got a DVD from Red Box and a six-pack of Michelob Ultra and called it a night. No, Derek truly pulled out all the stops and planned surprise weekend getaways to Keystone, afternoon picnics in the park near my house with my favorite bottle of wine, and Friday night dinners at some of the hottest restaurants in town that I'd never even been to before, although I was a native Denverite.

I felt like my life was a romantic movie montage—without Roxette playing in the background. I had literally never been this happy, even when I was in a "cute married couple" relationship. Derek and I had the capacity to talk about everything and nothing at all, which I now knew was the sign of a great relationship. In the past, I'd had a serious addiction to verbal diarrhea of the mouth whenever I was uncomfortable. But spending time with Derek helped me to learn how to enjoy companionable silences. I always made him laugh by asking him what his secret was since I was convinced that he couldn't be that perfect. He told me he was really messy, sometimes argumentative, and always forgot his dental appointments. Although his alleged "flaws" sounded like me on my best days, I was enjoying every moment we had together.

Even more importantly, I was happy to have him by my side as I made my grand debut at Amber's wedding the following Saturday. Of course, I'd be walking down the aisle with one of Amber's girlfriend's boyfriends— if you could follow that train of thought. But it was comforting that Derek would be there to sit with me at the head table and rescue me in case I got trapped in a "friendly" conversation with Adam's parents. I still hadn't seen them since I'd gotten back in touch with Amber due to the craze of balancing wedding planning with my already-full work schedule. But Amber often told me her parents said hello and wished me their best.

I was nervous about the initial meeting at the rehearsal dinner this Friday. I had already briefed Derek in great detail about how he was to do anything within his power—including punching me in the face—to stop me if, after a few drinks, I started talking to Adam's parents about his cheating. Derek was obviously also welcome at the rehearsal dinner since he was an old friend of the family. I really didn't think I would have been able to handle all of the wedding festivities without him.

The rehearsal dinner was to be held at the Falling Rock Tap House in downtown Denver, where Amber's fiancé Shawn used to work. Meaning he got an excellent deal on their back party room. The big silver lining to the awkward night ahead of me was that the Tap House specialized in—*you guessed it!*—beer. So at the very least, I could drink a few tall microbrews to put myself at ease.

I got more and more nervous as the week went on since I couldn't help imagining the worst case scenario when seeing Adam's parents after more than a year.

I envisioned myself saying, *"So...Have you adjusted well to having a dead son?"*

"I found a box full of your dead son's things, if you're interested in keeping them."

"Did you know your dead son was a cheater? How were your holidays?"

Or, when people asked how I knew Adam's parents, I would reply, *"I was married to their dead son."*

I don't know why I couldn't get the phrase "dead son" out of my head. It was blatantly rude. But I had thought about it so much, I was convinced I was going to slip up and say it anyway.

I spent the week working as hard as possible since I was going to take Friday off for the long wedding weekend due to all the details I was responsible for as the maid of honor. The only other time I'd held that role before was in April's wedding several years ago. But in that instance, her sister was such an anal control freak—who was also incredibly jealous she wasn't asked to be the maid of honor—that she passively-aggressively tried to take over all my planning duties to outshine me, which I was actually fine with.

Things were going surprisingly well working with Cherry, given we had a good six months of project partnership under our belts. The main tactic both of us used was to never, ever discuss anything closely related to personal lives. We talked about movies, celebrity gossip, and even politics. But we also made sure all those subjects never mentioned the word "cheating." That fact alone greatly limited most of our celebrity gossip topics, so we mainly talked about the latest box office hits at the movies, as if we were the female version of Siskel and Ebert.

I actually felt bittersweet about Cherry and I wrapping up our project in several months. As much as I didn't want to admit it, she was an excellent coworker. Since being a total slut had nothing to do with how well you worked, I could give her that one. This was also something I would never admit to anyone out loud, except maybe Derek if I was drinking heavily. But I was glad I'd done the stalking to meet Cherry in the first place. I may never know exactly what went on between her and Adam. Yet I also realized much of the problem was between Adam and I. Cute, adorable, and bubbly Cherry was just the symptom of a greater issue.

I'd learned such profound truths in my deep bout of depression when all I did was watch Dr. Phil and drink wine. But it really did ring true for me. I'm not saying it was my fault I got cheated on, by any means, because only an asshole would do that. Let's make that clear. But I had never wanted to admit to myself that things weren't as perfect as they'd seemed in my marriage. I would never know if I could have stopped Adam from having an affair, but I think our relationship would have had a much healthier chance if we had actually talked to each other about something other than work or our mutual friends. Just saying.

I wrapped up as much work as I could on Thursday evening and prepared to grab a quick bite to eat with Derek before going to bed as early as possible. The next day I had so many errands to run I'd had to make a twenty- item list, which included such tasks as picking up the wedding flowers, checking that the alterations on all of our dresses were done, confirming the hairstylist and makeup artist for the next day, and quadruple checking that the DJ had the right song list in the correct order for the reception. The funny part—that all maids of honor have to deal with—is that I wasn't getting paid for this heavy-duty wedding planning. On top of that, I'd actually *had to pay* three hundred dollars for my own very unfashionable and ill-fitting plum dress that I would never wear again. It was a conspiracy, I tell you.

Derek and I spent a few hours together eating at the Cherry Creek Grill until he could tell I was so stressed out and wound up he ordered me to go home and go to bed right away so I wouldn't be a total monster tomorrow—his words. What a sweetheart. I actually wouldn't be seeing him again until the next evening at the rehearsal dinner. Before I left, I made him run through our plan about how he was going to mentally or physically intercept me if I started to say inappropriate things about dead people in front of Adam's parents. He didn't feel totally comfortable with punching me in the face—as much as I encouraged it in case of an emergency.

So we agreed he would just try to interrupt the conversation and redirect it if I started getting weird. That put me slightly at ease so I was able to get a generous six hours of sleep that night—when you take into account all my tossing and turning and worrying and stressing and rethinking the wedding plans for the next day.

ভ৩ৎ৩

By the time my day of amateur wedding planning had rolled to an end the following day, I not only wished I had been equipped with a headset to bark orders at unknown people waiting in the wings, but I was pretty sure I had used up all the minutes on my monthly cell phone plan. Amber called me nonstop about things that didn't even make sense. I started out trying to politely reassure her. But by our last phone call, I ended it with, "Shut up, shut up, shut up—I'll see you at the rehearsal!"

If she was mad at me for chewing her out over the phone, she didn't show it at the rehearsal dinner. She ran up to me and gave me a huge hug, thanking me for everything I'd done for her. I had also shown up early to set up the tables with the colors and themed decorations for the wedding—plum and gray, A Night in Paris. Although I was nowhere near becoming a professional decorator, I thought my amateur attempt at interior design was pretty darn impressive.

I wove alternating plum and gray streamers over each and every table leg. I also placed large centerpieces of miniature Eiffel Towers next to fleur de lis notecards in large glass bowls in the center of every table so all guests could write a wish or a happy note for the bride and groom to have for later. Again, these were all cheesy wedding ideas I scraped off of the Internet, but Amber appeared to be more than pleased.

I was seated at the main table for the rehearsal dinner, next to Derek, with Adam's parents on my other side. I didn't have the balls to change my place card. I figured Adam's mom had probably put it there on purpose and would be deeply hurt if I tried to sit elsewhere. Besides, I didn't have anywhere else to go. All the tables were packed to the gills with Amber and Shawn's sorority sisters, fraternity brothers, coworkers, extended family, and even a few cashiers from their local grocery store —that's how friendly they were. If I didn't know Amber well, it would have made me sick.

Fortunately for me, Derek arrived ten minutes early to the dinner, as I had begged him to. I was afraid of being stuck there alone, vulnerable to any awkward conversations with Adam's parents. We sat down in our places at the table, and I had a clear view of the door as Adam's parents, Paul and Diana, arrived just a few moments later. They were bombarded by an onslaught of people they hadn't seen in years, so it took them nearly fifteen torturous minutes to get over to their seats next to me at the head table.

When they saw me, they appeared overjoyed, showering me with huge hugs and lip-sticky kisses on my cheek—from Adam's mom, not his dad. FYI. They also acted surprised and delighted to see Derek there as my date. They'd known him since he was "just a tiny guy, playing Little League," according to Adam's mom.

So far, our first post-dead-husband meeting seemed to be going well. But I was still highly skeptical.

Our dinner was served with excellent speed, thanks to the fact the groom had an in with the wait staff. I drank beer after beer until I couldn't remember how many I'd had. Derek tried to politely point out to me that at the very least, I didn't want to be hung-over at the wedding tomorrow, but I just laughed him off. What did he know anyway?

Finally, it came time for all of the sentimental speeches that took up hours and hours of the rehearsal dinner. Amber's dad kicked it off by saying how much he loved Shawn and how pleased he was to have him as an official member of the family, even though they already considered him to be their honorary son. A few of Amber's sorority sisters went next, giggling like crazy and repeating "Um" and "Like" so much it was difficult to understand what they were saying. From the basic gist of it, they told a cute story about Amber and Shawn meeting. But I didn't catch too many details.

After speeches from aunts, cousins, coworkers, and even a grocery store bagger, the room finally fell silent. A few heads turned in my direction. *Why were they looking at me?*

Oh! That's right. It was my maid of honor responsibility to give a beautiful speech that would bring the crowd to their knees. *Here I go*, I thought as I stood up from my chair, beer in hand.

"Hey, everyone," I said, clutching my beer to my chest with both hands like I'd won an award. "You may be wondering how I know Amber. I actually consider her to be my sister because we've been so close for so long. I was married to her brother, who is...dead."

At that point, Derek tugged urgently on the back of my skirt, but I slapped his hand away. I was on a roll.

"Anyway, I just want to thank Amber for always being like the younger sister I never had and for also not giving up on me when I turned her down to be her maid of honor the first time." The crowd laughed politely. "I just wasn't ready a few months ago to be in her wedding, but since then, I've realized how important family can be, whether they're your blood relatives or not." I tried to think of something else interesting to say. The crowd looked at me expectantly.

"Um, here's to Amber and Shawn! And many years of happiness...and wedded bliss and...enjoyment."

Enjoyment? What was I thinking? Why hadn't I taken the time to write out a speech beforehand like every other maid of honor on the planet? I'll tell you why. I was up to my ass in flowers, decorations, favors, and invitations. I just didn't have the time. Derek reassured me my speech wasn't as "bad as it could have been." Both of Adam's parents turned to me and thanked me sincerely for what I said. Adam's mom added, "We understand this was very hard for you. It means a lot that you're here today."

I sighed with relief. Derek squeezed my hand comfortingly. Although I would never be accused of being eloquent in delivering a valedictorian-esque maid of honor speech, more than anything, I was just relieved I hadn't said the words "dead husband" outright. The rest of the night was a blur. We wrapped up the fun festivities then a few of us in the bridal party lingered in the bar to chat and indulge in a couple of extra microbrews.

Derek and I decided to tear ourselves away at the modest hour of twelve a.m. I needed to get a good night's sleep to be ready bright and early at nine the next morning. Even though the wedding itself wasn't until five, there was an astounding amount of things that needed to be done on the actual day. Besides providing emotional support to Amber, all the bridesmaids were getting their makeup done, myself included. One of my beauty connections was a local makeup artist who gave us a twenty-five per cent discount. All the while, a hairstylist would alternate to make sure our hairstyles were curly, bouffant, and hair-sprayed to the max. You would almost think we were in Texas if you saw the up-do in store for me. It was that big.

After double checking that all the bridesmaids had made it to the bridal suite on time for hair and makeup, I set out on a frenzy of last-minute wedding planning—triple checking that the area for the DJ was set up, that all of the tables in the reception area had their place cards, and especially that the church was heavily decorated with plum and gray ribbons, plum flower petals, and a tasteful deep gray aisle runner for all of us to walk down on our way to the altar.

Last but not least on my checklist was taking Amber's emotional temperature to make sure she wasn't a nervous wreck. This was something April did for me on my wedding day, and it was greatly appreciated. I pulled Amber aside just as she was about to put the final touches on her hair and veil and step into her dress for her big moment.

"How are you feeling? Are you doing okay?" I asked earnestly, checking for any telltale signs, like shaking, hyperventilation, or a pale face that meant she was going to vomit from nerves. By this point, I was an expert.

"Yeah, but...I just feel weird," she replied in a quiet voice.

"What do you mean? It's not like you're a virgin or anything, right? There's nothing to be afraid of."

She smiled weakly. "It's not that." Amber took a deep breath. "I didn't want to say anything, but I just really wish Adam was here." Her eyes filled with tears, and her chin started to wobble. As horrible as it was to admit, I was most concerned she was going to ruin her bridal makeup that had a retail value of eighty dollars. *Pull it together*!

"Amber, I totally understand how you feel. You were my bridesmaid when Adam and I

got married, and I know you would give any-
thing for him to be here on your special day.
Just know we're all really proud of you, and
Adam would be proud of you too."

That seemed like the right thing to say. She
visibly relaxed and shut off the waterworks.
Although I wouldn't have wanted Adam anywhere near the vicinity today, I still understood the fact it must have been horrible for
Amber to lose her brother so early. No matter
what Adam had done to me, today was a day
he should have been able to be here for his sister.

Within moments it seemed, she was ready
to walk down the aisle. I fussed around her incessantly when I should have been touching up
my own hair and makeup, taking care that her
veil was just right, her train was behind her,
and her lips were as glossy as possible. When
it came time for the first kiss as man and wife,
Shawn was going to get a mouthful.

Amber looked positively radiant as she
waited for the big moment of the bridal march
to begin. Her father stood nervously by, waiting for the cue to finally give his little girl
away. As the maid of honor, I was one of the
last bridesmaids to go down the aisle. The best
man and I watched all the bridesmaids and

groomsmen march away to *Endless Love*. I thought it was a clever and much better take on the traditional wedding march, which bored me to tears. I wished Amber luck one more, time, telling her how beautiful she looked and how proud I was of her, before it was my turn to walk down the aisle in the processional.

I took the arm of the best man, and we both walked slowly to our places in the front. It felt strange being a part of another wedding with Adam's family. The last time we were all together like this, it had been my own. And we all know how badly that turned out.

I'd thought I would have had a horrible reaction to being a part of Adam's sister's wedding. But more than anything, I just felt happy for her and sincerely hoped she had what it took to be honest with Shawn and make her marriage work. I knew we would definitely be having some serious heart-to-hearts after she was a Mrs. so I could gently impart to her all I had learned about how vital it was to be honest in a relationship—hopefully without accidentally telling her the shocking truth about her brother's cheating.

As I made my way up the gray aisle, I looked to my right and saw Derek smiling at me. I wasn't going to say I wished it was us walking down the aisle together today. I didn't even know if I was ready for that just yet. But what I did feel was comfort, happiness, and a sense of peace—all things I'd never experienced in a relationship before. I had no clue about whether or not Derek was going to be the father of my future babies—or even if I was going to have future babies. But the one thing I did know was that things were finally right.

Just right.

THE END

About the Author

Chick Lit author Bethany Ramos is a full-time freelance writer through Elance.com, but her real passion can be found in writing chick lit, women's fiction, and even a children's book called *Lions Can't Eat Spaghetti*. Bethany works at home full-time writing her fingers to the bone, and she also co-owns her own coffee website, The Coffee Bump, with her husband Mark.

Ramos' Chick Lit fiction is inspired primarily by her sarcastic personality and love of a good laugh. And it doesn't hurt to throw in a few quirky idiosyncrasies that make her characters totally unique—something she is quite familiar with. When she's not spinning a new tale of Chick Lit drama at her computer, Ramos loves spending time with her husband and two yappy Chihuahuas, reading (surprise, surprise!), exercising, and watching trashy reality television.